Theology of Solidarity

A Study on the Theology of James Massey

Theology of Solidarity

A Study on the Theology of James Massey

Viju Wilson

2019

Theology of Solidarity: *A Study on the Theology of James Massey* — published by the Rev. Dr. Ashish Amos of the Indian Society for Promoting Christian Knowledge (ISPCK), Post Box 1585, 1654, Madarsa Road, Kashmere Gate, Delhi-110006.

Online Order: http://ispck.org.in/book.php

Also available on amazon.in

ISBN: 978-93-88945-33-2

Laser typeset by

ISPCK, Post Box 1585, 1654, Madarsa Road, Kashmere Gate, Delhi-110006
• *Tel:* 23866323/22

e-mail: ashish@ispck.org.in • ella@ispck.org.in
website: www.ispck.org.in

Contents

Contents

Preface

My close association with James Massey began in 2012 when I started my doctoral studies under him. I was fortunate to work under this well known theologian of the time, and enjoyed a wonderful academic journey till his death in 2015. He left us (me and the people who worked with him in different stages of his life) with wonderful memories and bold theological thinking. Before I met him as doctoral student, I had heard about him and read some of his books and articles. During my doctoral studies, I could read all his writings, and could interact with him regularly. We used to discuss many issues related to theology, church and contemporary society. Often, we used to agree and sometimes our discussions used to end without consensus though he did not completely ignore my disagreements. Whenever I disagreed with him, he used to convince me with his facts and figures and arguments, and used to suggest some readings. I had a comfortable academic journey with him though I had reservations on some of his views which are not serious enough to disagree with his theological position and framework. Short period of my association with James Massey, in fact, enriched my thinking and helped me learn new ways of reading the text and the faith.

He was a person committed to his faith, community and church. His wide knowledge on Dalits and Indian society made him different from many Indian theologians of his time. His boldness in articulating the cause which he upheld in his life is a challenge for Dalits and other oppressed communities in India. Though his articulations are simple in language, but they are profound and disturbing for those who want to maintain the status quo. He attempted to touch every issue Dalits face in Indian society.

When I read his writings and studied his theological views, I felt that his views are scattered in different sources which he produced throughout the years. Some ideas were developed in different periods and presented them with certain modifications. However, they supply valuable insights for developing new theologies in present time. They are also useful resources for engaging with Dalits and other marginalized communities. This awareness led me to present his theological articulations systematically. This work is both descriptive and reflective. On the one hand the narration of his reflections and ideas will motivate the Dalits and those who are involved in the struggles of their empowerment; on the other hand more studies will emerge on his theology. One of the problems I encountered in presenting his ideas is that he has used same information and refections for responding to different issues. Since, he modified and developed his ideas in different writings; multiple sources for same thought have been used in this work.

Though it contains his theological refections on different issues and concerns of Dalits, Minorities and other subaltern communities, this book is entitled as *Theology of Solidarity* because the idea of solidarity runs through his writings as a thread. Directly or indirectly the idea of solidarity is implied in his arguments and thoughts. In the context of the Dalit initiatives of empowerment, solidarity is an important virtue that has to be practiced as an expression of Christian faith. His contributions have to be acknowledged and his thoughts should be promoted to build up just and humane communities. In order to make his thoughts more meaningful, other scholars are also referred in some of the chapters in this work. He is one of the few theologians who contributed a lot to the Indian theology in the first one and half decade of 21st century. Hope that this work may help the readers understand his theology and initiate further studies on his theological contributions. I am grateful to ISPCK, Delhi for taking up this work for publication. Special thanks to my wife, Sonia and children- Sia and Vihaan for their love and support.

Dr. Viju Wilson
Union Biblical Seminary
Pune

Chapter 1

James Massey
*Bold Theological Voice
and Unshakable Convictions*

James Massey, a Dalit theologian with an ecumenical outlook, attempted to read the Christian faith and Scripture through the eyes of Dalits for bringing radical changes in the life of Dalits in India. He was one of the bold theological voices of his time. His scholarship and activism primarily aimed to empower the Dalits and challenge the non-Dalits to denounce the casteist mind-set that perpetuated the oppressive condition of Dalits. In his theological quest, he raised a different voice to contest the ideologies/theologies and the institutions which ignored the issues of social justice and human dignity. His theological convictions were shaped by his encounters with social institutions, religious systems and different ideologies of the time. He used every opportunity to express his theological conviction that 'God always stands with the oppressed.' Within this framework, he articulated the issues of Dalits and Minorities. His voice and convictions still continues through his theology and interpretations of the Scripture. Following sections briefly explain his biography, major influences in his thinking and his contributions to the church and society.

A Brief Biographical Sketch

Prof. Dr. (habil.) James Massey[1] was born to Rev. Jalal Masih and Mrs. Fazl Bibi on 11 May 1943 in a village called Zafferwal in Gurdaspur district in Punjab. He was born and brought up in a devout Christian family. Though born in a socially and economically backward family, his hard work and determination took him into different heights in church and society. He was respected for his ideological/theological positions, and the interventions he made for the empowerment of Dalits in India. He was one of the pioneers of Dalit Theology, and advocated for the human rights of Dalits and Minorities. He served the Indian Church in different capacities and contributed to the development of theological education in India. He was blessed with good educational opportunities which provided him space to grow in life and ministry. He started his schooling in a village school. Though the family and social condition was not favorable for higher education, he could overcome all obstacles in life and pursue college education. Upon the completion of B.A. from Punjab University, he joined for theological education, and passed B.D. (Bachelor of Divinity) Degree from the Serampore College in 1967. In order to be equipped in Punjabi language mainly for translating Bible he also received *Gyani* Degree from Guru Nanak University in 1972. He completed his M.A. from Punjabi University, and earned Diploma in Book Publishing from Oxford Brookes University. He was awarded PhD on the subject, 'The Doctrine of Ultimate Reality in Sikh Religion,' by the Johann Wolfgang Goethe University, Germany in 1990. He also received Post Doctoral Degree (Habilitation) in the discipline of Religious Studies from the same university in 1995. His post-doctoral study was on 'Dalits in India: Religion as Source of Bondage or Liberation with Special Reference to Christians.'

James Massey began ministry as a University Youth Director, Gass Memorial Centre at Raipur in Chhattisgarh in 1967. His interest in literature and publications took him to Christian Literature Centre, a publishing house in Jullunder, Punjab and worked there as an editor from 1969 to 1971. In 1977 he joined Indian Society for Promoting Christian Knowledge (ISPCK), Delhi as Publication Secretary. He served this historic and well known Christian publishing house in different capacities till 1996. He was the General Secretary of ISPCK for eleven years (1985-1996). In 1996, he was appointed as a Member of National Commission for Minorities for three years (1996-1999). He was also founder Director of Community Contextual Communication Centre (CCCC), an NGO committed to work among Dalits, Women and Slum Dwellers. In 2001, he started Centre for Dalit/Subaltern Studies (CDS), New Delhi a research institution for Dalit/Subaltern studies. He continued as founder director of CDS and CCCC till his death on 3 March, 2015. He is survived by his wife, Mrs. Kalawati Massey and daughters: Jyoti, Kiran and Ujwala.

While holding important responsibilities, James Massy was actively involved in the life of the Church and its institutions: both theological and secular. As an ordained minister of the Church of North India, he served his Church in different capacities. The Church was benefited by his resourcefulness and leadership potential. He was the chairperson of the Evaluation Commission of Church of North India (2006-2008) and the Honorary Secretary for the Commission on the Mission of the Church of North India (1996-2005). He also served his Church as the Member of Theological Commission (2005-2008) and the Honorary Secretary for the Liturgical Commission (1978-2001). He was also a member of Isabella Thoburn Collage Society, Lucknow, UP (2000-2006), and Baring Union Christian College Association and Baring Christian College Managing Committee (1993-2002), Batala, Punjab.

Theological education was an important area of interest and passion in the life of James Massey. Majority of his writings are theological in nature. He served theological institutions and the Senate of Serampore College in different capacities. He was a member of Bishop College Society and Board of Management (2006-2015) and a visiting professor at Vidyajyoti, New Delhi and Gurukul Lutheran Theological College, Chennai. He served the Senate of Serampore College as a member of the Senate, the Honorary Secretary for the Board of Theological Education (2005-2011) and the Chairperson, Committee for Programs and Church Relation (1994-2000). As a renowned Indian theologian, he was invited to give several lectures in some of the universities in Germany and South Korea. As a committed ecumenist, he was associated with ecumenical bodies like National Council of Churches in India (NCCI) and World Council of Churches (WCC). He was a member of the Faith and Order Plenary Commission, WCC (1999-2006) and a member of General Body (1987-2000) and the Chairperson of the Communications Unit (1996-2000) of NCCI. He also contributed to the works of para-Church organizations, Christian research institutions and civil societies. He was the chairperson for Delhi YMCA Committee on Dalits, Tribals and Human Rights (1999-2001). He worked as the Vice Chairperson of the Christian Peace Conference of Asia-Pacific (1998-2000) and as the President of Christian Peace Conference of India (1992-2000). He served as Treasurer of Christian Institute for the Study of Religion and Society (CISRS), Bangalore (1990-1996). As the Chairperson, he gave leadership to World Association for Christian Communication (WACC), Asia Region (1989-1996). His relationship with institutions in Germany led him to be part of Indo-German Social Service Society, New Delhi. He also served as General Secretary of Dalit Solidarity Peoples (DSP) and raised his voice for the cause of Dalits and their solidarity.

As a prolific writer, James Massey authored several articles and books and edited a number of academic works in English, Punjabi and Hindi. He presented many papers in seminars and consultations, and organized several regional, national and international conferences and seminars on Dalit Issues, Dalit Theology and Human Rights. His well known books are *The Doctrine of the Ultimate Reality in Sikh Religion; Dalits in India; Roots: A Concise History of Dalits; Minorities and Religious Freedom in a Democracy; Alternative Approaches to Education; Dr. B.R. Ambedkar: A Study in Just Society; A Contemporary Look at Sikh Religion; Ecumenism Means Justice; Dalit Theology: History, Context, Text and Whole Salvation; Masihi Dalit: Ik Itihasik Paripreksya* (Hindi); *Masihita Ik Paricaya* (Punjabi); *Rethinking Theology in India; Introducing Dalit Theology; Dalit Roots of Christianity, Theology and Spirituality; Caste-Class Victims and Their Assertion for Justice; Towards Dalit Hermeneutics; Dalit Bible Commentary* Vols- 2, 8, 9, 17, 10 (Old Testament) 3, 5, 6, (New Testament) etc.

Major Influences in the Thinking of James Massey

The theological thinking of James Massey was influenced by many factors which he encountered throughout his life. The life of his parents, particularly their service to the community and the church impacted him a lot in his future ministry and thinking. His father was a village pastor, who was formerly a Mazhibi Sikh. The influence of his parents in his life can be read from his testimony that "they... have been a continued source of inspiration to me in my work."[2] His experience as a Dalit boy who was born and brought up in a rural village, which was part of a larger society where caste system gripped every aspect of social life, challenged his thoughts and motivated him to involve in the issues of Dalits and other marginalized communities.[3] He explains his socially and economically deprived childhood days in this way, "His early childhood was like the other children of his age. Almost the children of his age from about 5-7 years onward start working or helping in the rich landlord's field or taking care of their animals. In return they get either some food or some fodder for their own animals, or if they are working on a regular basis their wages are fixed on six-months or yearly basis, or so many kilograms of grain."[4] Moreover, he lived in a village, named Zafferwal in the district of Gurudaspur, where both Dalit Sikhs and Dalit Christians lived together. They shared common social identity and common place of living which is called even today as *thathis*, housing location of Dalits. They equally experienced common social, economic and religious deprivation.[5] Such experiences might have supplied material for his fight for social justice, particularly for the rights and empowerment of Dalits.

Though he was a son of a village pastor, James Massey had bitter experiences from the authorities of his own Church. Though he was given a scholarship instituted for the children of pastors in the first year of his college education, it was stopped at the end of the academic year because his father was 'not in the good-books' of the Church authorities. This incident did not stop his studies. He met the educational expenses by taking up a part-time job in the college. The next level of his encounter with the Church authorities happened when he decided to go for theological education. Initially, his application was refused by the Church Council. Later, it was accepted with two conditions: no financial assistance for the studies and no guarantee for ministry opportunity upon the completion of the studies. Thus, he began his theological education with a lot of uncertainties. After much struggles and hardships, he completed his theological studies without any financial sponsorship from the Church. Even the Church refused to give him a village congregation after the studies.[6] Though he was unfairly treated by his own Church, he did not give up his faith in God and his calling for the ministry. He strongly believed in God's plan for his life. It was later proved right in each stage of his life.[7] His painful experiences with the authorities of the church later reflected in his critique on the ecclesiastical structures and the ministerial goals and priorities of the Church.

The work of CISRS (The Christian Institute for the Study of Religion and Society), Bangalore, contributed to the ideological formulation of James Massey, particularly in Dalit studies. The conference on 'Sikhism and Christianity in Punjab' conducted in Baring Union Christian College with the help of CISRS led him into the field of inter-faith dialogue, particularly Sikh-Christian dialogue. It is interesting to note that he did his doctoral research in Sikh religion. The national consultations on 'Dalit Theology' organized with the help of CISRS in 1980's brought James Massey into the area of Dalit theological thinking. His writings on Dalit theology began during this period. His well known book, 'Roots: A Concise History of Dalits,' was the result of the motivation he received from CISRS. He was also encouraged by the involvement of CISRS in organizing regional and national level programs for Dalit empowerment.[8] The ideological and practical support he received from CISRS is evident in his writings on the areas CISRS focused throughout the years.

James Massey was also influenced by the Punjabi language, Punjabi culture and Sikh religion. He began his schooling with Punjabi as the first language because during those days Native Punjabi was meant for the children from villages. Hindi was the first language of majority children from the city/town.[9] His schooling in Punjabi language must have created in him an interest in Punjabi language. The Punjabi language and Punjabi culture are two important ingredients of his *punjabiyat* (Punjabi Identity). This *punjabiyat* contributed to his thinking. His *punjabiyat* was also shaped by the cultural values and ethos that originated from Sikh religion. For him, it is quite natural that the religion of the majority people influences the general ethos and common identity of people in respective cultural context. In this sense, his ideological and cultural orientation had the influence of Sikh religion. He admitted that the study on Sikh religion enriched his Christian faith also. It even provided him energy and encouragement to question the social order based on caste system which perpetuated the discrimination of Dalits. Which accepting the influence of Sikhism in his thinking, he also observed that Christianity offered him a message of hope clearer and louder than any other religious traditions. The consciousness of his *Punjabiyat* led James Massey to write his first book, *Masihiat-Ek Parichaya* (Christianity: An Introduction), in Punjabi. He wrote this work in Punjabi thought form. He also authored a few other works in Punjabi. His Punjabi translation of the Bible (Pavitar Bible) can be considered as the upshot of his *Punjabiyat*.[10]

James Massey actively involved in the programs of Dalit Solidarity Peoples Movement, an inter-faith movement, founded to promote solidarity among Dalits. His engagement with Dalits of different religious traditions provided him a larger framework for theological reflections which focused on the solidarity of Dalits and the liberation of all Dalits.[11] He raised his voice for the rights of Dalits and minorities within the framework of the democratic and secular values.[12] The ideology of B.R. Ambedkar also influenced his theological thinking. Many of his writings and arguments are enriched by the thoughts of B.R. Ambedkar. As a member of National Commission for Minorities, he got numerous opportunities to know the issues and challenges of minorities, particularly Christians, in India. It was reflected in his actions and reflections in terms of protecting and empowering the minorities in the country. In sum, James Massey was a product of his time. His thinking and theology was influenced by many personal experiences, incidents, persons, ideologies, movements etc. They defined his creative intervention in the issues of Dalits and minorities in India.

Major Contributions

All ventures initiated by James Massey were ecumenical in nature. It was ecumenical in terms of outlook and involvement. He was able to carry out his vision of Dalit empowerment with the help of a team of dedicated men and women who stood with him in all new initiatives he had undertaken. Fr. S. Lourduswamy, Fr. T.K. John, Mr. Philip Jadhav, Sr. Dr. Shalini Mulackal, Fr. Monodeep Daniel, Mr. Deepak Seth, Mr. Pramod Kumar, Mr. Chitaranjan Nag, Mr. Imti Jamir, Mr. Nungsang Jamir etc were the people who accompanied him in the works he had undertaken since 2000. They belonged to Christian both Catholic and Protestant, Hindu and Buddhist religious traditions. Apart from them, there were many scholars and activists who joined with him and participated in the projects or programs he had executed. Most of his lasting contributions, except Community Contextual Communication Centre, came after the establishment of Centre for Dalit/Subaltern Studies in 2001. Though he achieved a name and fame in his field, it would not have been possible if Mrs. Kalawati Massey, his wife, had not scarified her career. His busy schedule and travel compelled her to limit her life as a house wife to take care of his three daughters and manage house hold affairs in his absence. She often used to remind James Massey of her sacrifice to stand with his vision of empowering Dalits in Indian society. Several times, I have witnessed such conversations.

Dalit Theology

James Massey was one of the pioneers of Dalit theology movement in India. He contributed a lot to the development of Dalit theology through his writings, lectures, presentations, and his institution,

Centre for Dalit/Subaltern Studies. He popularized it in national
and international forums and found it as a means of creating
solidarity among Dalits. When he was General Secretary of ISPCK,
he took initiatives to publish books on Dalits and other Subaltern
communities and promote their theologies. Thus, he attempted
to influence the theological perspective of Indian Christians by
publishing books on Dalits and Tribals. Dalit Solidarity Peoples was
another platform for him to promote Dalit theology and its praxis.
Most of his Dalit theological writings were articulations on the issues
Dalits faced in society. He always tried to interpret Christian faith in
the light of the life realities of Dalits. His critique on the mission and
ministry reflected the thinking and concerns of common Dalits. He
added a new chapter into the history of Dalit theological thinking
by publishing Dalit Bible Commentary (Thirty Volumes), a first
ever attempt in India. It has become a major resource for doing
Dalit Theology today. He also played a key role in incorporating
Dalit Theology as one of the optional subjects into the Bachelor
of Divinity (B.D.) curriculum of the Senate of Serampore College.

Centre for Dalit/Subaltern Studies (CDS)

Centre for Dalit/Subaltern Studies (CDS), initially known as Centre
for Dalit Studies (Theology)-CDT (T), was the fruition of the vision
that James Massey had nurtured for a long time. The immediate
motivation for taking an initiative to actualize his vision came
during his stay at Uganda Martyrs University, Nkozi, where he
presented a paper on Dalit Theology in an international seminar
organized by the Institute of Missiology-Missio, Aachen, Germany.
The liberation theologians who responded to his paper challenged
him to implement his vision of 'Centre for Dalit Studies.' He also
shared it with some of his friends like Dr. Frans J.S. Wijsen, Dr.
Erhard Kamphausen and Dr. Marco Moerschbacher. After coming

from Uganda, he shared his vision and prospects of implementing it with his colleagues such as Most Rev. Malayappan Chinnappa, the Rt. Rev. Dr. A. George Ninan, Fr. S. Lourduswamy, Sr. Shalini Mulackal and Fr. Monodeep Daniel. They encouraged him to work out the plan and strategies to accomplish the vision. He and Fr. Lourduswamy worked for almost 18 months to develop the vision, the program and the resources. They travelled to different countries and conducted consultations on 'Centre for Dalit Studies (Theology)' and attended conferences to get support from organizations and institutions. After much discussions and deliberations, 'Centre for Dalit Studies (Theology)' was inaugurated on 28 September 2001 in a function held at the Indian social Institute, New Delhi.[13] Today, it is known as Centre for Dalit/Subaltern Studies located at Matiala Village in Uttam Nagar, New Delhi.

The Centre for Dalit/Subaltern Studies was established with certain broader objectives: "(1) To engage in a constructive theological debate in the light of one's experience and through critical self-reflection and thereby develop a theology from Dalit perspective. (2) To encourage the Dalit thinkers, activists and educationists to undertake constructive Dalit study aiming at developing a common Dalit ideology. (3) To undertake research in the areas of theology from Dalit perspective, Dalit liberation, social transformation, justice and equality and other related areas. (4) To understand the attitudes of the Indian Church towards the Dalits in general and the Dalit Christians in particular, and accordingly suggest remedial measures and undertake activities necessary for the proposed change. (6) To raise the consciousness of all sections of Indian society in order to enable the process of establishing a just society. (7) To develop spirituality based upon the universal Father-Motherhood of God into its implications for the solidarity (both sister/brotherhood) of all human beings. (8) To offer basic (foundation) and advance academic courses in the areas of theology from Dalit perspective."[14] Though it was started as an institution primarily focused on the concerns of Dalits, the issues of other oppressed communities were also addressed in the later period.

Since its inception, CDS has been involved in various activities which facilitate the empowerment of Dalits and other Subaltern communities. It has coordinated and organized research seminars, national and international conferences to promote Dalit theological thinking and create awareness on the issues of the Dalit/Subaltern communities in India. It has initiated a lot of publications on Dalit, Tribal and Subaltern studies which have been listed in the syllabi of various courses under the curriculum of the Senate of Serampore College. As a member of the Board of Theological Education of Senate of Serampore College, CDS has contributed to the theological education in India. Through the Contact Program, CDS reaches out to Churches, different faith communities, institutions and challenges the people on the issues of Dalits in the country. The CDS also has initiated 'Correspondence Course in Dalit Education' to make people aware of the condition of Dalits with concrete data. It provided information about the history, struggles and movements of Dalits/Subalterns. It was primarily designed to conscientize Dalits and build up solidarity among them. In order to prepare Dalit/Subaltern leadership, CDS has started a PhD program in collaboration with Vrije University (VU) Amsterdam and Radboud University, Nijmegen of the Netherlands. It also aimed to develop resourceful scholars in the field of Dalit/Subaltern studies.[15] Through its different programs, publications and projects, CDS has contributed to the development of Dalit/Subaltern theological thinking in India, provided opportunities for new scholars in the field of Dalit/subaltern studies and raised a different voice for an alternative society.

Community Contextual Communication Centre (CCCC)

The Community Contextual Communication Centre, a NGO, was started to uplift the neglected and the poor sections in society. It mainly concentrated on the education of dropout children, women empowerment programs, advocacy programs on Human Rights, adult education, health awareness campaigns etc. It was through the programs of CCCC; James Massey found the praxis of his theological and ideological articulations. Many people were benefited because of the work of CCCC under his leadership.

Nav Jyoti Post-Graduate and Research Centre

Nav Jyoti Post-Graduate and Research Centre (NJPGRC) started as a joint venture of Centre Dalit Studies (CDS), New Delhi, New Theological College (NTC), Dehradun and Dharma Jyoti Vidya Peeth, Faridabad. As a federated faculty, it offers M.Th programs under Senate of Serampore College. James Massey played an important role in the formation of NJPGRC. He continued as the Chairman of this institution till his death. It provided another opportunity and platform for CDS to involve and contribute to the theological education in India.[16]

Christians of Scheduled Caste Origin in India: A Study of Their Socio-Economic, Cultural and Political Status

In his life, James Massey had made many interventions for the rights of Dalits, particularly Christians among them, and fought for their reservation and other privileges. He realized the need of a comprehensive study on the condition of the Christians of Scheduled Caste Origin (Dalit Christians) to convince the Central and State Governments which denied them scheduled caste status and reservation benefits since independence. Thus, *Christians of Scheduled Caste Origin in India: A Study of Their Socio-Economic, Cultural and Political Status* was emerged out of his passionate concern for the rights of Dalit Christians. This was the first national study on the conditions of Dalit Christians irrespective of denominations. It was organized at four regional levels: North, West, East and South. The main objective of the study was to obtain the concrete details about the socio-economic, cultural, political and psychological conditions of the Christians of Scheduled Caste Origin in India. James Massey gave leadership to the study as a joint venture of Centre for Dalit Studies, New Delhi, Commission for SC/ST/BC of the Catholic Bishops Conference of India, New Delhi and Delhi School of Social Work Society, Delhi. The field study was conducted under the supervision of Prof. Dr. Ratna Verma, Prof. Rekha Dutt and Associate Prof. Alka Kumar. He and Prof. Dr. T.K John edited the work and published it in 2012. He even submitted it to the Office of the Prime Minister of India and the leaders of political parties to make them known the life realities of Dalit Christians.[17]

Dalit Heritage and Liberative Traditions in India

According to James Massey, the Dalits had their own religious and cultural traditions before the establishment of Vedic Religion. Their ancestors were indigenous people of this land and enjoyed all privileges of a normal human being. With the arrival of Aryans, the conflict emerged between the traditions of Dalits and Aryans. In due course, most of the Dalit traditions and religious beliefs were either co-opted or destroyed by the dominant traditions brought and developed by the Aryans (Brahmins). However, he argued that the remnants of Dalit traditions and heritage exist even today. They must be documented and used as a source for Dalit theologizing. It might enrich Dalit literature also. This idea was converted into a study project of Centre for Dalit/Subaltern Studies. The main objective of this study was to explore the existing elements of Dalit heritage and traditions. The historical origin, forms and patters of respective Dalit traditions, its present status and social base, its role for building Dalit consciousness etc are other aims of this study. It was a field-based study conducted in the select villages in the select districts in 21 states of India, where there was highest concentration of Dalit population. Many field workers were employed for this project. Mr. Das, in the initial stage, and Mr. M.J Thomas worked as Chief Field Coordinators.[18] This study was published as a resource book on Dalit heritage in 2015.

Dalit Bible Commentary

Dalit Bible Commentary was one of the outstanding contributions of James Massey. As one of the pioneers and exponents of Dalit theology, he realized that another level of the development of Dalit theology required the reading of the Bible through the eyes of Dalits in India. As a project of Centre for Dalit/Subaltern Studies, it was begun in 2006. He coordinated the work with a team of eminent scholars who were committed for the cause of Dalit liberation. Theologians and Bible Scholars from different church traditions: Protestant and Catholic involved in this work. Thirty Volumes of Dalit Bible Commentary were successfully completed and published. It was guided by a bold vision that "Dalit Bible Commentary should enable Dalit sensibility to enter into dialogue with the Biblical word/text, making the Scripture more meaningful to their lives." It followed 'Dialogical-Contextual Approach' which facilitated the dialogue between Biblical World and Dalit World. The interpreters focused more on the meeting points of these two worlds. It was an exercise of interpreting 'Scripture through the eyes of disempowered people.'[19] One Volume Dalit Bible Commentary was also published. Today, Dalit Bible Commentary provides resources for new way of reading Bible contextually and for developing new Dalit theological discourses.

Journal of Subaltern and Cultural Theology

Journal of Subaltern and Cultural Theology is an academic journal of Centre for Dalit/Subaltern Studies. James Massey initiated to produce an academic journal with two objectives: 1) "To provide a common platform for reflection for the Indian theologians, especially younger ones, belonging to various subaltern communities, who have been victims of caste-class Indian social system, so that they are able to pave the way for liberation of their communities by asserting their rights for freedom and justice." 2) "To encourage active participation of subaltern theologians, thinkers, activists and educationists in a constructive theological debate in the light of their experiences and through critical-reflection, and thereby develop theology (ies) as an instrument of establishing a 'just society' based on the universal principle of 'justice' which means equality, liberty and fraternity."[20]

The scholarly acumen and committed life of James Massey can be discerned from the comments of his colleagues. Deepak Seth, a Hindu by faith, said: "I have known Dr. Massey now for over thirty years, during which period I often had the opportunity to share with him his thoughts regarding various subjects like Dalit issues, Minority Concerns, Sikhism, Christianity and Church in India. He would always discuss these topics threadbare to make the subject crystal clear to me so that I could appreciate the underlying complexities and problems arising out of these. I will not hesitate to say that much of my understanding of these issues, particularly regarding Dalits, Minorities and Reservations came from the discussions which I had with Dr. Massey and which invariably appeared in print at some later stage."[21] Kim Yong-Bock, Chancellor, Asia Pacific Centre for Integral Study of Life, Seoul, observed that "Dr. Massey is certainly one of the most important Dalit theologians today, reading the Bible-Christian Scriptures-with scholarly excellence for its radical implications for the subaltern communities in the entire world, and particularly for the communities in India. For him theology is the matter concerning liberation of Dalit community and of bringing radical justice to the oppressed."[22]

James Massey's ideological interventions, practical initiatives and theological thinking (following chapters of this book) provide us an image of his personality. He was literally a man of bold theological voice and unshakable convictions. He never compromised his theological position and the cause and the values he stood for throughout his life. He had clarity on what he said and argued. He was not ashamed to talk about the issues of Dalits and Minorities with any person of high/low stature. I have witnessed several times how passionately he used to explain the condition of Dalits and argue for their empowerment in the seminars, and with national and foreign visitors in his centre. His planning and execution of the different programmes of Dalit empowerment always reflected his theological vision and unshakable convictions. For some, he was a 'liberal' because of his theological views. But he was a person who had strong faith in God and always found motivation for his vocation in the Scripture. He never questioned the faith but articulated it in the light of the oppressed human realities. He boldly raised his voice for the liberation of Dalits and set a pattern for future Dalit scholars, activists and theologians.

Endnotes

[1] Following information about his life and ministry is taken from a booklet published by Centre for Dalit/Subaltern Studies (CDS).

[2] James Massey, *Dalits in India: Religion as a Source of Bondage or Liberation with Special Reference to Christians* (New Delhi: Manohar, 2009 Reprint), 5.

[3] Deepak Seth, "Preface," in Deepak Seth, ed., *From Truth to Truth, A Journey through Faiths: A Selection of Representative Essays by Dr. James Massey* (New Delhi: CDS and NOIDA: Academy Press, 2008), 6.

[4] James Massey, "Ingredients for a Dalit Theology," in *Indigenous People: Dalits*, edited by James Massey (Delhi: ISPCK, Reprint 2006), 341.

[5] James Massey, *Dalit Theology: History, Context, Text and Whole Salvation* (New Delhi: Manohar, 2013), 127.

[6] James Massey, "Ingredients for a Dalit Theology," 342-343.

[7] James Massey, "History and Dalit Theology," in *Frontiers of Dalit Theology*, Edited by V. Devasahayam (Chennai: ISPCK/Gurukul,1997), 165

[8] James Massey, "An Analysis of the Dalit Situation with Special Reference to Dalit Christians and Dalit Theology," *Religion and Society*, Vol 52/No 3-4 (September-December 2007): 57-86 at 58-59.

[9] James Massey, "Ingredients for a Dalit Theology," 342.

[10] James Massey, "Theology for a New Community: Looking Ahead," in *Theology for a New Community*, edited by James Massey (New Delhi: CDS, 2013), 314-315.

[11] James Massey, *Dalits in India: Religion as a Source of Bondage or Liberation with Special Reference to Christians*, 159.

[12] Deepak Seth, "Preface," in Deepak Seth, ed., *From Truth to Truth, A Journey through Faiths: A Selection of Representative Essays by Dr. James Massey*, 6.

[13] James Massey, "Centre for Dalit Studies (Theology): An Introduction," *A Theology from Dalit Perspective*, edited by James Massey and S. Lourduswamy (New Delhi: CDS, 2001), 100-107.

[14] A.M. Chinnappa, "Inaugural Speech by the President of CDS (T) at the Inaugural Function of Centre for Dalit Studies (Theology), ISI, New Delhi, 28th September 2001," in *A Theology from Dalit Perspective*, edited by James Massey and S. Lourduswamy (New Delhi: CDS, 2001), 7.

[15] James Massey, "Centre for Dalit Studies (Theology): An Introduction," 104 ff & *Annual Activity Report 2009-2010* (New Delhi: CDS, 2010), 12, 14, 33.

[16] *Annual Activity Report 2009-2010* (New Delhi: CDS, 2010), 15, 33-34.

[17] Viju Wilson, "Victims of Caste and Wounded Sheep of the Church," *Journal of Subaltern and Cultural Theology*, Inaugural Issue (June, 2013): 82-91 at 82.

[18] James Massey, General Editor, *Dalit Heritage and Liberative Traditions in India* (New Delhi: CDS, 2015), 24 & M.J. Thomas, "Dalit Heritage and Liberative Tradition in North India: Towards Breaking the Silence," *Journal of Subaltern and Cultural Theology*, Inaugural Issue (June, 2013): 92-98

[19] James Massey, *Dalit Bible Commentary: A Challenge Response* (New Delhi: CDS, 2011), 6 & Imti Jamir, "Scripture through the Eyes of Disempowered

People," *Journal of Subaltern and Cultural Theology*, Inaugural Issue (June, 2013): 74-81 at 74

[20] James Massey, "Editorial," *Journal of Subaltern and Cultural Theology*, Inaugural Issue (June, 2013), 7-12 at 7.

[21] Deepak Seth, "Preface," in Deepak Seth, ed., *From Truth to Truth, A Journey through Faiths: A Selection of Representative Essays by Dr. James Massey*, 5.

[22] Kim Yong-Bock, "Forward," in James Massey, *Ecumenism Means Justice* (Matiala, New Delhi: CDS, 2014), 7.

Chapter 2

Theology of Solidarity

The biblical faith is expressed through certain virtues. They are taught by God through historical actions and revelations culminated in the life and work of Jesus Christ. Solidarity is one of such liberating virtues that run throughout the biblical narratives. It is not presented as an abstract concept but as a concrete reality happened in human history. Divine Solidarity is best expressed by the liberating divine interventions in the life of different communities, and set an example in Jesus Christ for human beings to continue the virtue of solidarity in respective societies. The beauty of Divine Solidarity is the locations God had selected in human history. The life of the oppressed often became the site of God's Solidarity. It invites us to express our solidarity with the oppressed of the time. The life realities of Dalits in India stand as a site for expressing the virtue of solidarity today. This chapter attempts to reflect on the concept of solidarity in the theology of James Massey.

Biblical God: God of Solidarity

According to the Bible, creation was the first act of God's historical participation in human history (Genesis 1 & 2). The call of Abraham was another significant intervention of God in human history (Gen. 12). The life and message of Prophets also demonstrate how God intentionally engaged in human history.[1] Indeed, the Bible is the witness of God's action in human history. God even commanded the people of Israel through Moses that their history of slavery should be retold from generation to generation. It is clearly narrated in Deuteronomy 6:20-25. Memory of the past helps them know the nature and involvement of God in their history.[2] Based on the nature of God's participation in the history of humanity, Biblical God can be called as God of Solidarity.

The biblical God is God of Solidarity with humanity, particularly with the oppressed communities in history. God selected the history of a slave community (People of Israel) to reveal God's action of solidarity. God's involvement in their oppressive historical situations informs about God's participation in the histories of other nations through prophets, kings and ordinary people.[3] The exodus history of the people of Israel explicitly narrates the nature and purpose of God's solidarity with the oppressed peoples like Dalits. God's solidarity is expressed not in words or ideas but in actions. It is not theoretical but experiential in nature. In the exodus event, God became part of the painful experiences of the people of Israel and liberated them from the bondage of slavery. In fact, God intentionally participated in the struggles of an oppressed community. God's action in exodus story gives hope to the oppressed communities like Dalits that God of Solidarity takes side with the oppressed and leads them into liberation. The liberation God offers is an experience of wholeness. It touches every aspect of human life in society. It is not limited to religious realm alone. It embraces social, economic and political dimensions too.[4] The exodus event is one of the interventions of God in history in solidarity with humanity. There are many such liberating interventions in the history of other communities. If we read those events within the framework of God's liberating actions, God of Solidarity can be identified in them.

God's solidarity with humanity is expressed not only through God's miraculous actions but also through God's incarnational act. John 1: 14 explain how God expressed solidarity with human beings through an incarnational act. Jesus Christ is the climax of God's solidarity with human beings, particularly the oppressed. In Jesus Christ, human beings ultimately meet the God of Solidarity. The beauty of God's incarnational act is that Jesus Christ gave up His otherworldly status and identity and became one among the oppressed. For Dalits, Jesus became a Dalit to identify with the oppressed. He became poorest of the poor to express God's solidarity with humanity.[5] God's incarnational act in Jesus Christ shows that solidarity is an intentional self-emptying for the sake of others who are longing for salvific experience in this world and the world to come.

The nature of God's incarnational act proves that God prefers to be with the oppressed. In the very act of incarnation, God became an ordinary human being. The people whom God selected to facilitate the process of incarnation were also ordinary human beings. God selected Mary, a poor village girl to play an important role in the incarnational act. God became a human being through the womb of an ordinary girl. Joseph, who was engaged to Mary before the birth of Jesus, was a carpenter. In fact, Jesus was also known as carpenter's son. The birth place of Jesus also shows that God wanted not only to become an ordinary human being but also to be born in an ordinary situation. The selection of ordinary people, place and situation for incarnational act was not accidental but intentional. It basically points to the purpose of God's incarnation: solidarity with human beings, particularly with the poor and the marginalized in the world and be a model for human solidarity. God became ordinary human being to ensure justice and equality to those who are oppressed for centuries because of unjust religious and social structures. In the Nazareth Manifesto (Luke 4: 18) of Jesus Christ and his subsequent ministry, what we see is God who identifies with the poor and marginalized people like Dalits.[6]

God's incarnational act points to the need of human solidarity with the oppressed. As God identified with human beings, they also have to express their solidarity with fellow beings, particularly with the oppressed. The exodus event shows that the people of Israel were fully committed to solidarity with one another. The commitment to solidarity generates power to resist the forces of oppression. People get new energy to fight against disabilities if they are committed to identify with their fellow beings for the cause of community liberation. The exodus event also informs that solidarity has two dimensions-a commitment to God and a commitment to fellow human beings. Dalit liberation (liberation of the oppressed) also demands a commitment to God and a commitment to fellow Dalits (oppressed persons) irrespective of religious and ideological persuasions.[7] The consciousness of God's participation in the struggles for justice enhances the level of solidarity among the oppressed. What Dalits and other oppressed communities need today is solidarity among them to define their destiny and achieve their goal of complete liberation from the bondage of oppressive social structures.[8] Dalit solidarity helps to reclaim their rights and occupy their legitimate space in society. The liberating story of Exodus reminds every Christian to be committed to God and to the fellow beings, particularly the oppressed.

God's solidarity in the exodus story of liberation gives hope to all oppressed communities. God of Solidarity cannot be indifferent to the cry of the poor and the oppressed like Dalits. The participation of God in human suffering has not ceased with exodus story. It continues even today. God of Solidarity constantly participates in the struggles of oppressed communities and acts against the

Pharaohs of the present time. They are unjust social, political, economic structures and the people who maintain those structures in society. God of Solidarity is against any structure which is built on oppressive values. The liberation offered by God of Solidarity is the liberation not only from sin and guilt but also from bondage of oppressive structures.[9] While exodus event introduces 'God who is on the side of the oppressed;' God's incarnational act in Jesus Christ presents 'God who liberates the oppressed.' The former declares that God always takes definite side with the oppressed communities like Dalits; the latter tells the story of God who became human being to liberate the oppressed. Both interventions basically aimed at the liberation of the oppressed. The oppressed took the centre stage in those divine interventions.[10] It has to be noted that God of Solidarity "stood with the Israelites till they achieved their liberation."[11] Moreover, liberation of humanity, particularly those who are oppressed is the will of the God of Solidarity.[12] This, in fact, enhances the hope of the oppressed communities to achieve their goal of 'whole salvation.' The mission of the God of Solidarity was fully manifested in Jesus' mission.

Jesus' Mission: Mission of Solidarity

Jesus' mission was centered on his Nazareth Manifesto (Luke 4:18-19) which primarily addressed four categories of people: the poor, the captives, the blind and the oppressed. In his mission and ministry, Jesus was actually expressing his solidarity with them. The healing, comfort, encouragement, empowerment and liberation/ salvation were flowing out of his solidarity with the people whom he encountered, particularly the oppressed of his time. The context he dealt with was like the context of Dalits in India. In every stage of his mission, Jesus was encountering the life realities which resembled the life realities of Dalits. Like his life, Jesus' mission was also started in an ordinary village called Nazareth which was despised by the mainstream Palestinian society. Jesus announced his liberative mission agenda in this village. Nazareth was considered as a worthless and despised city (John 1:45ff; 6:42), known for the ignorant people who did not know the law (John 7:4) and who did not attract anybody's attention. It is possible that Jesus' manifesto was influenced by the life realities of people in Nazareth. The Nazareth manifesto tells us that before commencing his mission, Jesus was clear about where and with whom he was going to begin his Mission of Solidarity. The poor, the captives, the blind and the oppressed became the primary target groups in Jesus' mission of solidarity.[13]

The 'poor' are the first group of people whom Jesus considered for His liberative mission. This category includes not only 'economically poor' but also physically weak and socially outcast. It means they are not only economic category but also social category. For Jesus, they deserve immediate attention because their present poor state is the result of unjust social and economic structures perpetuated for centuries. Who are the poor in Indian context? The socio-economic definition of poor situates Dalits in the category of poor in India. They continue to be poor because of the centuries-old caste system which historically denied them right to own property and kept them as 'servants,' if not slaves, of the feudal lords. In India, majority economically poor are socially poor too. Therefore, Dalits occupy an important place in mission agenda of Jesus Christ.

The 'captives' are second target group in Jesus' mission. They should be considered more than general understanding of 'prisoners.' They are captives of different ideologies and structures in society. Ideological and structural captivity can be political, religious, cultural and social in nature (Luke 4:1-5; 7:36-50; 11:37-53; 20:20-26). In our context, those who perpetuate caste-consciousness are under the structural and ideological captivity of caste system. The real victims of caste captivity are Dalits who suffer from the caste-psyche of caste people. Third category is the 'blind' people. This group constitutes not only physically blind people but also those who are blind to the broken realities of others and to the true values of life. [14] In Indian context, Dalits are the victims of those who are blind to the values of justice and equality. Therefore, the liberation of caste people from social blindness brings changes in the life of Dalits. Jesus in his mission attempted to heal not only the physically blind but also the socially blind by expressing his solidarity with the oppressed in society. His solidarity with the oppressed 'opened' the eyes of the dominant who devalued the oppressed.

The 'oppressed' are fourth category of people focused in the Nazareth manifesto of Jesus. The oppressed refers to the people who are socially, politically, culturally and religiously subjugated by the dominant in particular context. The expression, 'oppressed' is translated as 'Dalit' in the Hindi New Testament published by Bible Society of India in 1967. 'Dalit' is the most apt rendering for the 'oppressed' because Dalits are primarily the victims of caste system which is the root cause of all forms of oppression in Indian context. They face multiple oppressions because of their caste identity.[15] Therefore, the mission agenda of Jesus Christ cannot be understood apart from the liberation of Dalits. The salvation/liberation offered by Jesus Christ is also the liberation from the bondage of different oppressions operative in society. At the same time, the Nazareth manifesto addresses both the oppressed and the oppressors. The captives and the blind primarily represent the dominant people who are prisoners of oppressive ideologies and structures, and are blind to the egalitarian values. The Nazareth manifesto ultimately aims to establish a liberated human society where both the oppressed and the oppressors are fully liberated from oppressed conditions and oppressive thinking respectively. In order to achieve the goal of liberated human society, Jesus Christ emphasized the equality of human beings in his teachings and attempted to empower the marginalized through his actions of solidarity. He boldly challenged the claims of the dominant in society and brought the dominated into the centre stage of his teachings and actions. For him, domination was not the will of God. Therefore, he always opposed the oppressive behavior of the dominant.[16] It places Jesus' mission more closely to the Dalits in India. Moreover, Jesus risked his whole life to carry out his mission agenda. He had to pay the price for his solidarity with the poor and the oppressed.[17] Jesus' mission of solidarity prioritized not only to enlarge the social space of the poor and the excluded ones but also to transform the dominant groups.[18]

The mission of solidarity began with the announcement of the 'Jubilee Year or the Year of Lord's favor.' It was an announcement of radical transformation that would initiate God's reign on earth. It envisaged not only radical economic changes (Lev.25:10) but also fundamental change in the cultural, social and political structures (Luke 4:19) which perpetuated oppressive outlook in society. Reign of God was actually begun with the announcement of the Year of Lord's favor and subsequent ministry of Jesus Christ. Now, it is the responsibility of Jesus' followers to take forward his mission started by announcing the Year of Lord's favor.[19] The year of Lord's favor (liberation) becomes a reality in the life of the oppressed if actions of solidarity are initiated.

The mission of solidarity cannot be done without breaking the barriers of race, gender, color and caste. Jesus showed us how to break those barriers. Solidarity breaks the barriers and paves the way for new beginning, new order, new outlook and new world. He always promoted a new social order contrary to the existing order which was racial, oppressive and patriarchal. He taught through parables and stories that caste/race/gender based social order produces unjust social equations/relations in society. It not only divides the society but also establishes the hegemony of one group over the other.[20] The story of Good Samaritan (Luke 10:25-37) is an attempt to reverse the social order which considered Samaritans were impure and not qualified to be the neighbors of Jews. The Samaritans were considered socially inferior and were treated as 'untouchables' in Jesus' time. They were excluded from the social relations of Jews. In fact, they were Dalits in the first century Palestinian society. Like Samaritans, Dalits were/are also categorized as socially inferior people, and were called as 'untouchables.' The caste people never considered Dalits as their neighbors. As Jews never used the cups and bowls used by the Samaritans, so the caste people promoted two tumblers practice-one for the untouchable and other for the touchable caste- in public places. In the story of Good Samaritan, the third person, a Samaritan played the role of a good neighbor. He cared the wounded and saved his life. Today, he also stands as a model for human solidarity with the socially wounded. Through this story, Jesus argued that Samaritan who was considered as impure could be a good neighbor. This was a call to reverse the social order maintained by the Jews of his time. It is also a call to reverse the caste -based social order in India. In his dialogue with the Samaritan woman (John 4: 1-41), a Dalit woman in Indian context, Jesus Christ attacked the patriarchal social order which prohibited a public conversation with a woman, particularly a Samaritan woman. Jesus promoted a social order where women also get space to interact and share their feelings and thoughts. Jesus not only attempted for new social order but also an economic order. In the Parable of Laborers (Matthew 20: 1-16) Jesus introduced an alternate economic order which provides equal opportunities of employment and equal wages.[21] In the globalised economic order, while the caste people occupy high profile job opportunities, the qualified Dalits either have to satisfy with low profile jobs or to face unemployment. In India, private enterprises are owned by caste people who prefer their own men and women for important assignments. Moreover, Dalits are employed as laborers of big projects, but are given low wages. In the present economic order, Dalits are deprived of equal employment opportunities and equal wages. Thus Jesus' economic order of laborers is significant in today's context where Dalits face unemployment and exploitation of their labor by private enterprises and multi-national companies.

Jesus' visit at Zacchaeus house (Luke 19:1-10) is a practical expression of His mission of solidarity based on the principles of love, humility, hope and critical thinking. He reached out to the people who were considered as sinners in society. Jesus took a critical position which was contrary to the existing social thinking. Jesus' approach transformed the mind-set of the rich tax collector[22] who otherwise would have continued his allegedly fraudulent way of tax collection which economically exploited the poor. The mission of solidarity liberates the oppressed and transforms the oppressors and the sinners.

In short, the Nazareth manifesto explains the content of Jesus' mission. His mission was primarily a mission of solidarity with the oppressed. It reminds his followers, particularly the Church, to redefine the nature of its mission in the light of the mission of solidarity. The Church has to prioritize solidarity with the socially, economically and religiously oppressed peoples in her mission ventures. Along with the transformation of whole society, the empowerment of the oppressed, the natural outcome of the mission of solidarity has to get special focus in today's mission programme. For Dalits, Nazareth manifesto places them in the centre of Jesus' mission of solidarity in India. Their liberation is an accomplishment of Jesus' mission in contemporary society. In the mission initiatives, they must be educated about their rights and enable them to stand for their liberation. Their liberation is actually the liberation of their oppressors too because Dalits will be not completely liberated unless radical transformation does happen in the caste psyche of caste people. Both happen in the process of doing the mission of solidarity.

Theology of Solidarity and Whole Salvation

Human life is multi-dimensional reality. It cannot be limited either to the physical realm or to the spiritual realm. It is a beautiful combination of both dimensions if we don't go for strict compartmentalization. The experience of salvation/liberation also has to be understood within the framework of the holistic view of life: viewing human life as a whole. Salvation is not a compartmentalized reality in human life. It touches every aspect of one's life. Therefore, physical/material liberation is as equally important as spiritual liberation. Every human life needs salvation which is wholistic in nature. The idea of spiritual salvation, other worldly salvation, may not motivate the people who are involved in the journey of struggles for liberation in this world. Even if they seek out only spiritual salvation, they cannot escape from the question of life in this world. Therefore, while seeking spiritual salvation, they must attempt to eliminate the physical oppression which hinders their experience of salvation in this world. Salvation in this world refers to a dignified life which experiences freedom, respect, justice and peace. The historical interventions of biblical God and the nature of Jesus' mission inform us that Divine Solidarity with humanity is ultimately aimed to achieve the whole salvation-the salvation in this world and the world to come. It is an experience of freedom from both physical and spiritual bondages. The Bible, in fact, teaches about the whole salvation of entire creation. In the Old Testament, salvation is understood as freedom from any physical factor or condition which prevents the celebration of life in its fullness. It can be deliverance from physical illness, natural disaster, oppressive life situations, captivity etc. The liberation of Israelites from the bondage of Egyptians is the best example of the Old Testament understanding of salvation. For the Israelites, the freedom from captivity was a salvific experience because slavery restricted the progress of their personal and community life. The liberation from Babylonian captivity, for them, was also an experience of salvation. The beauty of these salvation experiences was that they experienced the Solidarity of God in their enslaved conditions. Indeed, this Divine Solidarity enabled them to initiate the process of liberation. The salvific experiences of Israelites define salvation as this-worldly reality, and it cannot be limited to personal realm alone.[23] It is an experience of personal and community freedom from the life-negating powers in society. Therefore, this-worldly aspect of salvation cannot be ignored in the practical understanding of biblical salvation.

In his mission of solidarity, Jesus adopted a wholistic approach to the salvation of humanity. The very purpose of Jesus' life and mission was to achieve the whole salvation/liberation of people. The change he wanted to bring was wholistic in nature: personal and societal. This was the rationale behind his mission of solidarity. For that, he addressed not only to the spiritually blind but also to the physically oppressed. In order to achieve the aim of whole salvation, he touched the social, economic, religious and social aspects of life.[24] His life and mission, an epitome of divine solidarity with humanity, attempted to liberate people from both spiritual and physical bondages. He did not compartmentalize the salvation experience, but upheld a wholistic view of it in his teachings and actions. The social, political and economic empowerment of people, particularly the oppressed among them is part of the whole salvation offered by God in Jesus Christ. Jesus' mission undoubtedly proves it. While Jesus emphasized holistic salvation in terms of physical and spiritual aspects of life, he also offered salvation for every one-both the oppressors and the oppressed (Dalits). This is another dimension of whole salvation. Whereas the oppressed lost their dignity and humanhood because of oppressive mechanisms, the oppressors lost their divinely created humanity because of their involvement in the process of exploiting the oppressed. Therefore, both need salvation. For Dalits, the oppressors need to be liberated from their oppressive caste psyche which perpetuates the exclusion of Dalits. The salvation is both physical and spiritual, and involves both the oppressed and the oppressors. They aim for a liberated society, based on Christ-event of redemption, where everyone will be in the process of liberation.[25] Dalits need whole salvation which saves them in every area of their lives. For them, salvation becomes holistic if it brings community liberation than individual liberation. In a caste society, they primarily aim for a salvation experience in which they are completely liberated from the bondage of caste hegemony. It is a community experience which goes beyond faith and ideology.[26] Whole salvation basically emphasizes human development along with spiritual empowerment. Spiritual liberation alone does not help Dalits to live dignified life. In a society where Dalits are deprived of their status because of the lack of economic and social empowerment, holistic human development becomes an essential element of their salvation experience.[27] Human development along with spiritual liberation will only enable the Dalits to begin their liberation process[28] towards whole salvation. If salvation is only limited to physical or spiritual realm, then it is 'partial' salvation. Christian understanding of salvation is 'whole salvation' which addresses 'this-worldly' and 'other-worldly' concerns of human life. The work of Divine Solidarity revealed in Jesus Christ affirms the Whole Salvation of humanity, particularly the oppressed and points to the mission of the Church on this earth: Mission of Solidarity.

Divine Solidarity through Human Solidarity

God expressed liberating Solidarity through human beings in history. Therefore, human solidarity for liberation can be considered as a manifestation of divine solidarity in the world. Divine Solidarity was/is for the whole salvation of human beings, particularly the oppressed among them. It demands human beings to express their solidarity with fellow beings, particularly those who strive to celebrate their lives in fullness. Theology of Solidarity invites the oppressed communities like Dalits to experience Divine Solidarity through their solidarity for achieving the liberation and upward social mobility in this world, which will continue in the world to come. The solidarity leads them to empowerment and privileged condition. It also gives them the confidence to resist the oppressive forces. In social life, Dalits basically strive for equal social standing which eventually leads them to power and privileges. For them, dignified life comes first in the pursuit of holistic empowerment. Instead of succumbing into the trap of caste people who always want the oppressed communities divided, Dalits irrespective of sub-caste and creed need to stand in solidarity to achieve their goal of whole salvation. Community solidarity generates power within and creates the space in society.

The political power has facilitated economic empowerment and social mobility of certain communities in India. Dalits, who constitute the sizable number of voters in many constituencies, often fails to prove their strength in electoral politics. This constituency has strong political potential in society. Unfortunately, Dalits are ideologically and politically divided and unable to wield the political power and influence the corridors of power. It calls for Dalits to build up solidarity which can pave the way for their political empowerment. It can enlarge the political space of Dalits and makes them politically powerful constituency in society. Political power is a necessity because it facilitates constructive interventions to deliver social justice. The solidarity which led to the liberation of the people of Israel was political in nature too. God sided with them to demand their legitimate right of being free from the bondage of Pharaoh. This same God challenges Dalits to take bold steps of political solidarity to end the life of exclusion.

The Dalits are historical victims of exploitative economic structure maintained by the caste system. On the one hand they were not allowed to own economic resources like land; on the other hand, their jobs were considered as polluted. The caste-based economic outlook still contributes to the economic disempowerment of Dalits. Arundhati Roy once observed that "When you look at India, through the prism of caste, at who control the money, who owns the corporations, who owns the big media, who makes up judiciary, the bureaucracy, who owns the land, who doesn't-contemporary India suddenly begins to look extremely un-contemporary."[29] The 'un-contemporary' reality is that the socially poor (Dalits) continue to be economically poor in India. It demands Dalits to come together and stand for economic justice. Jignesh Mewani, a Dalit leader, rightly observed that both social justice and economic justice are equally important in Dalit assertions[30] (Solidarity Assertions). In order to achieve economic empowerment, Dalits, particularly educated and successful among them, should take bold initiatives in the form of establishing educational institutions, generating job opportunities by starting industrial units, community development programs etc. God of Solidarity invites the empowered Dalits to primarily identify with their disempowered brothers and sisters who deserve preferential considerations. Dalit solidarity for social, political and economic empowerment is an expression of Divine Solidarity which works for the whole salvation of the oppressed communities. Theology of Solidarity reminds us the need of identifying with the oppressed as Biblical God expressed solidarity with an oppressed community in history. Any form of solidarity becomes a channel of Divine power if it is expressed for the cause of liberating those who live a disempowered life. Every Christian is called to become an embodiment of Divine Solidarity.

Endnotes

1 James Massey, *Dalit Roots of Christianity, Theology and Spirituality* (New Delhi: CDS, 2008), 39-42.

2 James Massey, *Dalit Roots of Christianity, Theology and Spirituality*, 35-36.

3 James Massey, "History and Dalit Theology," in *Frontiers of Dalit Theology*, edited by V. Devasahayam (Chennai: ISPCK/Gurukul, 1997), 179-180.

4 James Massey, "A Review of Dalit Theology" in *Dalit and Minjung Theologies: A Dialogue*, edited by Samson Prabhakar and Jinkwan Kwon (Bangalore: BTESSC/SATHRI, 2006), 7-8.

5 James Massey, "A Review of Dalit Theology," 8.

6 James Massey, "Mandal Commission Report: A Christian Perspective," *Religion and Society* Vol XXXVII/No. 4 (December, 1990): 40-49 at 44.

7 James Massey, "A Review of Dalit Theology," 9.

8 James Massey, "History and Dalit Theology," 181.

9 James Massey, *Ecumenism Means Justice* (Matiala, New Delhi: CDS, 2014), 21-22.

10 James Massey, *Dalit Theology: History, Context, Text and Whole Salvation* (New Delhi: Manohar, 2013), 177.

11 James Massey, *Dalit Bible Commentary, Old Testament Vol. 5, Judges* (New Delhi: CDS, 2012), 85.

12 James Massey, *Dalit Bible Commentary, Old Testament Vol. 10, Ezra, Nehemiah and Tobit* (New Delhi: CDS, 2013), 33.

13 James Massey, *Ecumenism Means Justice*, 24.

14 James Massey, *Dalit Theology: History, Context, Text and Whole Salvation*, 207-208.

15 James Massey, *Ecumenism Means Justice*, 26.

16 James Massey, *Dalit Theology: History, Context, Text and Whole Salvation*, 209.

17 James Massey, *Ecumenism Means Justice*, 27.

[18] James Massey, *Dalit Bible Commentary, New Testament Vol. 3, The Gospel According to Luke* (New Delhi: CDS, 2007), 160.

[19] James Massey, *Ecumenism Means Justice,* 26.

[20] James Massey, *Ecumenism Means Justice,* 35.

[21] James Massey, *Dalit Theology: History, Context, Text and Whole Salvation,* 210.

[22] James Massey, *Dalit Theology: History, Context, Text and Whole Salvation,* 211.

[23] James Massey, *Dalit Bible Commentary, Old Testament Vol. 9, 1 & 2 Chronicles* (New Delhi: CDS, 2012), 138-139.

[24] James Massey, "Mandal Commission Report: A Christian Perspective," 45.

[25] James Massey, *Ecumenism Means Justice,* 37.

[26] James Massey, *Dalit Theology: History, Context, Text and Whole Salvation,* 211.

[27] James Massey, *Dalit Bible Commentary, Old Testament Vol. 17, Jeremiah, Lamentations, Baruch* (New Delhi: CDS, 2012), 115-116.

[28] James Massey, *Dalit Bible Commentary, Old Testament Vol. 17, Jeremiah, Lamentations, Baruch,* 157.

[29] Saba Naqvi, "We need Ambedkar-Now urgently..." *Outlook* (10 March 2014, New Delhi), 29.

[30] *The Hindu* (Vijayawada, Friday September 23, 2016), 10.

Chapter 3

Caste, Religion and Exclusion

In India, socio-economic-political standing of a community is decided by many factors. Among them, caste plays a 'historical' role in the advancement of communities. While caste identity opens up new opportunities of progress for some communities; it works against the prospects and possibilities of others in the process of empowerment. Some make use of their numerical strength and bargain with political system, and create their space in society. Whereas religious identity works for some to improve their socio-economic-political standing; it does not do the same job with others. There are many communities which could not come up in the socio-economic and political ladder of the society because of their caste identity and religious affiliation. The Christians of Scheduled Caste Origin (also known as Dalit Christians) is one of such communities neglected and excluded in various spheres of the societal life due to their caste and faith identities. This chapter takes an effort to highlight and reflect on the excluded life-realities of Dalit Christians in contemporary society. While engaging with other sources, this chapter heavily depends on *Christians of Scheduled Caste Origin in India: The Study of Their Socio-Economic, Cultural and Political Status*, a study jointly conducted by Centre for Dalit/ Subaltern Studies, New Delhi, Commission for SC/ST/BC of the

Catholic Bishops Conference of India, New Delhi and Delhi School of Social Work Society, Delhi. It was carried out under the leadership of James Massey. This study has brought out the present standing of the Christians of Scheduled Caste Origin in social, economic, political and educational realms of life.

Caste and Religion: Factors of Exclusion

In India, 'exclusion' has its historical roots in the institution of caste. The creation story narrated in the hymn, *Purushasukta* in *Rigveda* is considered as the source of the institution of caste. It spells out four orders, namely *Brahman*, *Rajanya* (Kshatriya), *Vaisya* and *Sudra,* respectively originated from the four parts of the *Purusa,* the embodied spirit: the mouth, the arms, the thighs and the feet. Occupationally, they represented the priest, the king, the tradesman and the laboring man correspondingly. Later these four orders evolved into numerous castes.[1] The classification in creation story was the beginning of exclusion in Indian society. It not only assigned particular vocation to the people of different orders but also excluded the people from taking up other's line of work. For instance, it excluded non-Brahmins to become priest and non-Kshatriyas to become kings. The Sudras are fully excluded from doing these two jobs. The Hindu literatures like *Manusmriti* further strengthened the idea of 'exclusion' by prescribing more social regulations. It can be noticed in *Manusmriti* x: 51-52, "But the dwellings of *Kandalas* and *Svapakas* shall be outside the village...their wealth (shall be) dogs and donkeys. Their dress (shall be) the garments of the dead, (they shall eat) their food from the broken dishes, black iron (shall be) their ornaments, and they must be always wandered from place to place."[2] These verses show the negation of dignified life and the creation of excluded communities in society; and virtually gave momentum to place more communities in the box of exclusion/ excluded life.

'Purity and Pollution,' one of the essential features of caste system, intensified the life of exclusion. In the earlier days, the twice-born castes[3] used to take *pakka* food (cooked in ghee) only from certain castes. They never used to accept any kind of food from some castes but if necessary only water. At the same time, they never used to take even water from some castes.[4] It shows that by following the caste rules, the high castes excluded the low castes in the social relations. In ancient Kerala, there were two kinds of pollution: atmospheric pollution and pollution by touch. Atmospheric pollution was caused by the approach of Nayadi, Pulayan, Kanisan and Mukkuvan (fishermen) less than 72 feet, 64 feet, 36 feet and 24 feet respectively. The Muslims, Syrian Christians and foreign Hindus constituted the second category of pollution.[5] Except Brahmins, certain fixed distances and manners were stipulated to all castes to avoid pollution. In Travancore Kingdom in ancient Kerala, a Nair was allowed to approach a Brahmin but not to touch him. The Ezhavas and the Nadars had to stand at distance of 36 steps from a Brahmin. A Pulayan was not allowed to approach a Brahmin less than 96 steps. The Nadars and Ezhavas were permitted to approach a Nair at the distance of 12 steps. A Pulayan had to keep 66 steps off from a Nair. Though it was not acceptable all over in the country, a Syrian Christian was allowed to touch a Nair. But a Nair would not eat with a Syrian Christian. The Pulayas and Pariahs used to approach other castes within fixed distance, but never allowed to touch. The shadow of these slave castes was also considered as object of pollution.[6] This is just a representative example of the caste-ridden Indian society in the early period. The rules of purity-pollution kept out or excluded mainly the low castes (presently Other Backward Classes-OBCs) and the untouchables (presently Scheduled Castes or Dalits) from the mainstream of the society. Their privileges and rights were defined within the framework of purity and pollution.

Their societal advancement (social-economic-religious) was made impossible by the purity-pollution notion of the caste. Indeed, they were excluded from dignified life. Thus, the mechanism of caste created excluded communities historically.

The technological revolution and high profile entrepreneurial and managerial progress of 21st century have not altered the attitude of Indian mind that is immersed in caste consciousness.[7] Mandal Commission Report is right when it says "In India caste system has endured for over 3000 years and even today there appears no symptoms of its early demise."[8] The historical role of caste in creating excluded communities is continuing persistently. It is to be noted that the historical victims of caste still face exclusion in one form or the other in the socio-economic-political-religious context of India today.

Religion is another factor which creates excluded communities. According to the Constitution of India, our nation is Sovereign Socialist Secular Democratic Republic.[9] It does not have a state religion, and all religions are constitutionally treated equal. Article 15 (1) denounces any kind of discrimination on the ground of religion, "The State shall not discriminate against any citizen on grounds only of religion, race, caste, sex, place of birth or any of them."[10] Article 25 (1) guarantees religious freedom, "Subject to public order, morality and health and to the other provisions of this Part, all persons are equally entitled to freedom of conscience and the right freely to profess, practice and propagate religion."[11] Though these two articles are well meant in the content, they could not stop creating excluded communities. Best example in this regard is the Constitution (Scheduled Castes) Order, 1950 commonly known as 'Presidential Order 1950'. According to this Order, Scheduled Caste status (SC status) can be given only to the person who professes Hindu religion. Later, it was amended by the Parliament to extend the SC status to the Sikh in 1956 and to the Buddhist in 1990.[12] Thus, at present, the Dalits who belong to Hinduism, Sikhism and Buddhism only can avail SC status. It means the Dalits who belong to Christianity, Islam etc do not come legally or constitutionally under the category of Scheduled Castes. Therefore, they cannot be benefitted by the welfare schemes of government, reservation and legal protection given to the Scheduled Castes.[13] The Constitution of India says there must not be any discrimination in the name of religion, but the Presidential order 1950 excludes Dalit Christians, Dalits Muslims etc from getting the privileges of Scheduled Caste status.

The secular fabric of the nation is threatened by the surfacing of majority religious nationalism in the contemporary socio-political context. Hindutva ideologists and political outfits define nationalism in terms of majority religion (Hinduism). It excludes the religious minority communities such as Christians and Muslims from the mainstream of the society and creates communal divisions. The anti-conversion bills passed by various states are part of the strategy of majority religious nationalism. They are against the spirit of Constitution, and curb the religious freedom of the citizens.[14]

It is true that caste and religion create excluded communities in different spheres of life in Indian society. While some face exclusion solely because of their caste identity, others by the religious identity. Still some face exclusion due to caste and religious identities. Among them, Christians of Scheduled Caste Origin (Dalit Christians) are most affected in the Indian society. They face exclusion from different corners within the church and society.[15] Before discussing about their experiences of exclusion/excluded life, it is important to have a glance on the present context of Christian community in India whose frame of mind and involvement are crucial for the holistic empowerment of Dalit Christians.

Christian Community in Changing Context: Quantity, Quality, and Identity

St. Thomas, one of the disciples of Jesus, is traditionally believed to have brought the Christian faith in India in 52 AD. Catholic, Protestant, Evangelical and Pentecostal missionaries came in different periods, and established their respective ecclesiastical systems and traditions. The people from different social backgrounds became Christians throughout the centuries. The missionaries and the native Christians established Churches, schools, colleges, hospitals etc as part of their missions in different parts of the nation. Consequently, Christianity emerged as one of the religious traditions/communities in India. As it stands today as one of the minority religious communities in the changing context of 21st century India, it's condition is not encouraging in terms of its existence and witness, particularly in relation to the advancement of the Christians of Scheduled Caste Origin, more than half of its members.

Quantitative Decline

According to the Census of India 2011, the Christians constitute only 2.3% (2.78crores) of the total population of India.[16] 46% of Indian Christians live in five southern states. Seven north eastern states and Goa are home to 30% of Christians. Rest of the country accommodates 24% of the Christian population.[17] When we analyze censuses of 1981, 2001 and 2011 there is decline in the number of Christians. In 1981, Christians were 2.42 % of total population. In 2001, it came down to 2.34%. In 2011, the percentage remains the same. It means within 30 years, according to the government data, there is no growth in Christianity. One of the main reasons for the 'official' decline is dual-religious membership. For example, a number of Dalit Christians keep 'Hindu identity' in their official documents for getting Scheduled Caste privileges. Many of them have returned to Hindu fold also.[18] Of course, the mission organizations can claim otherwise. There may be truth in their claims too. Even if we believe the claims of mission organizations, the present growth does not do justice to the economic and human resources spent till the date. The geographical presence of Christianity-more in Southern and North Eastern States and less in Northern States- does not support the growth stories.

But whatever may be the claims and disclaims on the quantity, one can not negate the fact that the growth of Christianity is declining at least in the official records. It has its own ramifications. In the 'vote bank politics' context where quantity (number) plays a role for considering the demands and concerns of a community, the decline in quantity may not enthusiastically attract the attention of the political class of any ideological spectrum to the needs of Christian community, particularly the Dalit Christians. The political groups/ parties, which mainly depend on the official data on numbers, are well aware about the quantity of Christians and their inability of becoming pressure group. The role of quantity clearly reflects in the statement of George Joseph quoted by B.R. Ambedkar in his discussion on 'Does the Indian Christian Community count in India?' "Christians do not count, because they are small in numbers."[19] It implies that to be counted for anything in India, number is a matter. If one thinks in line with quantity, it can be inferred that the decline of Christians in number at least in 'official records' and the consequent lacking of political pressurizing directly affects the attempts of Dalit Christians to get Scheduled Caste (SC) status. The Dalit Sikhs and Dalit Buddhists were able to achieve the SC status because of the political bargaining with numerical strength of respective religious communities. The Christian community fails either to disprove the official records on its quantity if it is contradictory to the actual strength or to become politically pressure group in the present context for raising united voice for Dalit Christians.

Decline in Qualitative Faith Life

The quality in life and witness is fundamental to the Christian faith. Here, quality is understood in terms of outlook and action informed by the teachings of Jesus Christ. The early missionaries sacrificed their lives and upheld the quality of Christian faith in word and in action. As stands today, qualitative Christian faith life has been questioned in different spheres. First of all, Christian community in India is a divided house more than ever in its history. Christians are divided in such way that they cannot unite in near future. It is not a secret that the denominations are not able to come together sincerely at least in the programme/issue level. This division actually contradicts the idea of Christian community as Body of Christ. B.R. Ambedkar articulated the division within Christianity long back in this way:

> The Indian Christian is a disjointed-it is a better word than the word disunited-community. All that it has in common is a common source of inspiration. Baring this one thing which they have in common everything else tends to keep them apart. Indian Christians like all other Indians are divided by race, by language and by caste. Their religion has not been a sufficiently strong unifying force as to make difference of language, race and caste as though they were mere distinctions. On the contrary their religion which is their only cement is infected with denominational differences. The result is that the Indian Christians are too disjointed to have a common aim, to have common mind and to put a common endeavour...In short, the term Indian Christian is just a statistical phrase. There is no community feeling behind this phrase. Indian Christians are not bound together by what is consciousness of kind, which is the test of the existence of a community.[20]

This 'disjointness' challenges the prospects of Christianity in the 21st century. Secondly, the Christians lost their witness in service sector. Majority of the Christian educational institutions actually serve the elite Hindus and Christians. They are inaccessible to the poor in society. It reminds us the life of Jesus who empowered the poor with his teachings (knowledge) freely. With a few exceptions, Christian hospitals are also unaffordable to the poor. This tendency is a blatant negation of the ministry of Jesus who healed the sick freely. It does not mean that hospitals should not charge, but they can be made affordable to the poor. Moreover, the institutions such as schools and hospitals do not serve the mission purpose too. As Ambedkar said,

> Even today, hundreds and thousands of high caste Hindus take advantage of Christian schools, Christian colleges and Christian hospitals. How many of those who reap these benefits become Christians? Every one of them takes the benefit and runs away and does not even stop to consider what must be the merits of a religion, which renders so much service to humanity.[21]

This is very much true in our context. Thirdly, the Christians in the government sector as high officials and administrators are not untouched by the culture of bribe. Fourthly, denominations and dioceses are either formed or functioned on the basis of caste or ethnic origin. Fifthly, gender prejudices prevail in community life and ministerial space. It is against the biblical teaching that men and women are created in the image of God. Sixthly, politicians and representatives of the people belong to the Christian community are being caught in corrupt cases. Finally, the morality of Christian leaders including Bishops, priests, pastors etc is being questioned in today's society. In short, today, the Christian community cannot claim qualitative faith-life informed by the teachings of Jesus Christ. Quality of faith is tested in the actions which negate discrimination, immorality and stereotyping within and outside the community. The lack/decline of qualitative faith life discourages the Christians as a community to involve intentionally in the life-realities and the problems of Dalit Christians in society.

Caste/Ethnic Identity over Faith Identity

The nature of the present existence of Christian community in India leads to the question that whether faith decides their identity or caste or ethnic origin defines their identity? Logically, the identity of Christians should be defined by their faith. Unfortunately, his/her identity is defined by caste/ethnic origin along with faith. Therefore, at present, we have not Christians as such in the strict sense of the term 'Christian,' but Reddy Christians, Nadar Christians, Syrian Christians, Dalit Christians, Tribal Christians etc. Irrespective of denominations, this identity formation has been promoted and maintained. In fact, the faith identity is being replaced by caste identity. It is also unfortunate that faith identity alone will not work out in terms of genuine fellowship and communion in Christian community today. Amartya Sen is right when he says, "A strong-and exclusive-sense of belonging to one group can in many cases carry with it the perception of distance and divergence from other groups. Within-group solidarity can help to feed between-group discord."[22]The caste identity within faith community and the inability to affirm faith identity beyond caste/ethnic barriers place the Christian community in predicament in terms of identity, witness and unity. The tendency of placing/preferring caste identity over faith identity creates visible or invisible divisions and exclusions within the faith community, and dissuades the Christian community to identify with the cause of the Christians of Scheduled Caste and their development in the society.

It can be noted from the above discussion that the present Christian community which is quantitatively and qualitatively declining, denominationally divided and preferring caste/ethnic identities is not able to be genuinely sided with the Christians of Scheduled Caste Origin. This badly affects the attempts of Dalit Christians to remove their excluded life realities.

Christians of Scheduled Caste Origin in India: Excluded by Caste and Religion

As per the available data, 16.6% of Indian population is Scheduled Castes (SC).[23] It is calculated in the recent census that only 21.9% of SC houses are made with concrete roof. 58.2 % of their houses are floored by mud. 46.6% houses have only one room.[24] This description is a minute aspect of the *unequal* life condition of Dalits in India. They are the real *unequals* in society. They are the victims of the interplay of caste, religion and politics in the contemporary society. Among them, the Christians of Scheduled Caste Origin suffer more discrimination and exclusion. Christians of Scheduled Caste Origin have been historically discriminated and disadvantaged by the Church and the Government.[25] Though they constitute majority of the Indian Church their caste identity works against their advancement in the Church, particularly in the multi-racial churches, due to the casteist mind-set of the ecclesiastical authorities. Because of their faith affiliation, they are excluded from all constitutional rights and privileges, and welfare programmes and policies of the Government which they are entitled to enjoy as people of Scheduled Caste Origin. Indeed, they are in identity crisis, discriminated, less heard in the corridors of power, and less conscientized of the reasons for their present condition and predicament.

Christians of Scheduled Caste Origin: Life of Exclusion

Though the exact numerical strength of the Dalit Christians is uncertain due to the lack of systematic study, most of the scholars place their proportion between 50 and 75% of the total Christian population in India.[26] However, it is generally observed that the

Christians of Scheduled caste origin constitute majority of the Indian Christians.[27] They mainly come from the communities previously branded as 'untouchables' in society. It has been viewed that conversion has not fulfilled their dream of dignified life and identity. It has not changed their social status in the eyes of non-Dalits particularly, the upper castes in society and within the church. Still, they carry the stigma of low caste origin.[28] Often, they are addressed along with their caste names in pejorative sense. They bear the pain and humiliation in silence.[29] The co-religionists regard them as 'socially inferior.' It is strange to note that they are considered first as Dalits and then as Christians within and outside the faith community.[30] While they are defined and treated within the framework of caste in the Church and society, they are excluded by fellow Dalits and Government due to their faith affiliation. In fact, they experience discrimination and exclusion: in the society, within the church, among the Dalits and by the Government. This leads them to the identity crisis: whether faith or caste defines the identity. For them, both block their advancement in life, and negate adequate space in society and church. The ill-treatment within the church makes it more painful for them than in the society. The Dalit Christian housings are segregated from that of the high castes in many of the Christian villages or locations. It is not uncommon that there are separate church buildings and cemeteries for the Christians of Scheduled caste origin.[31] Though faith identity prevents them to get privileges and resources from the government, they live as risk-takers of faith on strong foundation.[32] The discriminated life realities of Dalit Christians lead to the point that they live a life of exclusion as they lived before changing their faith. With conversion, they might have got new religious identity along with other identities, but not the 'milk and honey' in form of equality, dignity and recognition as promised by the new faith.

Education as Tool of Empowerment: Still a Dream

Like other disadvantaged communities, Christians of Scheduled Caste Origin are denied of equal education opportunities to equip themselves in life with right perspective and to develop job skills in the changing economic scenario. It thwarts their materialistic and social empowerment. In the education sector, many of them face discriminations such as negation of admissions, ill-treatment, separate seating arrangements, refusal to give drinking water, refusal to serve lunch/ mid meals etc. Though literacy rate is reasonable, majority of them are either dropouts or discontinue before they reach high school. Graduates among them are very small in number, and still less people have taken up technical education.[33] This miserable situation is mainly due to the lack of economic resources, limited access to higher educational facilities and unaffordable education system.[34] Who are the culprits for this condition-Church or Government? Both are responsible in their respective capacities. As Christians, Christians of Scheduled Caste Origin put their trust in the schools and colleges run by the Church. Instead of providing quality education to the Dalit Christians, they serve mostly the upper caste Hindus and Christians who can manage to pay for the same. One cannot negate the fact that though the church manages best schools, Dalit Christians still cannot achieve quality education to develop quality life which consequently leads to community empowerment.[35] Compared to non-Dalit co-religionists Dalit Christians are educationally backward.[36] The Government is also equally responsible for the unequal educational status of Dalit Christians. Since the Christians of Scheduled Caste Origin are not entitled for reservation benefits, they are excluded from various scholarships of Government for higher education. While education functions as a tool of empowerment for other communities, it is a daydream for the Dalit Christians to be materialized. Therefore,

Government and church should develop education policies and programmes which consciously incorporate the Christians of Scheduled Caste Origin. The church should take a moral stand that she will not serve the influential minority at the cost of neglecting the powerless and voiceless majority through her educational institutions.

'Outcaste' in the Economically Liberalized Context: Disempowered

The caste system, which defined the status of Dalits Christians in society and church, continues to decide their economic condition also. Like their forebears, the Christians of Scheduled Caste Origin carry the stigma of economic deprivation even today. The caste people treated the ancestors of Dalit Christians as slaves, squeezed their labor power, and deprived them of land and resources. The economic deprivation of their forebears directly or indirectly has influenced the present situation of Christians of Scheduled Caste Origin.[37]

Most of the Dalit Christians are economically poor suffering poverty, misery, etc.[38] Majority of them is landless agricultural laborers or casual laborers.[39] Though very few of them are employed in government and in private sectors, majority of such employed are working in sweeper or last grade categories in Municipal Corporation, hospitals and banks. Those who are working as plumbers, electricians, drivers, or cooks have to be satisfied with a meager amount of salary. Majority of them are not able to meet the daily expenses with the income they get through ordinary jobs. A very few educated people are in the so-called comfortable positions, but not in key places. They face discrimination even from their subordinates.[40]

Regarding the possession of land, majority of Dalit Christians possess less than one acre land. That too is dry land.[41] The living conditions of Dalit Christians in the rural areas are same with the fellow Dalits of other religious groups.[42] Majority of them do not have proper housing and are deprived of civic amenities. They don't have regular income to meet the basic needs and the educational expenses of their children. Most of the banks are not ready to provide them loan for education or housing or other job-oriented initiatives. They are trapped in debts by money lenders. Often they are not given proper salary in rural areas. They are exploited in mines, construction sites and other sectors where hard labor is needed.[43] Moreover, caste prejudices discriminate them in job opportunities. In fact, they face occupational segregation in economically liberalized society.[44] On the one hand, lack of education restricts them to do only agricultural jobs; on the other hand, they are forced to do their traditional jobs even if they have proper education. It is sad to note that neither church nor Government is sincerely concerned about the economic emancipation of Dalit Christians. They continue their journey as economic 'outcaste' in the economically liberalized global context of 21st century. They are not able to taste the cake of so-called national economic growth along with others. They are 'outside' the box of development due to the lack of education and negligence of government machineries. Hence, the economic empowerment of the Christians of Scheduled Caste Origin should become one of the main priorities of church and Government to end their economic deprivation.

Participation in Political Process: Outside the Camp

In a democratic country like India, participation in politics and decision making process is imperative for the advancement of any community. It is a known fact that all government decisions, policies and welfare programmes are 'political' in nature. Those who are in the decision making bodies/ structures are either politicians or bureaucrats/government officials who naturally plan and execute the programmes in line with the policies of political parties/coalition in power. Decisions, which they take, are sometimes positive for certain communities/groups and negative for others. Therefore, participation in decision making process plays an important role in the development of any community, particularly disadvantaged community like Christians of Scheduled Caste Origin.

The Dalit Christians are politically discriminated in all levels of the political process of our nation. They are excluded because of their caste identity and faith-affiliation. They experience political discrimination in different forms. In many rural / urban locations, their presence in the local political meetings/campaign is not appreciated by the upper caste people. Either they are excluded from the list of candidates in local/assembly/parliament elections or forced to withdraw from the contest. Even if they are getting elected in the decision making bodies, they are often silenced by the upper caste members. Their voice is less valued. Political discrimination of Dalit Christians does not end with their exclusion from decision making process and election. The worst is the violation of fundament political right guaranteed by the Constitution of India: Right to Vote. Many times, they were threatened to vote in favor of particular political party or candidate, and even obstructed to cast their vote. Moreover, many of their names are not in the voter list. Even if they overcome those casteist political hurdles, the maximum political position they may achieve is Panchayat membership. It is not only high caste Hindus but also caste Christians obstructs the political participation of the Christians of Scheduled Caste Origin.[45] In sum, the political entry of Dalits Christians is mainly blocked by Caste and Faith. Since, they are not entitled for reservation; they cannot try their political fortunes in the reserved constituencies. His/her faith-identity works against reservation benefits. While an upper caste Christian can get elected either in a Christian dominated or general constituency, a Dalit Christian cannot even think to become a candidate! They are outside the 'political camp.' The political parties and church should take bold steps to bring the Christians of Scheduled Caste Origin into the mainstream of political process and to empower them politically to raise their voice and participation in the decision making process.

Christian Women of Scheduled Caste Origin: A 'Bent' Life

The Christian Women of Scheduled Caste Origin are more subjugated and discriminated than men of the same category. As women of Scheduled Caste origin they face discrimination from caste Hindus and Christians (both men and women). As women they also go through the restrictions imposed by the socio-religio-cultural prejudices within and outside the community.[46] They are more vulnerable among the Christians of Scheduled Caste Origin. The personhood of Dalit Christian women is an epitome of discrimination. Their discriminated life is due to the inter-connected mechanism of unjust caste hierarchy, biased gender sensitivity and imbalanced class formation and faith identity. They are devalued more than 'caste' women.[47] Most of them are illiterate. Uneducated Dalit women are even neglected by women of advanced Dalit families. The Christian Women of Scheduled Caste Origin do not get the benefits of the welfare programmes of government as enjoyed by other women in society. They seldom get chance to participate in the political process. They are exploited in the job markets, and are forced to be satisfied with a small amount of 'salary.'[48] Indeed, their life is 'bent' with restrictions, burdens and prejudices within the family, society and Church.

Christians of Scheduled Caste Origin and Church: 'Wounded Sheep' and 'Uncaring Shepherd'

Numerically, Indian Church is Dalit Church because majority of her members are drawn from Scheduled Caste Origin.[49] Several factors have contributed to their conversion to Christianity: aspiration for dignified life, emancipation from the bondage of caste, educational help etc. Though some changes have taken place in their lives because of conversion, now they feel that the church has left their 'just cause.' For them, church is not taking bold initiatives to promote their well being.[50]

The 'casteist mentality' is deeply rooted in the psyche of the majority Indian Christians.[51] Therefore, the Christians of Scheduled Caste Origin experience discrimination in various levels within the Church. Their status is same inside and outside the Church. They are consciously excluded from the decision-making bodies and prominent positions in the church, particularly in the multi-racial churches/denominations. Most of the top-positions are occupied by the non-Dalit Christians.[52] Dalits Christians allege that Church needs them only for conversion, but not for leadership. They also feel that their brothers and sisters in other religious traditions, especially Dalit Hindus, have improved their economic and social status thanks to the reservation policy and other welfare programmes of government.[53] These feelings come out of their 'wounded' psyche resulted by the negligence of the church towards their advancement. Who is responsible for their discrimination? They would say the church leadership, the 'uncaring shepherd' in whom they have kept their trust and hope. In spite of the various forms of discrimination experienced in the Christian community, still they adhere to the faith which has given them hope of liberation from the chains of the caste 'demons.'[54] The church is morally and theologically responsible to take audacious steps to redress their grievances. She must rise up to their expectations and intentionally engage with their discriminated and disempowered realities.[55] In true sense, the church only can wipe out their tears. She must be able to fight on behalf of them to get deserved benefits such as reservation and participation in the various development programmes of the government.

Scheduled Caste Status and Reservation: An Issue of Justice

Reservation has been a tool for the socio-economic upliftment of the weaker sections in Indian society. Scheduled Caste Status and Reservation are interrelated in the mechanism for the preferential treatment of Dalits in government jobs, welfare programmes, higher education etc. According to the Presidential Order of 1950, scheduled caste status can be given only to the Hindus who are formerly considered as untouchables. Later, it has been extended to Dalit Sikhs and Dalit Buddhists through constitutional amendments.[56] Though the Dalit Christians are given a few benefits under the OBC category, they have been denied of the Scheduled Caste Status due to their faith identity. Dalit Christians' demands of Scheduled Caste Status and Reservation have been positively reflected in the Commissions appointed by the Government to study reservation related issues. Kaka Kalekar Commission (1955) and Mandal Commission (1980) have unmistakably pointed out the fact of caste discrimination among the Christians, and have categorically recommended Scheduled Caste Status for Dalit Christians. Ranganathan Committee Report has suggested that socio-economic backwardness should be criteria of reservation. It is a welcome sign for the Christians of Scheduled Caste Origin, who are ensnared in the legality of the Presidential Order of 1950.[57] But how far it will be materialized/ fulfilled is a big question before the Dalit Christians who face continuous discrimination from the government. It is pitiable that the democratic government takes action on the report about the community which can influence the political power structures with their vote-bank politics! It is incontestable that objections or obstacles raised against the reservation are matters of politics and pragmatism rather than principle of justice and equality.[58] Unfortunately, Dalit Christians are not able to become a pressure group. On the one hand, they are ideologically and politically divided; on the other hand they are discouraged to be united by the upper caste political leadership and the denominational leadership.

The issue of Scheduled Caste Status and Reservation is a justice issue. Christians of Scheduled Caste Origin have been denied of justice because of their religious faith. By this denial, fundamental right of the profession of any religion guaranteed by Indian Constitution has been violated. This violation is basically a human right violation also. It is a violation of the principles of natural justice and fairness too.[59] The cause of Dalit Christians is less addressed by the government and the church.[60] Of course, some attempts have been made by organizations/groups to address the issue politically and judicially. But those efforts are not fully supported by the entire Christian community. The Indian Church is neither able to be united nor to garner political support for the cause of Dalit Christians.[61] It is unfortunate that the Dalit Christians are even opposed by their brothers and sisters in other religious traditions. Lack of such solidarity also adversely affects their demand for reservation. If the issue of scheduled caste status and reservation is understood with the perspective of justice in the context of the life-realities of Dalit Christians, nobody can deny their genuine demand for the same. It is the responsibility of the church and the society, including legislative, executive and judicial machineries of this great nation to address the issue of justice involved in granting scheduled caste status and reservation for the Dalit Christians.

The Engagement of Church/Faith Community

The Christians of Scheduled Caste Origin are one of the most excluded communities in India. Two factors, 'Caste' and 'Religion' contribute to their excluded situation in society. At the same time, two main agencies, the church and the government, are equally responsible for the present situation of Dalit Christians, and they must take initiatives to end the life of exclusion. However, the role of Christian faith communities in empowering the Dalit Christians

The Indian Church is more aware of its minority-cum-upper caste/class consciousness. She fails to remember that it is the weaker sections of the society like Dalit Christians who need the service of the "Servant Church." Often the church uses her minority rights and other privileges to serve its upper caste elites (both Christians and those from other faiths) in society. Instead of expressing solidarity with the poor, the church consciously or unconsciously takes side with the rich and the affluent. She may be concerned about how she can feed other's children by making her own children orphan! Nothing wrong to feed other children, but church must remember that her children can also expect same attention she extends to other children.

Church as a community of Jesus must primarily concentrate on the rights of the oppressed people groups like Dalit Christians who are really disempowered in all aspects of life. It does not mean that Church should stand only for their cause. But in the context of excluded life-realities of the Dalit Christians, church should re-think on who is her real priority in delivering her services: educational, medical, developmental programmes and advocacy? Who needs really her solidarity? Whether the people who still live a life of exclusion and marginalization or the people who enjoy the basic fundamental rights? For Dalits, the church of present context must become the church of solidarity with Dalits, which is rooted in the commitment to the well-being of the millions of people who are striving for dignified life. The socio-economic-political witness of the church in pluralistic context cannot be fruitful if it does not identify with the life of the oppressed in society. The church needs to be led by the consciousness of solidarity with the Dalits. The foundation of this consciousness of solidarity is Jesus who identified with the least one in the society. He did not exclude anyone but attempted to create space for them. It is the responsibility of the so-called 'minority' Church to work for the unorganized majority powerless people (Christians of Scheduled Caste Origin) who are not in the mainstream of the society. Their issues should become the concerns of the church today.

The nature of the exclusion of the Christians of Scheduled Caste Origin in society and church informs that they are the 'victims' of caste and are the 'wounded' sheep of the church. Their victimization must come to an end; and their 'wounds' must be healed. As a human community, their condition also has to be changed in the changing context of India. For that, there should be change in the pattern of thinking among the Indian Christians. There should be combined efforts of both Dalits and non-Dalits in the Christian community to transform the excluded life realities of Dalit Christians. On the one hand non-Dalits should shun their 'superior mentality' and embrace the value of inclusion and consider Dalit Christians not as Dalits but as Christians; on the other hand Dalits should continue their journey of struggle to come out of the imposed 'Dalitness'-social, political, religious, economical. The God of Solidarity demands the non-Dalits to express their solidarity with Dalits who long for fullness in life. The successful Dalit Christians also need to come forward and stand with their fellow brothers and sisters who still face different forms of exclusion in society. Moreover, the church should consciously develop the policies which will make sure the educational and job opportunities to Dalits in her institutions. She should set up income generating programmes for their economic empowerment. The democratic governments must formulate policies and programmes including reservation which would help the Dalit Christians in their journey towards wholistic empowerment. The life of exclusion can be defeated by the initiatives of solidarity and the life of solidarity modeled in Jesus Christ.

Endnotes

[1] Ralph T.H. Griffith (tr. & cr.), *The Hymns of the Rigveda*, New Revised Edition, Reprint (Delhi: Motilal Banarsidass, 1986), 603.

[2] G. Buhler (tr.), *Sacred Books of the East Edited by F. Max Muller Vol. 25, The Laws of Manu* (Delhi: Motilal Banarsidass, 1988), 414.

[3] Twice-born (*dwija*) castes are those which belong to the first three *varnas*-Brahmin, Kshatriya and Vaishya. M. N. Srinivas, *Social Change in Modern India* (New Delhi, Orient Longman Limited, 2000), 8.

[4] G.S. Ghurye, *Caste and Race in India* (London: Routledge and Kegan Paul, 1932; Reprint of Fifth Edition, Bombay: Popular Prakashan, 1994), 7.

[5] William Logan, *Malabar Vol I* (Madras: Government Press, 1887; Reprint, Trivandrum: Charithram Publications, 1981), 144-145.

[6] G.S. Ghurye, *Caste and Race in India*, 9-10; A. H., *Day Dawn in Travancore* (Kottayam: C.M.S Press, 1860), 8-9 & Samuel Mateer, *Land of Charity* (London: John Snow & Co, 1871), 28 & 31.

[7] Felix Wilfred, *Asian Public Theology* (New Delhi: ISPCK, 2010), 30.

[8] *Reservations for Backward Classes, Mandal Commission Report of the Backward Classes Commission, 1980* (Delhi: Akalank Publications, 1990), 19.

[9] *The Constitution of India* (Ministry of Law and Justice, Government of India, 1989), 1.

[10] *The Constitution of India*, 7.

[11] *The Constitution of India*, 12.

[12] S. Lourduswamy, *Towards Empowerment of Dalit Christians* (New Delhi: Centre for Dalit/ Subaltern Studies, 2005), 106-107 & 109-110

[13] Satish Deshpande and Geetika Bapna, *Dalits in Muslim and Christian Communities* (New Delhi: CDS, CBCI and NCCI, 2010), 52.

[14] Faizan Mustafa and Anurag Sharma, *Conversion: Constitutional and Legal Implications* (New Delhi: Kanishka Publishers, 2003), 107-114.

[15] S. Lourduswamy, "Catholic Church and Dalit-Tribal Movements in India," in *Rethinking Theology in India*, edited by James Massey and T.K. John (New Delhi: Manohar and Centre for Dalit/Subaltern Studies, 2013), 183.

[16] *Indian Currents* XXVII, no. 36 (September, 2015): 26.

[17] *Indian Currents* XXVII, no. 36 (September, 2015): 28.

[18] James Massey, "Christianity to be Renewed? Rethink Theology," in *Rethinking Theology in India*, edited by James Massey and T.K. John (New Delhi: Manohar and Centre for Dalit/Subaltern Studies, 2013), 29-30.

[19] *Dr. Babasaheb Ambedkar: Writings and Speeches* Vol 5, compiled by Vasant Moon (Bombay: Education Department, Government of Maharashtra, 1989), 448.

[20] *Dr. Babasaheb Ambedkar: Writings and Speeches* Vol 5, 476.

[21] *Dr. Babasaheb Ambedkar: Writings and Speeches* Vol 5, 444.

[22] Amartya Sen, *Identity and* Violence (New Delhi: Allen Lane (Penguin Books), 2006), 1-2.

[23] http://www.indianexpress.com/news/scs-sts-form-25—of-population-says-census-2011-data/1109988/ 09/11/2013. According to the Census of 2001, SC population is 16.3% *Census of India 2001, Primary Census Abstract Scheduled Castes* (New Delhi: Office of the Registrar General and Census Commissioner, India, 2001), xlvi.

[24] *Census of India 2011, Tables on Houses, Household Amenities and Assets for Scheduled Castes* (New Delhi: Registrar General and Census Commissioner, India, 2012), xliii-xlvi.

[25] Felix Wilfred, "Editorial," *Jeevadhara* Vol. XLI/No.241 (January, 2011): 3-5 at 3.

[26] Satish Deshpande and Geetika Bapna, *Dalits in Muslim and Christian Communities*, 60 & 108 (reference no 5.)

[27] K.E. Rajpramukh, *Dalit Christians of Andhra* (New Delhi: Serials Publications, 2008), 80.

[28] Camil Parkhe, *Dalit Christians: Right to Reservations* (Delhi: ISPCK, 2007), 1-3; James Massey and T.K. John, eds., *Christians of Scheduled Caste Origin in India*, 14; K.E. Rajpramukh, *Dalit Christians of Andhra*, 80-81.

[29] S. Lourduswamy, "Catholic Church and Dalit-Tribal Movements in India," 185 & S. Lourduswamy, *Towards Empowerment of Dalit Christians, Equal Rights to all Dalits*, 20-21.

[30] Satish Deshpande and Geetika Bapna, *Dalits in Muslim and Christian Communities*, 128.

[31] James Massey and T.K. John, eds., *Christians of Scheduled Caste Origin in India*, 16; Indukuri John Mohan Razu, "Towards a Critical Theology of Risk Taking: The Changing Landscape and Discourse," in *Rethinking Theology in India*, edited by James Massey and T.K. John (New Delhi: Manohar and Centre for Dalit/Subaltern Studies, 2013), 362.

[32] K.E. Rajpramukh, *Dalit Christians of Andhra*, 81; Felix Wilfred, "What Can 'Upper Caste' Christians Learn from Dalit Christians?" *Jeevadhara* Vol. XLI/ No.241 (January, 2011): 66-76 at 72-73.

[33] James Massey and T.K. John, eds., *Christians of Scheduled Caste Origin in India*, 75-82.

[34] S. Lourduswamy, "Catholic Church and Dalit-Tribal Movements in India," 186.

[35] S. Lourduswamy, "Dalit Christians: Has Anything Changed?," *Jeevadhara* Vol. XLI/No.241 (January, 2011): 7-13 at 12-13; S. Lourduswamy, *Towards Empowerment of Dalit Christians, Equal Rights to all Dalits*, 26-27.

[36] Satish Deshpande and Geetika Bapna, *Dalits in Muslim and Christian Communities*, 133.

[37] Camil Parkhe, *Dalit Christians: Right to Reservations*, 4.

[38] Felix Wilfred, "What Can 'Upper Caste' Christians Learn from Dalit Christians?" 66-76 at 68.

[39] Satish Deshpande and Geetika Bapna, *Dalits in Muslim and Christian Communities*, 131-132.

[40] James Massey and T.K. John, eds., *Christians of Scheduled Caste Origin in India*, 83-86.

[41] James Massey and T.K. John, eds., *Christians of Scheduled Caste Origin in India*, 87-90.

[42] K.E. Rajpramukh, *Dalit Christians of Andhra*, 81.

[43] James Massey and T.K. John, eds., *Christians of Scheduled Caste Origin in India*, 92-93 & 98-99 & S. Lourduswamy, *Towards Empowerment of Dalit Christians, Equal Rights to all Dalits*, 29-30.

[44] Satish Deshpande and Geetika Bapna, *Dalits in Muslim and Christian Communities*, 129.

[45] James Massey and T.K. John, eds., *Christians of Scheduled Caste Origin in India*, 132-135.

[46] Felix Wilfred, "Create Opportunities for Dalit Christians," An Interview with Archbishop A.M. Chinnappa, *Jeevadhara* Vol. XLI/No.241 (January, 2011): 77-84 at 79.

[47] Bama, "Dalit Christian Women Today, Their Struggles and Prospects for Future," *Jeevadhara* Vol. XLI/No.241 (January, 2011): 35-44 at 35-36; Shalini Mulackal, "Women: Theology and Feminist Movements in India," in *Theology in India*, edited by James Massey and T.K. John (New Delhi: Manohar and Centre for Dalit/Subaltern Studies, 2013), 166.

[48] James Massey and T.K. John, eds., *Christians of Scheduled Caste Origin in India*, 136-142.

[49] S. Lourduswamy, "Dalit Christians: Has Anything Changed?," 7-13 at 11.

[50] James Massey and T.K. John, eds., *Christians of Scheduled Caste Origin in India*, 149f; K. Jesurathnam, "Yerraguntala Peraiah: An Honorable Dalit Christian Missionary," *Journal of Subaltern and Cultural Theology* (2013): 20-24 at 22-23; S. Lourduswamy, "Catholic Church and Dalit-Tribal Movements in India," 190.

[51] Pauline Chakkalakal, *Discipleship, A Space for Women's Leadership* (Mumbai: Pauline Publications, 2004), 28.

[52] K.E. Rajpramukh, *Dalit Christians of Andhra*, 80; Indukuri John Mohan Razu, "Towards a Critical Theology of Risk Taking: The Changing Landscape and Discourse," 348.

[53] James Massey and T.K. John, eds., *Christians of Scheduled Caste Origin in India*, 155f.

[54] Francis P. Xavier, "Anatomy of Humiliation and Signs of Hope," *Jeevadhara* Vol. XLI/No.241 (January, 2011): 26-34 at 27-28 & 34.

[55] Felix Wilfred, "What Can 'Upper Caste' Christians Learn from Dalit Christians?" 66-76 at 74; S. Lourduswamy, *Towards Empowerment of Dalit Christians, Equal Rights to all Dalits*, 23-24.

[56] S. Lourduswamy, *Towards Empowerment of Dalit Christians*, 106-110; Camil Parkhe, *Dalit Christians: Right to Reservations*, 31-34.

[57] James Massey and T.K. John, eds., *Christians of Scheduled Caste Origin in India*, 163-170 & 224-226; S. Lourduswamy, *Towards Empowerment of Dalit Christians, Equal Rights to all Dalits*, 21-22.

[58] Satish Deshpande and Geetika Bapna, *Dalits in Muslim and Christian Communities*, 135.

[59] Camil Parkhe, *Dalit Christians: Right to Reservations*, 7; Satish Deshpande and Geetika Bapna, *Dalits in Muslim and Christian Communities*, 136.

[60] *People's Reporter* Vol. 26/No. 24 (Mumbai, December 25-January 10, 2014), 1 & 24; S. Lourduswamy, "Catholic Church and Dalit-Tribal Movements in India," 187-188 & 202-207.

[61] S. Lourduswamy, "Dalit Christians: Has Anything Changed?" 7-13 at 11-12.

Chapter 4

Freedom of Religion, Communal Politics and Minorities in India

Crime happens in different forms. Many factors contribute to the criminal activities in society. We identify crimes with different names according to their nature and consequences. Every individual/community irrespective of faith and culture face some form of crime. Often, people take precautions to protect themselves from the consequences of possible crimes. Criminal elements really pose great threat to the harmonious life in a plural society. One of the recent trends of criminal behavior in India is mob violence. It is carried out in the name of religion, caste, ethnicity etc. Intolerance is the root cause of mob violence. It is painful that people of different religious traditions are poisoned by the ideologies of hate and exclusion. The worst form of mob violence happens in the name of religion. Now, it is easy to mobilize crazy mob in the name of religious sentiments and unleash violence against other religious communities. Minorities are major victims of mob violence in India. According to the report of the Pew Research Centre in 2015, India is one of the worst countries for religious tolerance in the world.[1] Even after two years, this information stands validated.

Mr. Hansraj Ahir, Union Minister of State for Home informed the Lok Sabha that there were 822 incidents of communal violence in the country in 2017. In these incidents, 111 people were killed and 2384 were injured.[2] Religious intolerance begets crimes in the form of the physical attacks and direct and indirect violation of religious rights. For the minorities, major form of crime they face is violation of religious rights in different levels. It prevents their upward social mobility and keeps them in constant fear. Violation of Rights is basically a crime. When a right is violated, then a crime is committed. This chapter narrates various dimensions of the violation of religious rights and Christian response to the issues of minorities in the context of religious intolerance.

Violation of Religious Rights

India is a Sovereign Socialist Secular Democratic Republic.[3] Though the original meaning of 'secularism' denotes a complete separation of religion and the state, Indian secularism in a strong religiously pluralistic situation refers to the equal support and acceptance of all religions by the state.[4] Dalai Lama once said, "...India is a living example of religious harmony and secular ethics. The Indian Constitution is based on secularism."[5] But today, though not fully, the secular society is polarized in terms of caste and religion. Religious polarization appears to be more disastrous than any other sort of division. It contributes to religious intolerance which in turn creates crimes against the minorities. In the context of the political use of religion, the very idea of secularism has been distorted. It also has been interpreted in terms of 'minority appeasement.'[6]

Communal polarization in the name of religion and consequent violence is an important threat to the Indian secular fabric. It threatens our pluralistic heritage and destroys communal harmony. Even after 72 years of independence, communal tensions continue throughout the nation. It is viewed that for Muslims, "communalism is a much bigger issue than corruption."[7] The communal tensions are the signs of intolerance and mistrust among the communities. The vote bank politics adds fuel to the fire of communal polarization and violent crimes. The post-Babri Masjid violence in Uttar Pradesh (1992), post-Godhra violence in Gujarat (2002), and recent one in Muzaffar Nagar in Uttar Pradesh (2013) etc. are examples of the desperate attempts of politicians to keep intact or increase their vote bank through 'the politics of hatred.'[8] According to T.R.S. Subramanian, Cabinet Secretary of India from 1996-1998, "India's vote banks are still based on religion and community rather than performance and economic interests. This can be exploited by parties, as seems to have happened in Muzaffarnagar, where Samajwadi Party wants to solidify its Muslim vote and BJP and RLD their upper-caste and Jat vote banks."[9] The communal polarization in electoral politics is blessed and initiated by the politicians. In the pretext of protecting minorities, they also create minority vote banks. This often leads to counter-polarization of Hindu voters which mainly benefit BJP and its allies.[10] It has also to be noted that whether the massacre of Muslims in Gujarat in 2002 or the anti-Sikh riots in Delhi in 1984[11] or the Niyogi Committee Report on the Missionary Activities in Madhya Pradesh in 1965[12] or the reconversion of Christians and the destruction of Churches to build temples in Dangs District in Gujarat in 1997[13] are the outcome of the larger agenda of communal politics which criminally polarizes the society. The continuation of communal riots, tensions, grouping even on simple or local issues, shows that the forces of communalism have won, to a large extent, in polarizing the people in religious lines. The result is defining people religiously in all aspects of life that 'you are Hindu, Muslim, Christian, Sikh...Not Indian.' Now, it is not national identity, but religious identity matters in Indian polity. For instance, in electoral politics, wherever mixed religious communities in equal or slightly different proportion exist, majority religious sentiments of the particular constituency are evoked. In the case of one religious community constitutes majority in a constituency, caste or denomination or sect card is employed to ensure electoral victory. We are polarized! This polarization is not an innocent process but a product of calculated and vicious agenda which begets crimes against the minorities.

Today, the violation of constitutionally guaranteed religious rights, particularly 'the right to profess, practice and propagate the religion' of the minorities, is common phenomenon throughout the nation. The situation is such that Christians in many states celebrate their festivals in fear and anxiety. Though the state offers protection in public sight, it is not able to control the fringe elements/ groups which spew venom of hatred against the minorities and perpetuate unlawful activities against them. According to James Massey, religious rights are violated in two ways: direct and indirect. Direct violation comes in the form of physical attack, destruction of worship places, disruption of religious meetings etc. It is undertaken by violent mobs with the secret connivance of ruling class who often conveniently disclaim their involvement. Indirect violation happens in the form of administrative delay, denying permission to build worship places and conduct religious meetings, withdrawing police protection, etc. The indirect violation always comes from the state administration. Regarding the violation of religious rights, particularly violence against minorities, it is important to note that it happens in everywhere irrespective of states and ruling political parties. In India, all religious minorities have faced different forms of the violation of their rights in different periods. It can be direct or indirect violation of their rights. The continuous violation of religious rights shows that violation of religious freedom has become a national problem. It is an irony that though Constitution guarantees 'freedom of conscience' and protection against discrimination on the grounds of religion, the Presidential Order of 1950 and the Freedom of Religious Acts passed by different states directly contradict those constitutional provisions. While the Article 15 of the Constitution prohibits any kind of discrimination on the basis of religion, the Presidential Order of 1950 excludes Christians and Muslims of Scheduled Caste origin from availing the privilege of scheduled caste status which is essential for getting the benefits of reservation and social welfare programs of government. It is purely a direct violation of their religious right. We are proud of the Article 25 of the Constitution which allows every citizen to exercise the freedom of conscience in relation to the choice of his/her religion. But the freedom of religion acts passed by the states with strict regulations on conversion actually curtails the freedom of religion. They really restrict the freedom of citizens. The Uniform Civil Code is another challenge to the minorities including Christians.[14] It has to be noted that protection of the rights of religious freedom plays an important role in unifying the country.[15] But the State as protector of rights has haplessly become perpetrator of the negation of rights. The direct or indirect violation of religious rights does not happen without overt or covert support of the states. If the state is strong in its conviction regarding the protection of the rights of people, no force can commit any form of violation.

The proponents of Freedom of Religion Acts argue that these laws are necessary to stop the forced conversions. Though it sounds good, those laws are promulgated to target minority religious communities, particularly Christianity which attracts the people, mainly those who are in the lower strata of society. Most of the criminal cases charged in the light of newly framed religious laws are against the Christians though none of them are convicted so far.

All such cases are registered on the basis of false allegations leveled by the certain communal organizations. Often proper investigations are not conducted before filing the cases. At this juncture, it has to be noted it is not Christianity alone involved in mission and conversion. All religions have their preachers, mission activities, and carryout direct or indirect conversion strategies. But the freedom of religion act is rarely applied to all religions except Christianity and Islam. Moreover, there is higher fine and punishment for the conversion of Scheduled Castes (Dalits) and Scheduled Tribes (Tribals) as if they do not have capacity to take right decision on the choice of their religion.[16] When a Dalit becomes a Christian s/he loses his/her privilege of Scheduled Caste Status. Apart from reservation benefits, s/he is not entitled to get special protection guaranteed by the Protection of Civil Rights Act, 1955; Protection of Civil Rights Rule 1977 and SC and ST (Prevention of Atrocities) Act, 1989 passed by the Parliament.[17] Two things have to be noted in this legal embarrassment. One is Dalits are not allowed to choose any religion without restrictions even though the Constitution guarantees it. Secondly, Christian/Muslim Dalits are discriminated just because they have exercised their fundamental rights. This is a paradox of freedom. As minorities Dalit Christians face extreme discrimination in the name of religion. The restriction or violation of fundamental rights through legal enactment is a crime against the people. What is Christian response to the violation of religious rights including minority rights?

Firstly, Christian involvement in religious awareness programs and inter-community dialogues must be encouraged. They must have an awareness of the religious situation of the country and their religious rights. It will help them to be sensible to the context which becomes religiously more sensitive in the present time. They must have initiate inter-community dialogue programs which facilitates mutual understanding of faiths. In a society where intolerance in the name of religion gets momentum, inter-community dialogues can promote religious tolerance and develop an atmosphere in which religious freedom of every citizen is respected and crimes against the minorities are stopped. Secondly, Christians must come together beyond denominational boundaries. What is needed is program centric unity or solidarity than organic unity/ solidarity. Denominations are not going to be dissolved into one entity. While maintaining individual identity the denominations can unite on program level and respond to the issues of religious freedom. A consciousness of one body though spread in different denominations can bring Christians together to protect their rights in this land. Thirdly, Christians must take steps to develop organized programs or protests to put pressure on law enforcement authorities to punish the culprits who directly or indirectly involve in communal violence. Preliminary legal education must be given to the believers and pastors. They also should be educated of minority religious rights. At the same time, Christians can join hands with other communities or civil societies which stand for the justice of the victims of religious conflicts. Fourthly, there has to be rethinking in some of the methods of evangelism carried out by some mission organizations and individuals. Aggressive evangelism often leads to communal tensions which affects not only social relations between different communities but also lives of poor Christians. This suggestion is not to dilute the command of Jesus Christ but to design relevant mission programs that will not create communal tensions and crimes. Fifthly, Christians must participate in political process and use their political influence for advocating the rights of religious freedom. It should not be a communal pressure group which stands for particular community. If Christians stand for the protection of the religious rights of all citizens, they also will be protected in society. Sixthly,

Christians should stop presenting the common issues related to the Christian community, such as Christian Personal Law, denial of the equal rights of Dalit Christians, violation of the educational rights of minorities, the question of increasing atrocities on Christians, as issues of a denomination or section. They must be treated as issues of whole Christian community. The ruling class, who belong to the majority religion may not even understand denominational differences, may ignore the issue if they come to know that particular issue is raised by one of the denominations among the Christians. A divided bargaining does not generate any result. If there is a united action in presenting the issues of Christian community, it will automatically reflect in the approach of administration. It can at least reduce the negative ramifications of the policies and programs concerning the rights of minorities. Finally, Christians must join hands with other minorities to respond to the common issues concerning the rights of minorities. They should respond even when the rights and freedoms of another minority community are violated. They should also express their solidarity with minorities who are persecuted or discriminated in the name of their faith.[18] The protection of religious freedom has to be considered as part of their religious life which is founded on the life and work of Jesus Christ who taught the values of love, freedom and justice.

Interplay of Religion and Politics

Indian political society has always witnessed the interplay of religion and politics. Since independence, the level of such interplay has been increasing from less harmful to an uncontrollable stage. Today, it has reached into a dangerous level in which communalization of politics is complete in India. Recent general and state elections have witnessed blatant attempts to communally polarize the voters. A communally divided society has already been created by the politics of communalism in India. The founders of this nation attempted to create an alternative society based on the principles of justice, equality, liberty and fraternity. They never thought that communal politics would replace secular politics in which religion had no role in the democratic process of election. They envisioned a society where the values of justice, liberty, equality and fraternity would prevail over caste hegemony and religious majoritarianism. But today, communal politics has become a threat to the secular polity of the nation. It is a challenge for all citizens irrespective of religious affiliation.[19] Christians have a role to play in the communally charged context. They have to approach the issue of communal politics based on the values and teachings of Christian faith.

Christian faith demands its followers to have an inclusive approach in all aspects of life. It does not teach them to exclude or discriminate anyone just because of his/her religion. Therefore, Christians cannot journey with communal politics which also causes crimes in society. They have to follow different approach which is holistic in nature. On the one hand Christians have to engage in all aspects of life including politics; on the other hand they cannot be exclusive in approach. Their political engagement has to be driven by the traditions of prophets and Jesus Christ. The Bible gives some insights regarding the nature of Christian political engagement (Isa 61:1-3, Lk 4:18-19). The Book of Isaiah provides a model of political engagement, i.e., 'Prophetic Politics' (Ch 9, 11, 53). This model demands two things: firstly, the protection of the poor and weak against the domination of ruling class. Prophetic Politics stands against economic exploitation, political discrimination and social marginalization which are illegal in nature. It does not support any political dispensation which neglects the poor and the weak. It means Christian political engagement must be prophetic involvement and must stand for the weak and the poor. They must raise the issues of poor against the tendency of using the poor to get communal political mileage. Secondly, prophetic politics reminds that God is the true sovereign of the state and the ruler is subjected to the sovereign God. It means the ruler has to rule according to the will of sovereign God who protects the rights of every citizen particularly the minorities and the poor. If the ruler does not fulfill his/her responsibility, prophetic politics requires that ruler must be reminded of his/her duty in relation to his/her subjects. The Christian political engagement needs to remind the ruling class about their democratic role when the nation faces the threat of communal politics which sides with a particular religious community and promotes their interests and involves in criminal activities. 'Messianic politics' is another model for the political engagement of Christians. It is an extension of 'prophetic politics.' Isaiah talks about a messianic ruler (Is 11: 4-5). Christians believe that Messiah or Messianic ruler about whom Isaiah prophesied is Jesus Christ. He is also portrayed as 'the suffering servant' (Is 53). The life and ministry of Jesus on this earth informs that Jesus stood for an alternative model of politics. He did not conform to the politics of his time, which was exploitative and oppressive in nature. His 'politics' was informed by his consciousness that he was a 'suffering servant' who came to serve others even though He was Messiah. He attempted to create a new socio-political order which challenged the dominant political ethos and practices. He aimed to form a 'just society' based on justice and righteousness. Jesus' engagement in society had political significance also. Though he did not directly attempt to get political power, his actions and teachings were shaping the social-political and religious mind-set of the people. He confronted the political class of the society by becoming a 'suffering servant' who expressed his solidarity with the poor and the weak. He was showing them that political class must engage

with the issues of people in society. Jesus' servant approach actually
disturbed the dominant political class. Therefore, this must be the
approach of Christians who engage in politics. They have to become
suffering servants who stand with those who are peripheralized in
society.[20] Jesus' messianic politics demands every citizen and ruler
to be 'suffering servant' who attends the issues of people irrespective
of caste and creed. This servant approach to politics is missing in
the world today. The absence of such approach is the main reason
for communal politics. Once politics is understood as means of
serving people, it cannot be played with communal interests.

Christian faith also demands its adherents to support democratic
system. The values of democracy are inherent in the Christian
understanding of human beings, world and political order. Now
the question is whether political democracy-election, formation of
government etc- alone can establish just order in society. In other
words, can we say that political democracy means the existence of a
'just society'? India is a democratic country which adopted political
democracy based on equality, justice, freedom. But the irony is that
different forms of inequality still exist in the country. Dalits, Tribals
and other backward communities experience unequal social realities.
The existence of social inequality in political democracy shows that
people live a life of contradictions. Though political democracy
claims to establish a just society through democratic process,
social inequality continues to prevail in society. Therefore, political
democracy is incomplete without achieving social democracy.[21] In
the Indian context, social democracy, the establishment of a social
order in which everyone is equally valued in social life is very much
important because caste still holds the thinking of majority citizens.
It must be the basis of political democracy. Social democracy is
a biblical mandate too. The prophets of Old Testament and Jesus
Christ emphasized the need of social equality. They questioned the

ruling class who ignored the social conditions of the poor, the weak and the minorities. Christian political engagement must focus on social democracy while attempting to support and strengthen the political democracy in India. The question of social democracy can prevent the eruption of communal politics.

Political education is another area where Christians must be focused in their political engagement in the context of the communalization of politics. Firstly, they should take initiatives to educate fellow Christians about the democratic values, Indian political system, ideological base of political parties, constitutional rights and duties etc.[22] Secondly, political education should be extended to fellow citizens particularly the weaker sections of society who are used and implicated in communal conflicts and crimes. Political education can make citizens aware of the threat of communal politics. Therefore, political education must become part of Christian witness in society. The Christians also must shun communal politics and support secular politics with social democracy.

Minority Rights and Issues of Minorities

According to India Census 2011, Hindus constitute 96.63 crores (79. 8%) of Indian population, Muslims- 17.22 crores (14. 2%), Christians- 2.78 crores (2.3%), Sikhs- 2.08 crores (1.7%), Jains-0.45 crores (0.4%), Buddhists-0.84 crores (0.7%), Other Religions- 0.79 crores (0.7%), Religion Not Stated – 0.29 crores (0.2%). This religious demography shows the diversity of Indian society. Every religious community is socially and politically dominant in the areas where they are majority. Though the Hindus constitute majority of the population, they are not homogenous in tradition and culture. While acknowledging the beauty of India's religious and ethnic diversity, one cannot evade the inherent problems, particularly the communal polarization and violence, in the pluralistic society. Conflict is natural in a society where different religious communities co-exist. It may arise in the name of identity, policies of government, sharing of resources and opportunities, religious and political views etc.[23] But harmonious life in a plural society depends on good governance and informed tolerant citizenry. Though the Constitution of India has clear provisions for the protection of minorities and their institutions, often they are targeted by communal groups and unable to exercise their rights. They face many problems even though everything looks alright in public domain.

The minorities, particularly Christians, run many educational institutions in India. The Constitution of India allows them to establish and run institutions. They cater quality education to all irrespective of religious traditions. But they face excess interference of various educational and administrative departments of the government. This is one of the main problems minorities face today. Instead of helping and encouraging them in developing the education sector, unnecessary political and administrative involvement in the pretext of education policies, employment rules and other regulations notified by the government keep them in anxiety and distract them from taking new initiatives. The excess interference is a violation of Article 30 of the Constitution. Communal minded officials and rulers purposely interfere to tarnish the reputation of the institutions developed by the minorities. Many institutions are targeted to help private individuals who run educational institutions. Another problem the minorities, particularly the Christians face is the encroachment of their properties by the local landlords or government departments. In many places, minorities own prime properties in commercial locations. The business people or landlords either intimidate the minorities to sell the property to them or try to get it in low rate or bring them into legal battle. There are cases of encroaching Christian graveyards and Muslim Waqf Board properties. These are different forms of crimes against the minorities. Every encroachment has direct or indirect political and administrative support. This happens in spite of having a Constitution which allows the minorities to establish and manage their religious institutions and own movable and immovable properties.[24] It is unfortunate that there are members in minority communities, particularly those who are in charge of minority properties, play the role of brokers to get the minority properties for the land lords and business people.

There are welfare programmes introduced by state and central governments for the social, economic and educational advancement of different communities. But the scope of those development programs is very much limited as far as the minorities are concerned. On the one hand specific development and welfare programmes for the minorities are less in number; on the other hand there always exits confusion regarding the inclusion of minorities in many welfare programs. Often the government officials are helpless because of the absence of clear guidelines with regard to the implementation of welfare programmes in relation to the minorities. Though there is National Minorities Development and Finance Corporation (NMDFC) for the development of minorities in India, its benefits do not reach the minorities. The non-corporation of state governments makes the minorities deprived of the benefits of NMDFC. Moreover, the procedure involved to get the benefits also keep the minorities, majority of them are poor, away from such institution.[25] Administrative delay in delivering the benefits is a crime committed against the minorities. The ideology of the ruling party also plays a big role in implementing the welfare programs for minorities. If the ruling party is communal, then the implementation will be dead slow. There will be minority programs in advertisement but not in actual practice. The communal politics even defines minority welfare programs as 'minority appeasement.'

National Commission for Minorities (NCM) is a central statutory body formed by an act of Parliament for monitoring the affairs of minority communities in India. It monitors the implementation of welfare programs for minorities, the violation of their rights particularly minority rights etc. Every state is also required to form State Minority Commission. Both national and state minority commissions are mandated to address the issues of minorities within their jurisdiction. But the problem the minorities face with regard to the minority commissions is that most of the state minority commissions are either defunct or unable to properly function. There are mainly two reasons. Firstly, majority states show less interest to form the commissions with full membership. Even if members are appointed, they are politically appointed. It is not necessary that they arise above the political ideology and address the issues of minorities. Secondly, state minority commissions are often not allotted sufficient funds to carry out the responsibilities. Except NCM, state minority commissions don't have statutory status. It also affects the functioning of state minority commissions. They should be strengthened with powers and well defined functions so that they can contribute to the welfare of minorities in the country and protect their rights. The work of minority commissions has to be considered as part of social justice enforcement mechanism.[26] The success of state minority commissions depends on the political outlook of the state government also. If the state is ruled by a communal party, then even the formation of state minority commission can be deferred indefinitely. It is actually a crime against the minorities. The formation of minority commissions can create a sense of protection among the minorities. At the same time, The National Commission for Minorities "has to represent the people to the government, not government to the people, if it has to fulfill the statutory role given to it in the Act of 1992."[27] It must not work an extension of particular government, but as a defender of minority rights.

Communal violence is another major problem faced by all minority communities. As noted earlier, every minority community has experienced the pain of communal violence. Communal violence is not limited to one or two states. It has become a national issue today. History teaches us that communal violence can happen under the rule of any political party irrespective of ideology. Communal violence is faced not only by the national minorities but also by the majority religious community which is minority in some states. After every communal conflict, it is common today to form a judicial commission or to send minority commissions to examine the situation. They come up with suggestions to prevent communal violence in future and recommend different legal remedies. But the sad part of the story is that recommendations in majority cases are not implemented. Even if any commission points out the culprits, either action is not taken or commission report is rejected. The problem is that the state governments do not have political will to implement the recommendations. Often, they are afraid to touch the culprits who belong to the majority community in respective context. Lack of political will to book the culprits further gives encouragement to the criminal elements in society.[28] Majority victims of communal violence are minorities. Communal violence causes internal migration and keeps the minorities in constant fear. A state with strong political will and commitment to the rights of minorities only can prevent the communal violence.

The minorities are common phenomenon throughout the world. The majority communities cannot simply eliminate them from respective countries or regions. The problems they face are part of the imagination that the minorities will gradually absorbed into majority religious, cultural, social system. If minorities live on this earth, it is God who created them and enable them to survive. The minorities exist from the ancient times. In fact, diversity is divine creative agenda. The Bible provides the stories of minorities in different kingdoms. The story of Jews in Egypt is the best example of the existence of minorities. Though they had gone through painful experiences after they demanded freedom their existence as a minority community actually contributed to the diversity of Egyptian society. The existence of minorities primarily affirms the principle of diversity. The biblical story of Babel Tower (Gen 11: 1-9) speaks about the importance of diverse cultures, ethos, values, and languages in society. When Babylonian imperial power attempted to build up one world order against the divine order which recognizes differences, God destroyed the plan by confusing the language of the people who were involved in the project. The different languages emerged out of confused state is the evidence of God's approval of different languages whether spoken by majority or minority. The Babel Tower project aimed mono-language, mono-culture, and possibly mono-religion. It can be read as absence of diversity and absence of minority. A context becomes diverse when a minority culture or a faith emerges into visibility. In the story of Babel Tower, we see a God who wants a society to be heterogeneous rather than homogenous. The Day of Pentecost (Acts 1:1-13) also affirms diversity. When the Holy Spirit came upon those who gathered there, they began to speak in different languages known by others who witnessed the outpouring of the Spirit. It means God loves the diversity of languages in society. The existence of different languages points to different communities including minorities.[29] The Day of Pentecost tells not only the importance of diversity but also the need of unity. Though they spoke different languages, they were united in vision and mission. The principle of 'unity in diversity' is very much evident in our constitution also. While recognizing different cultures, languages, people groups and faith, it strongly emphasizes national unity. It conveys the fact that the principle of diversity cannot endanger the unity of nation.[30] In fact, diversity is both biblical and constitutional principle. God does not want human beings to create a society without diversity which is contributed by the existence of minorities. By protecting the minorities, we honor and acknowledge the divine principle of diversity. The violation of the rights of minorities is the violation of the divine plan of diversity. In short, crime against minorities in the name of their faith is actually crime against God who created them.

The land known for its tolerance has no space for religious intolerance. India is that land which has been nurturing the value of tolerance for many centuries though there had been some aberrations in the past. The statement of Swami Vivekananda at the Parliament of World's Religions, Chicago in 1893 summarizes the mind of ancient India. "I am proud to belong to a religion which has taught the world both tolerance and universal acceptance. We believe not only in universal toleration, but we accept all religions as true. I am proud to belong to a nation which sheltered the persecuted and the refugees of all religions and all nations of the earth."[31] But today, the land of tolerance is becoming the land of religious intolerance because of communal bigots who politically capitalize the religious sentiments of people. The religious intolerance manifests in different forms and violates the rights of minorities. An element of crime is involved in every violation of religious and minority rights. In the context of increasing crimes against minorities, Christians must join hands with the communities, organizations, civil societies who stand for the cause of creating a just society where both minorities and majorities co-exist and share the resources equally. Christian educational institutions should be made as centers of creating new generation who respect the rights of every citizen of the land. As followers of Jesus Christ, Christians have to strive for building up a humane and tolerant society because tolerant society is a sign of the Kingdom of God. The strength of a majority community is tested by its commitment to the protection of a minority community. This protection is one of the expressions of divine solidarity with humanity. The minorities are not burden but beauty to the social body of a nation created by God. Crime against them is a scar on the body of a nation.

Endnotes

[1] http://www.pewforum.org/2017/4/11/global-restrictions-on-religion-rise-modestly-in-2015-revesing-downward-trend/

[2] www.firstpost.com Feb 6, 2018.

[3] *The Constitution of India,* Ministry of Law and Justice, Government of India, 1989, 1.

[4] Wendy Doniger, "The Hindu Code in Vanishing Ink," *Outlook* (24th February 2014, New Delhi): 16-18.

[5] *The Times of India* (March 21, 2014, New Delhi), 6.

[6] Wendy Doniger, "The Hindu Code in Vanishing Ink," 18.

[7] Tanweer Alam, "Top Myths About Muslims," *The Times of India* (March 21, 2014, New Delhi), 20.

[8] Aroon Purie, "From the Editor-in-Chief," *India Today* (September 23, 2013), 1.

[9] Kunal Pradhan, "Riot for Vote," *India Today* (September 23, 2013), 26.

[10] Kunal Pradhan, "Riot for Vote," 25.

[11] Pavan K. Varma, "A Deeply Sorry Game," in *The Times of India* (15th February 2014, New Delhi), 20.

[12] Prem Anthony, "Church, State and the Civil Society," *VJTR*, Vol 78/no 2 (March, 2014): 166-182 at 174.

[13] Prarthna Gahilote, "Some Old Footfalls?" *Outlook* (24th February 2014, New Delhi), 14.

[14] James Massey, "Religious Rights and Democratic Institutions of India with Special Reference to Christians," in *From Truth to Truth, A Journey through Faiths: A Selection of Representative Essays by Dr. James Massey*, edited by Deepak Seth (New Delhi: CDS and NOIDA: Academy Press, 2008), 210-213; James Massey, *Caste-Class Victims and Their Assertion for Justice* (New Delhi: CDS, 2013), 41-42; James Massey, "Minority Rights," *NCC Review* cxxi/2 (February-March, 2001): 119-144 at 139.

[15] James Massey, *Minorities and Religious Freedom in a Democracy* (New Delhi: Manohar & CDS, 2003), 114.

[16] James Massey, *Caste-Class Victims and Their Assertion for Justice*, 44; James Massey, "Minority Rights," 119-144 at 140.

[17] James Massey, "Religious Rights and Democratic Institutions of India with Special Reference to Christians," 214-215; James Massey, "Dalits and Human Rights," *Religion and Society* Vol 49/No 2& 3 (June and September 2004): 1-9 at 4-5.

[18] James Massey, "Religious Rights and Democratic Institutions of India with Special Reference to Christians," 215-216; James Massey, *Minorities and Religious Freedom in a Democracy*, 147.

[19] James Massey, "Inter-Play of Religion, Politics and Communalism in India," in *From Truth to Truth, A Journey through Faiths: A Selection of Representative Essays by Dr. James Massey*, 224.

[20] James Massey, "Inter-Play of Religion, Politics and Communalism in India," in *From Truth to Truth, A Journey through Faiths: A Selection of Representative Essays by Dr. James Massey*, 225.

[21] James Massey, "Inter-Play of Religion, Politics and Communalism in India," in *From Truth to Truth, A Journey through Faiths: A Selection of Representative Essays by Dr. James Massey*, 226.

[22] James Massey, "Inter-Play of Religion, Politics and Communalism in India," in *From Truth to Truth, A Journey through Faiths: A Selection of Representative Essays by Dr. James Massey*, 226.

[23] James Massey, *Minorities and Religious Freedom in a Democracy*, 42.

[24] James Massey, *Minorities and Religious Freedom in a Democracy*, 65.

[25] James Massey, *Minorities and Religious Freedom in a Democracy*, 66.

[26] James Massey, *Minorities and Religious Freedom in a Democracy*, 95.

[27] James Massey, *Minorities and Religious Freedom in a Democracy*, 160.

[28] James Massey, *Minorities and Religious Freedom in a Democracy*, 111.

[29] James Massey, *Minorities and Religious Freedom in a Democracy*, 139; James Massey, *Caste-Class Victims and Their Assertion for Justice*, 28.

[30] James Massey, *Minorities and Religious Freedom in a Democracy*, 140; James Massey, "Minority Rights," 119-144 at 137.

[31] https://www.ramakrishna.org/chicgfull.htm

Chapter 5

Dalit Theology: Some Methodological Reflections

Theology is primarily an attempt to understand and interpret the faith meaningful to the context. Dalit theology is one of the contextual theologies emerged in India in 1980s. It articulates the hopes and aspirations of Dalits and opens new avenues of expressing the faith in society. The life realities of Dalits, an oppressed community, have become an interpretative tool and source in Dalit theologizing. Many scholars have contributed to the development of Dalit theology. James Massey, one of the pioneers of Dalit theology movement, has also articulated on the nature, goal and method of doing Dalit theology. Though he shared the common vision and mission of Dalit theology, he attempted to widen its scope and implications by bringing fresh insights into it. Some of the methodical issues which James Massey addressed in his Dalit theologizing are explained in this chapter.

Origin

Dalit theology is an attempt to interpret Christian faith in the light of the life realities of Dalits in India. It is emerged out of the past and present discriminated experiences of Dalits and their struggles against casteism, and their aspirations for social justice in Church and society.[1] The liberation of Dalits from the oppression of caste mechanism is the focal point of Dalit theologizing.[2] The body-mediated experiences of Dalits are the primary epistemological source of Dalit theology. Though Dalit theological thinking began to appear in 1980's, according to John Webster, the seeds of Dalit theology were already sown in the address given by Rev. John Subhan, a convert from Islam, in All Religions Conference for Dalit leaders held at Lucknow in May 1936. His speech was on 'The Goodnews of Christ for the Depressed Classes' that was influenced by the theology of the social gospel.[3] However, the development of present Dalit Theology begins with 'Towards a Shudra Theology,' an address delivered by A.P. Nirmal at the United Theological College, Bangalore in April, 1981.[4]

According to James Massey, the first phase of Dalit theology was developed in 1980s. During this period, pioneers of Dalit theology movement articulated the vision, need and goal of Dalit Theology. One of the contributing factors for the emergence of Dalit theological thinking was the involvement of many Dalit and non-Dalit Christian thinkers in Dalit movements of that time. Dalit movements of 1970s also influenced the Dalit theological thinking of this phase. In the second phase (1990s), debate and discussions were concentrated on the role and sources of Dalit theology. The attention was also given to reflect on Dalit identity, Dalit history and Dalit solidarity. During this period, the expression, 'Dalit' was defined as an 'oppressive state' of Dalits throughout the centuries in caste society. They named themselves with the condition of their historical victimhood. The 'theology' in Dalit theology was interpreted as pointer to the role of Christian faith/theology in the life of Dalits to come out of their 'oppressed condition.' CISRS played an important role in this period to organize consultations and initiate studies in developing Dalit theologizing. It also joined with Dalit movements to conduct regional and national level programs to promote the cause of Dalits and their initiative of theological thinking. The third phase, started from 2000, has witnessed new developments such as emergence of more Dalit theological literature, instituting Dalit theology departments and establishing research institutes such as Centre for Dalit/Subaltern Studies, New Delhi. They addressed new challenges posed by globalization in the life of Dalits and initiated efforts to develop Dalit hermeneutical principles.[5] During these phases, Gurukul Lutheran Theological College and Research Institute, Chennai, played an important role in elevating Dalit theology as an academic discipline. It was the first theological college that established a full-fledged department of Dalit Theology in India. Through its academic initiatives, Dalit theology was recognized as an optional subject both in the B.D. and M.Th. programs under the Senate of Serampore College.[6]

Goal and Role

According to James Massey, theology "is the local expression of the experiences of local people of their faith."[7] In this sense, for him, Dalit theology is a faith expression of the "living experiences of Dalits." It is rooted in their experiences of oppression, poverty, suffering, injustice, illiteracy, and denial of identity.[8] Dalit theology helps the Dalits locate their experiences in theological context[9] and facilitate their liberation by questioning the oppressive values which perpetuated their social captivity.[10] The ultimate goal of Dalit theologizing is to enable Dalits to recover their original status, 'the divinely undivided humanity of the created world.' They are normal human beings created with God-given rights and privileges enjoyed by others.[11] Caste system separated them from others and placed them in inferior status. The role of Dalit theology is to build solidarity among Dalits to combat the forces of social oppression.

Solidarity generates power to challenge the dominant strategy of perpetuating divided humanity. Theological foundation for solidarity is biblical God who is the God of Solidarity who always sided with the oppressed in human history. God of Solidarity demands commitment to God and to the fellow Dalits. This dual commitment is expressed in solidarity. For Massey, this solidarity must be the subject of Dalit theology. In fact, Dalit theology is also a faith reflection on the solidarity between God and Dalits, and among themselves. This solidarity is guided by the aspiration of Dalit liberation and motivated by the assurance of the participation of God in their struggles and the life of Jesus who stands as model for vertical and horizontal solidarity.[12] The dual solidarity of Dalits only can lead them into whole salvation. Dalit theology provides theological resources for achieving the goal of whole salvation, and thereby contributing to establish 'just society.'[13] In the process of theologizing, according to James Massey, Dalit theology has to bring out the Dalit roots of Christianity in India. It helps them claim their ministerial and leadership space in the Church. Dalit theology, being a counter theology, also needs to offer an alternative vision for the oppressed communities who have been influenced by traditional Indian theologies.[14] He also cautions that Church, as an institution, has always opposed any change in the theological thinking of people in the past. Still, she is not fully open to new theologies like Dalit theology. It is also a fact that faith communities do not enthusiastically receive any theology which questions the structures and practices of the Church.[15] The goal and role of Dalit theology informs that it is an action-oriented faith refection which seeks to achieve full liberation of Dalits in society.

Critique of Indian Christian Theology and Missionary Theology

Classical Indian Christian Theology, according to James Massey, is not relevant to the majority Christians who come from socially marginalized communities in India. Its irrelevancy lies in its formation. It was emerged out of the religious and cultural experiences of upper caste Christians whose main concern was to appropriate the Christian faith within the framework of Brahmanic religiosity and philosophy. The classical Indian Christian theologies never embodied the experiences and faith narratives of majority Christians whose social status was very low in the caste hierarchy.[16] Since the pioneers of this movement such as Brahmabandhav Upadhyaya, Sadhu Sunder Singh, Nehemiah Goreh, H.A. Krishna Pillai, Narayan Vaman Tilak, A.J. Appasamy, P. Chenchiah, V. Chakkarai, etc were upper caste Christians, the experiences of majority Christians did not form the content of their theological articulations.[17] While the immediate concerns of the caste Christians was the indigenization of Christian faith-the interpretation of Christian faith in Brahmanic Hindu thought forms, the lower caste Christians were concerned about their survival and livelihood in society. Instead of addressing the issues of these poor Christians, the pioneers of Indian Christian theology attempted to respond to the religious and philosophical questions of the time. The need of Dalit Theology emerged in the context of the failure of Indian Christian theology to respond to the life realities of Dalits. It was realized that a new theological expression based on the experiences of Dalits only could address their issues and facilitate their liberation from the social and theological captivity.[18]

Like Indian Christian theology, traditional missionary theologies promoted by the European missionaries also did not address the issues of Dalits and other oppressed communities. Being rooted in pietistic theological interpretation of Christian faith, missionary theologies focused on second birth, personal holiness and otherworldliness. They emphasized individual salvation which is futuristic and otherworldly. Since pietistic theology was emerged as a theological expression of the rich in Europe, particularly in

Germany, missionary theology rooted in pietism failed to address the issues of the poor in India.[19] The early missionaries who were born out of pietism introduced a missionary theology which was unconnected to the realities of majority Indian Christians, particularly the Dalits. Whatever they introduced into India still influences the minds of Indian Christians.[20] In fact, missionary theology introduced in India was not fully contextually relevant. We needed a theology which must have responded to the contextual realities like caste-based social order and its ramifications in the life of people who belonged to the lower strata of society. Missionary theologies failed to understand the fact that no theology could be relevant to the Indian context if it did not address the issue of caste.[21] Instead of encouraging the people to shun caste consciousness, missionary theologies either compromised with caste system or ignored the challenges of caste. This was the result of the influence of pietism. Dalit theology was emerged as a response to the continuing influence of missionary theologies which motivated the Dalits in terms of otherworldly life more than affirming 'this-worldly-cum-otherworldly life.'

James Massey is also critical of 'Public Theology' or 'Asian Public Theology.' It devalues the contextual theologies which, according to Public theologians, are more relative than universal, and having no absolute claims. For Max L. Stackhouse, one of the proponents of Public Theology, contextual theologies are expressions of the experiences of certain communities which do not have universal appeal. He argues that public theology addresses the issues of 'a new public' surfaced in the context of globalization and aims to the emergence of global civil society. Though he criticizes contextual theologies, public theology is also emerged out of American and European contexts. The Asian public theology shares the views of 'Public Theology' in the west. It focuses on the questions and issues of the people in general, and is interreligious in nature. Felix Wilfred, a pioneering voice of Asian Public Theology, explains the nature of the involvement of Asian Public Theology. For him, it deals with all issues in public sphere, but may not specifically touch the issues of the poor. Within the interreligious framework, he argues for the role of every religion in public sphere. Though Asian Public Theology deals with the issues of subaltern communities, main attention is to address the issues of people in general. By promoting interreligious approach to engage with public sphere, Asian Public Theology encouraging dominant religious traditions which are least concerned about the societal issues of oppressed communities like Dalits.[22] The need of Dalit theology comes in the context of the 'public' nature of issues addressed in the public theology. It is not necessary that 'a new public' will consider a Dalit issue as a public issue. Dalit theology informs that every issue faced by Dalits is a public issue because it is the product of the outlook of a social order created by caste system which influences entire society.

According to James Massey, the goal of new theological expressions should be to build up just and humane communities in society. Both the dominant and the dominated should equally participate in this process. While the dominant confess their role for unequal social condition and get rid of their oppressive mind set, the oppressed forgive those sins emerged out of unjust social and economic systems and involve in the process of creating a new human community and a new culture of participation, sharing, fellowship etc.[23] Dalit theology aims to achieve this goal by motivating the people to destroy the walls of separation created by caste in Indian society. Dalit reading of Christian faith contribute to this process of liberation.

A Comment on Methodology

In the initial period of doing Dalit theology, according to James Massey, many of the pioneers including him were not following a particular methodology. Though they were aware of the need of a methodology in developing new theological formulations, they did not think of a well designed methodology to be followed in their articulations. However, they placed pain and pathos of Dalits as point of departure for Dalit theological thinking. For Massey, in the beginning stage of Dalit theology, methodology was not their main concern but the condition of Dalits in church and society and their struggle for liberation. This liberative impulse constituted the rationale for Dalit theology. When he wrote his first article on Dalit theology, 'Ingredients for a Dalit Theology,' Massey says, "I hardly had any thought of methodology." Though the absence of methodological guidelines slowed down the process of Dalit theologizing, the pioneers could articulate the vision and goal of Dalit theology in the early decade of the development of Dalit theology. Gradually they began to focus on methodological issues, and attempted to develop systematic thinking on the life realities of Dalits in church and society.[24] Since then, different Dalit theological methodologies have been emerged, and enormous literatures have been added to the Dalit theological thinking.

Nature of Dalit Theology

The expression 'Dalit' in Dalit theology basically defines the nature and goals of Dalit theology. 'Dalit' as an identity derives from the condition in which the people who identify themselves as Dalits live in for centuries. This condition is imposed upon them by the people who perpetuated caste as a tool of domination and symbol of hegemony. On the one hand, caste system placed them in inferior position, on the other hand created division among them by naming them based on the assigned jobs. But their past informs them that before caste system was introduced, they were undivided humanity enjoyed freedom in all aspects of human life. Dalit theology attempts to empower Dalits to reclaim the lost identity and dignified life.[25] The nature of Dalit theology can be discerned from the five specifics explained by James Massey. Firstly, Dalit theology is primarily intended to conscientize Dalits of their present condition in church and society. It has to make them aware that they belonged to a casteless community existed on the principle of equality. It is the caste system which pushed them into the condition of discrimination and stigmatization. The process of conscientization helps the Dalits to learn that their present condition, particularly their inferior status in the caste system, is neither divinely ordained nor self-created, but imposed on them by a humanly created institution-caste system. Dalit theology enables them to contest the caste system which prevents their upward social mobility, and equip them with a new perspective and thinking which lead them to whole salvation.[26] Secondly, Dalit theology confronts the non-Dalits who perpetuate caste mind-set and give off caste feeling against Dalits. It tells them that by practicing caste and oppressing Dalits, they are also losing their original divinely created humanity. The liberative process initiated by Dalit theology includes the liberation of non-Dalits, the liberation from casteism, too. It explains the inclusive nature of liberation promoted by Dalit theology. The liberation of both Dalits and non-Dalits constitutes the agenda of Dalit theological thinking.[27] Thirdly, Dalit theology questions the conscience of the church and Christian community influenced by the traditional theologies that produce passive faith communities. It also challenges the faith communities to confront the oppressive political, economic, social, religious, cultural structures and take a stand with the Dalits who constitute majority of Christian population in India.[28] Fourthly, Dalit theology encourages common believers to actively participate in the struggles of Dalits. They are influenced by the otherworldly theological thinking which keeps them passive towards the pertinent human issues of this world. Dalit theology counters this theological orientation and inspires them to follow Jesus Christ who expressed his solidarity with least ones in society.[29] Fifthly, Dalit theology stands for the whole salvation of Dalits and non-Dalits. It attempts to facilitate salvation/liberation of Dalits in this world and in the world to come according to the Christian faith. The salvation which focuses only on otherworldly life is partial salvation, which is not Biblical understanding of salvation. Since Dalit theology aims to achieve casteless faith communities and societies, it takes a theological position based on the redemptive work of Jesus, which was made for entire humanity, both Dalits and non-Dalits that liberation becomes wholistic when Dalits are liberated from caste oppression and non-Dalits are liberated from caste consciousness. Thus, Dalit theology facilitates everyone to reclaim original divinely created human state which is not oppressive but liberative in nature.[30] Though Dalit theology primarily stands for the liberation of Dalits, its inherent nature explains that the liberation of Dalits contributes to the liberation of non-Dalits and the birth of new human and faith communities in society.

Sources of Dalit Theology

Like any other contextual liberation theologies, Dalit theology derives its life from certain sources. They provide data for building up a theology which reflects the theological thinking of an oppressed community in India. Though primary sources come from Dalit world, Dalit theology draws liberative insights from ideologies, religious traditions and various academic disciplines. James Massey argues that Dalit history constitutes the primary source of Dalit theologizing. He focused on the history which tells the past identity of Dalits before the arrival of Aryans. The dominant histories always portrayed Dalits in inferior social position and made them to accept an identity given by the caste system. The history of Dalits before the origin of caste tells that once they were normal human beings who owned land, natural resources and enjoyed human dignity and freedom. They were the original dwellers of this land. Therefore, the history of Dalits must be rewritten to recover the status of Dalits and contest the dominant narrations of Dalit identity. On the one hand Dalit theology challenges the hegemony of caste by drawing insights from the history of Dalits in pre-Aryan period; on the other hand it attempts to reconstruct the history of Dalits to reclaim the lost human dignity. The recognition of history as source of theologizing comes from the Bible (Deuteronomy 6:20-25; I Corinthians 1:26-28). It is a mandate to remember the past while articulating the faith in the present context.[31] The past identity of Dalits as the people who enjoyed freedom and dignity provides rationale for the very purpose of Dalit theology.

Dalit experience is another important source of Dalit theologizing. It is an experience of pain and pathos a Dalit experiences as an individual and as a member of a community. At the individual level, s/he experiences discrimination and humiliation in social gatherings, work place, educational institutions etc. S/he faces physical assault, social boycott at the instances of inter-caste marriages and prohibition from certain sacred places. However, a Dalit woman experiences more pain than a Dalit man because of her gender and caste. Though individual humiliation cannot be separated from community level of humiliation, Dalits experience pain as a community when they begin to resist the caste oppression and discrimination. They face physical assault, burning down of homes and villages, public sexual harassment of their women, social boycott and negation of basic amenities such as water, road, electricity etc. The caste hegemony always attempts to suppress

Dalit community awakening by dividing them on the basis of sub-caste and religion.[32] These past and present experiences not only provide resources for developing theologies but also ask theological questions of freedom, liberation/salvation, justice etc. The search for the answers to the questions emerged from the experiences of Dalits pave the way for the birth of new theological formulations.

Dalit theology emerges out of a dialogue between Scripture and the context of Dalits. The Scripture presents the Gospel of Jesus Christ which is liberative and empowering for Dalits in their journey of struggle. A Dalit theologian interprets the Scripture in the light of the life-realities of Dalits. In this process, the Word of God gets embodied in the Dalit context and lives among them as liberating force.[33] As a source, the Scripture comes after the context of Dalits. Dalit theologizing starts from Dalit realities and get into the Scripture. When the Scripture is read in Dalit context, it is read with a perspective. The new reading brings forth new meaning of the text. The Scripture provides numerous liberative ideas and thoughts on every day human life. When they are interpreted in relation to Dalit life, new theological discourse is evolved.[34] In addition to Dalit history, Dalit experience and Scripture, Social Sciences also can function as sources of Dalit theology. They provide data on caste system and its various manifestations in society. This is very much important for a theological articulation which challenges caste system and its impact on Dalits. The tools of analysis in social sciences help to understand the pertinent issues of Dalits in society. The data on these issues supply material for new theological reflections.[35] A study on the beliefs, values, customs, traditions and institutions of particular society also can provide resources for Dalit theologizing. In this attempt, liberative elements can be analyzed and interpreted in relation to Dalit life.[36] Dalit theology becomes meaningful to all Dalits if it reflects the liberative values and percepts of other religious traditions too. For example, the Christian understanding of God can interact with beliefs on God in other religious traditions. This will help in strengthening Dalit theological understanding of God. The liberative insights from other religious traditions can become a source for developing a sound theology for Dalit liberation. It may also contribute to the solidarity of Dalits irrespective of faith affiliations.[37] The sources of Dalit theologizing not only provide material for making a theology but also remind the need of discovering new sources for taking Dalit theology into another level of its growth. No source is absolute. New challenges require new sources for developing relevant theological responses.

Who has to do Dalit Theology?

Dalit theology, according to James Massey, must primarily be articulated by Dalit themselves. Since it is emerged out of their painful historical experiences and of their hope for liberated life, an authentic Dalit theology can be produced by Dalits alone. They are the primary epistemological source for this theology. They are the content of Dalit theology. Though non-Dalits who are genuinely committed to the cause of Dalit liberation can also participate in the process of Dalit theologizing, their theology will be a 'theology about the Dalits.' It will not be 'a theology of the Dalits' which comes out of the lived experiences of Dalit realities.[38] The difference between these two theologies is that while the former is the result of an acquired knowledge of the non-Dalits the latter is the product of the experiential knowledge of the Dalits. A true Dalit theology emerges from the knowledge and experience of Dalits who are involved in the struggles for the liberation of Dalits.[39] It does not mean that non-Dalits are completely excluded from doing Dalit theology. However, in order to maintain 'Dalit identity' of Dalit theology priority must be given to the 'experience' of Dalits over the 'knowledge' of non-Dalits in the process of developing Dalit theology. The emotional identity of Dalits with Dalit theology and the 'solidarity in action' of the non-Dalits with Dalits together bring out a theology which is Dalit in essence and liberative in nature. The Dalit theologizing of non-Dalits become genuine if they express their solidarity with the Dalits and participate in the struggles for liberation.[40] The roles of both Dalits and non-Dalits in Dalit theologizing ultimately should lead to the structural change in society, and contribute to the building up of just and humane communities where every human being is respected as the image of God. Dalit theology strives to achieve that goal.[41] At the same time, for James Massey, a Dalit theologian must always be reminded of a few things: firstly the aspiration of Dalits for their whole salvation; secondly Biblical God is on the side of the oppressed like Dalits and emboldens them to challenge the oppressive forces in society; thirdly, Jesus Christ is the model for participating in the struggles of Dalits for liberation.[42] S/he also must have 'faith commitment' to enter into the process of Dalit theologizing. It has to be reflected in the personal commitment to God, the fellow Dalits and the society.[43] It is the faith commitment which takes him/her to the world of Dalits and provokes him/her to articulate the faith in the light of Dalit life realities. A theology of liberation is born in the encounter between the faith and the world of Dalits. Dalits who experience and know this world of pain, struggle, sorrow and resistance can contribute better than non-Dalits.

Dalit Bible Commentary

Dalit Bible Commentary was one of the initiatives taken by Centre for Dalit Studies under the leadership of James Massey to interpret the Bible in the light of Dalit life realities. It was intended to make Scripture more meaningful in the life of Dalits and non-Dalits in Indian society. It followed a dialogical approach in interpreting the text. It facilitated Dalit context/life to enter into dialogue with the biblical text and context. Dalit Bible Commentary looked at the Bible through the eyes of Dalits and tried to inculcate new consciousness in reading the Scripture. It informs that sensitivity to the Text and the Dalit context is the primary requirement for interpreting the text from Dalit perspective. When the text is interpreted in Dalit context, the interpreted word, the incarnated word, become liberating word for Dalits,[44] and a new theology is born. In the dialogue between Dalit world and biblical world, interpreter has to locate the points of convergence and relevance between these two worlds. For example, the Dalit world and the biblical world enter into dialogue in the process of interpreting Luke 2:8-20. In this story, the shepherds are portrayed as people who first heard the angelic announcement of the birth of Jesus Christ. A reading from Dalit perspective informs that both the shepherds in the biblical world and the Dalits in India have certain commonalities in terms of their job and social status. The Greek term for 'shepherd' is *poimen*, which means 'to care.' In Punjabi language, one who looks after the animals is called *palee*. Majority of them are Dalits. In fact, both are involved in almost same occupation. In the biblical world, the shepherds were 'abhorrent to the Egyptians' (Gen 46:34). Caste system and its purity-pollution mechanism made the Dalits 'abhorrent' to the caste people. The shepherds worked on contract basis (Gen 31:41) as a Dalit *palee* works even today. Most of the time, a shepherd was compelled to live outside the village (Lk 2:8) because of the requirement of job. Like a shepherd, a Dalit was/ is also supposed to live outside the main village because of his caste identity and so-called impure job. Though shepherds were considered as inferior in the biblical world, they were the first recipients of the news of the birth of Jesus. Moreover, most of the patriarchs in the Old Testament were shepherds. David was a shepherd. One of the titles given to Jesus in the Bible was 'Son of David.'[45] This type of dialogue (Dalit world and biblical world) strengthens their (Dalits) hope of empowerment and generates new energy in their lives to work for it. Dalit Bible Commentary is basically Dalit theology. It is an interpretation of scripture (contents of faith) facilitated by the dialogue between Dalit world and biblical world.

As a theology that emerged out of the experiences of an oppressed community, Dalit theology mainly responds to the issues and concerns of Dalits in India. It envisions the liberation of Dalits from the oppression of caste and offers them a perspective to contest the dominant narratives that make them subjugated in society. Dalit theologizing affirms the theological value of Dalit experiences and encourages them to read the Scripture through their eyes. Dalit theology is also an expression of the assertion of their identity, history and values. As a theology of solidarity, it not only theologizes the experiences of Dalits but also motivates them to build up solidarity among them to achieve the goal of whole salvation/full liberation.

Endnotes

[1] M.E. Prabhakar, "Introduction," in *Towards a Dalit Theology*, edited by M.E. Prabhakar (Delhi: ISPCK, 1989), 2.

[2] M.E. Prabhakar, "The Search for a Dalit Theology," in *Towards a Dalit Theology*, edited by M.E. Prabhakar (Delhi: ISPCK, 1989), 44.

[3] John C.B. Webster, *The Dalit Christians: A History* (New Delhi: ISPCK, Revised and Enlarged Version 2009), 275.

[4] Arvind P. Nirmal, "Introduction," in *A Reader in Dalit Theology*, edited by Arvind P. Nirmal (Reprint, Chennai: GLTC & RC, 2007), iii.

[5] James Massey, "A Review of Dalit Theology" in *Dalit and Minjung Theologies: A Dialogue*, edited by Samson Prabhakar and Jinkwan Kwon (Bangalore: BTESSC/SATHRI, 2006), 3, 6-11; James Massey, "Vision and Role of Dalit Theology," in *A Theology from Dalit Perspective*, edited by James Massey and S. Lourduswamy (New Delhi: CDS, 2001), 69.

[6] Arvind P. Nirmal, "Introduction," iii.

[7] James Massey, "Ingredients for a Dalit Theology" in *A Reader in Dalit Theology*, edited by Arvind P. Nirmal (Reprint, Chennai: GLTC & RC, 2007), 145.

[8] James Massey, "Ingredients for a Dalit Theology" 147.

[9] James Massey, "A Review of Dalit Theology," 7.

[10] James Massey, "History and Dalit Theology," in *Frontiers of Dalit Theology*, edited by V. Devasahayam (Chennai: ISPCK/Gurukul, 1997), 181.

[11] James Massey, "An Analysis of the Dalit Situation with Special Reference to Dalit Christians and Dalit Theology," *Religion and Society*, Vol 52/No 3-4 (September-December 2007): 57-86 at 83.

[12] James Massey, "An Analysis of the Dalit Situation with Special Reference to Dalit Christians and Dalit Theology," 84.

[13] James Massey, "Dalit Theology: Response to Dalit Context," in *Dalit Issue in Today's Theological Debate*, edited by James Massey and S. Lourduswamy (New Delhi: CDS, 2003), 129.

[14] James Massey, "Dalit Roots of Indian Christianity," in *Frontiers of Dalit Theology*, edited by V. Devasahayam (Chennai: ISPCK/Gurukul, 1997), 203.

[15] James Massey, "Ingredients for a Dalit Theology," 150.

[16] James Massey, "Need of a Dalit Theological Expression," in *Confronting Life: Theology out of the Context*, edited by M.P. Joseph (Delhi: ISPCK, 1995), 196; James Massey, *Dalits in India: Religion as a Source of Bondage or Liberation with Special Reference to Christians* (New Delhi: Manohar, 2009 Reprint), 170.

[17] James Massey, "Need of a Dalit Theological Expression," 197.

[18] James Massey, *Dalits in India: Religion as a Source of Bondage or Liberation with Special Reference to Christians*, 172-173.

[19] James Massey, "Christianity to be Renewed? Rethink Theology," in *Rethinking Theology in India: Christianity in the Twenty-first Century*, edited by James Massey and T.K. John SJ (New Delhi: CDS & Manohar, 2013), 26.

[20] James Massey, "Dalit Theology: Response to Dalit Context," 121.

[21] James Massey, "Christianity to be Renewed? Rethink Theology," 27.

[22] James Massey, "Christianity to be Renewed? Rethink Theology," 42 45.

[23] James Massey and T.K. John, "Common Task for Tomorrow," in *Rethinking Theology in India: Christianity in the Twenty-first Century*, edited by James Massey and T.K. John SJ (New Delhi: CDS & Manohar, 2013), 456-457.

[24] James Massey, "Revisiting and Resignifying the Methodology for Dalit Theology," in *Revisiting and Resignifying the Methodology for Dalit Theology*,

edited by James Massey and Indukuri John Mohan Razu (New Delhi: CDS & Bangalore: UTC, 2008), 51-55.

[25] James Massey, *Dalit Theology: History, Context, Text and Whole Salvation* (New Delhi: Manohar, 2013), 215-216.

[26] James Massey, *Ecumenism Means Justice* (Matiala, New Delhi: CDS, 2014), 99.

[27] James Massey, "Vision and Role of Dalit Theology," 78.

[28] James Massey, *Dalit Theology: History, Context, Text and Whole Salvation*, 223.

[29] James Massey, "Vision and Role of Dalit Theology," 79.

[30] James Massey, *Ecumenism Means Justice*, 100.

[31] James Massey, "History and Dalit Theology," 174-176.

[32] James Massey, *Ecumenism Means Justice*, 91-92.

[33] James Massey, "Revisiting and Resignifying the Methodology for Dalit Theology," 61.

[34] James Massey, *Dalit Theology: History, Context, Text and Whole Salvation*, 154.

[35] James Massey, *Ecumenism Means Justice*, 92.

[36] James Massey, "Revisiting and Resignifying the Methodology for Dalit Theology," 59.

[37] James Massey, *Ecumenism Means Justice*, 94.

[38] James Massey, "Centre for Dalit Studies (Theology): An Introduction," *A Theology from Dalit Perspective*, edited by James Massey and S. Lourduswamy (New Delhi: CDS, 2001), 102.

[39] James Massey, "A Review of Dalit Theology," 12.

[40] James Massey, "Centre for Dalit Studies (Theology): An Introduction," 103.

[41] James Massey, "A Review of Dalit Theology," 13.

[42] James Massey, "Vision and Role of Dalit Theology," 76.

[43] James Massey, *Dalit Theology: History, Context, Text and Whole Salvation*, 154.

[44] James Massey, *Dalit Bible Commentary: A Challenge Response* (New Delhi: CDS, 2011), 7-9.

[45] James Massey, "Introduction," in *Dalit World-Biblical World: An Encounter*, edited by Leonard Fernando S J and James Massey (New Delhi: CDS and Vidyajyoti College of Theology, 2007), 13-14.

Chapter 6

Church, Mission and Ministry

The idea of 'Church' is metaphorically illustrated by different biblical images such as 'Body of Christ', 'People of God' and 'Bride of Christ'. It was gradually developed as a doctrine, and the study of the doctrine of Church later came to be called as 'Ecclesiology'. The term 'ecclesiology' is derived from the Greek word, *Ekklesia,* which means 'an assembly', 'called out' etc. Throughout the centuries, the doctrine of 'Church' has been explained and interpreted in different ways according to the changing context of the time. Isidore of Pelusium of 5th century interpreted Church as "the assembly of saints joined together by correct faith and an excellent manner of life."[1] For Augustine of Hippo, Church is "a mixed body" of both saints and sinners.[2] Martin Luther understood Church as the place where the 'Word of God is preached, believed, confessed and acted upon.'[3] These ecclesiological understandings developed in specific contexts, particularly the engagement of Christian faith with the existing ideological and philosophical thinking of the time. Dalit ecclesiological articulations are evolved out of the experiences of Dalits within the Church and in the larger society, and their encounters with the 'elitist' and 'casteist' image of the Indian Church. Thus, the present existence of the Christian community and the condition of Dalit Christians is the locus of Dalit ecclesiological thinking. In this chapter, ecclesiological and missional/ministerial refections of James Massey are briefly narrated. His is placed along with other scholars to make his views more vivid and engaging.

Indian Church as 'Church of the Poor'

The history of the Indian Church starts from St. Thomas, one of the disciples of Jesus Christ, who is believed to have introduced the Christian faith in India. After his arrival in AD 52, many missionaries from different church traditions came and propagated the faith, and established their ecclesiastical orders. Gradually, people from different social backgrounds became members of the church throughout the centuries. The missionaries and the native Christians equally contributed to the establishment of churches and the formation of Christian communities throughout the nation. Socially, majority Christians come from Dalit, Tribal, Adivasi and Other Backward Class (OBC) communities. If membership of the Indian Church defines the image of the Church, then Indian Church is basically 'Church of the Poor' or 'Community of the Poor' because majority of its members are socially and economically poor. However, contradictory to its existence, the church exhibits an 'elitist image' or 'elitist identity' in society.[4] This image is built upon its institutions, which are mainly benefited by the elite sections in society, the church buildings, the mission compounds and a small number of its members who have achieved upward social and economic mobility. In fact, theologically and sociologically, Indian church has to be called as the 'Church of the Poor/Marginalized."[5] The social composition of the members and the missional and theological position of the church validate this contextual image. The elitist image/identity of the church, particularly in terms of structure or hierarchy, is inherited from the Christendom model of the church which emerged during the period of Constantine the Great. The church began to imitate the power structure and life of the Roman Empire without considering its identity derived from Jesus. The priestly class became royal class and began to call themselves as princes of the church and appear in imperial robes. The present church still follow the Christendom model which maintains elitist image in society. The 'Church of the Poor' does not exclude anyone but takes a stand which affirms the preferential option for the Indian poor. It is a church which stands in solidarity with them. The foundation of this image is Jesus Christ, the prophet-servant, who lived for the poor in society.[6] The elitist image tends to ignore the concerns of Indian poor and limits their space in the church.

Church as a New Community

The creation story in the Bible narrates the divine vision of a new community (Gen 1-2) which exists in harmony and peace. But the first community could not remain in its original state due to the misuse of the freedom given by God. (Gen 3). As the story of human community unfolds in the Bible, we see that in the process of restoring human community into its original status, God chose a particular community named Israel and gave them two main tasks: internal transformation and become an agent of transformation for the rest of the humanity (Gen 12:1-3). In order to achieve the tasks given to them, God gave them certain rules including Ten Commandments (Deut 5:1-22). The ultimate purpose of these rules was two-fold: the right relationship with God and with fellow human beings. Hence, a new community as intended by God at the time of creation would be formed again. The praxis of the vision of a new community is authentically seen in the life and work of Jesus Christ. He rejected the existing socio-religious structures of the community life in his time and introduced an alternative form of community. He taught the basic foundations of a 'new community.' He denounced exclusion and attempted to build up an alternative community based on the vales of love, justice, equality and freedom.

He embraced the people who were considered as socially inferior and laid the foundation for a new community beyond any class (caste) or gender. The equal and inherent value of every human being was upheld in his teachings. His view of equality was against the dominant binary of 'superior' or 'inferior' in community life, which is contradictory to the will of God. By calling people, Jesus was calling them to be part of a new community. They were actually called to involve in the process of building up a new community where mutual empowerment happens. Jesus firstly appointed twelve disciples and later, he selected another seventy to engage in the work of building up a new community. (Lk 10:1-12). His life and work is the foundation of this new community. And the church stands as a sign of the new community which Jesus inaugurated on the earth.[7] It has to exist as a community where none is excluded on social and economic grounds, but accomplishes the divine vision of a new community, an alternative community in life and witness in society. For Dalits, Church is a new community of solidarity, hope, acceptance, love, equality, justice, social healing and empowerment. This is the location where their social capital and network for upward mobility is developed. The church as a 'New Community' must take bold initiatives to facilitate the upward social mobility of Dalit Christians in society. It does not mean that church should stand only for their cause. However, they deserve 'preferential treatment' because of their historical victimization that deprived them of their social and cultural capital.

Mission and Ministry

Christian faith is a missional faith. Every Christian is called to share the Gospel of Jesus Christ in respective context. This mandate is derived from the Great Commission of Jesus Christ, upon which the idea of Christian mission is grounded and developed. Some understand Christian mission as the propagation of the Gospel of Jesus Christ while others consider it as witnessing to Jesus' life through actions, particularly human empowerment initiatives based on Nazareth manifesto. When we understand Christian mission in the light of Jesus' life and work, it is evident that Christian mission basically aims to accomplish the holistic salvation of entire creation. Different perspectival readings have contributed to the discourses on the nature and purpose of Christian mission. Though mission and ministry are often compartmentalized in academic discussions, both have same aim to be achieved: salvation/liberation of entire creation in this world. Both facilitate the process of empowering human community spiritually and socially. For Dalits, there is no difference between mission and ministry. One has to complement another in the process of their liberation/salvation in this world and the world to come. However, the life-realities of Dalits inform us that they are historical targets of mission and ministry. They often remain as 'objects' than 'subjects' in mission and ministry ventures.

Mission and Ministry: Change in Perspective

Indian Christianity is the product of mission endeavors starting from St. Thomas in the first century to the European missionaries and native Christians till today. The Indian constitution, which guarantees religious freedom with propagation of the faith, provides legal protection to the Christian mission. The mission organizations and the mission departments of different denominations make use of their resources to propagate the faith among different people groups. The question often raised by Dalits is, what is prioritized in mission and ministry of the Church: quality or quantity? It is a fact that majority of Christian mission and ministry activities aim to increase the number of converts than the quality of those converts. Quality here refers to the spiritual and social advancement of the converts. The social condition of the majority Dalit converts tells a different story of missional/ministerial engagement. Pope Francis said "I am convinced of one thing: the great changes in history were realized when reality was seen not from the centre but rather from the periphery. It is a hermeneutical question: reality is understood only if it is looked at from the periphery, and not when our viewpoint is equidistant from everything..."[8] A look from periphery (Dalit location) informs that their social and economic status has not been adequately changed even after their conversions. Still majority of them are in slums or colonies or in their old *Cheries*. In fact, they experience "standstill condition"[9] in terms of social and economic mobility. This is not to negate the contributions of mission workers in the life of Dalits, but to say that they have not yet come to the socio-economic-educational standing of their brothers and sisters in other religious traditions and co-religionalists. This failure is the point of departure for new missional and ministerial ventures. We do not ask the question, whose responsibility is to bring the new converts into another level of his/her life in society? Asking such question will initiate the process of making a shift in the perspective of mission and ministry. If it is asked, the answer would be: the collective effort of Christian faith communities in the respective context. They often forget their responsibility because of the influence of 'other worldly' missional theologies taught throughout the generations. The 'other worldly' missional theologies[10] teaches that the Christians should mainly (read 'only' also) aim for the salvation in another world which is yet to come. This one-sided understanding is contradictory to the Biblical vision of mission and ministry. The words of M.M. Thomas are antidote to 'otherworldly' affirmation of Christian mission and ministry, "Humanization is inherent in the message of salvation in Christ."[11] Saving the lives of people, particularly the Dalits also means helping them to live as dignified and empowered human beings with God-given rights and privileges. According to Samuel Amirtham, "Jesus' proclamation of the Good news is evangelization, which means that those who are in various kinds of bondage, in prisons of poverty and powerlessness, under the bonds of ignorance and superstitions and the victims of oppression and injustices are free."[12] Therefore, there should be a change in the perspective of Christian mission and ministry: a shift from quantity to quantity-cum-quality and from partial empowerment to wholistic empowerment. For Dalits, mission and ministry should result in the establishment of Christian communities empowered in all aspects of life. An authentic missional and ministerial affirmation of faith leads to the experience of liberation/salvation in this world and the world to come.

Pain-Pathos of People: Site of Christian Mission and Ministry
Dalit theologizing locates Christian mission and ministry in the site of the *pain-pathos* of Dalits and other marginalized communities. It is the site where Christian mission and ministry have to find its meaning in public space. For Dalits, responding to the *pain-pathos* of those involved in the struggle is a ministerial and missional engagement. Its efficacy depends on how much those involved in mission and ministry knows the *pain-pathos* and the wounded psyche of the margins and the vulnerable in society.[13] This is also an experience of locating God in the life realities of the marginal people like Dalits.[14] Dalit theologizing explains two aspects of missional and ministerial involvement: locating God in the pain-pathos of people and empowering them to fight against their condition of wretchedness. The former naturally leads the witnessing community to the latter. The legitimacy of *pain-pathos*-centric mission and ministry comes from a missional God who always stands on the side of the oppressed as happened in the event of Exodus. It reminds the missional community that divine missional intervention occurs in the sites of *pain-pathos* and resistance. God's liberating presence appears in the sites where there are attempts to

break the chains of bondage, be it social, political, religious, etc.[15] God, who involved in the Exodus event, calls the struggling people in any part of the world as "my people." It is a sign of the missional engagement. This God unconditionally involves in the struggles and painful realities of margins and enters into partnership with them.[16] This is the rationale of Dalit understanding of mission and ministry. The divine missional intervention in the life of oppressed masses is multi-dimensional in nature. It touches social, political, economic and religious aspects of life. God stands with the margins and the vulnerable till they achieve their liberation from oppressed conditions.[17] It explains the very nature of biblical mission and ministry. Moreover, God empowers them to initiate the process of salvation/liberation. The divine empowerment enables them to fight against their stigmatized and wretched life situations. Therefore, Christian mission and ministry need to facilitate the 'whole salvation' of the margins. The missional and ministerial interventions must empower the margins to shake off their social, economic, political and religious bondages and experience the 'whole salvation.'[18] In short, for Dalits, mission and ministry starts from the sites of the *pain-pathos* of margins and ends with their 'whole salvation.' In other words, it is a journey from 'pain-pathos' to 'whole salvation.'

Mission and Ministry as Dialogue with Life realities and Issues of Dalits

According to James Massey, "Christian mission and ministry among Dalits is primarily a dialogue with their life realities and issues. Missional and ministerial engagement with them must not be seen as a gift or charity."[19] This dialogue is intended to restore their dignity and identity in society. The caste system pushed them into the condition of 'no-people' and deprived them of original identity and dignity. Therefore, missional and ministerial vocation must be designed to have an intentional dialogue with the pertinent issues of

Dalits. The mission as dialogue finds its foundation in God who is dialogical in nature. As missional God, the biblical God is dialogical God too. This God initiates dialogue with people and participates in human history. The biblical God's dialogue with people happened in two levels: His incarnational act in Jesus and the life of Jesus. The intimate dialogue happened in the second level-God's dialogue with humanity through the works and teachings of Jesus Christ. In this level, God expressed his full solidarity with the people, particularly the Dalits of his time. In the incarnational act, the dialogical God sacrificed his other-worldly identity and took on the identity of the poor. He interacted with the life-realities of people who were religiously, socially and economically disempowered in society. They were the main dialogue partners of this dialogical God on this earth. The beauty of his dialogue was that many were empowered and restored back to the normal human life.[20] Jesus' mission and ministry was actually God's dialogue with people who were in need of the liberating touch of the Divine. For Dalits, this must serve as the foundation of Christian mission and ministry.

God's dialogue with the people through Jesus Christ, particularly the incarnation act, provides insights for Christian mission and ministry among the Dalits. Firstly, the incarnational act demands the church to initiate dialogue with the issues of Dalits in India. Along with the propagation of faith among the people, the church must also rediscover its mission as participating in the struggles of Dalits and other marginalized communities. It means the propagation of faith and the ministry of empowerment should complement each other. If the former is not accompanied by the latter, the church's 'incarnational act' remains incomplete. Secondly, the Church must redefine the concept of the people of God. As Jesus embraced the margins of his society as the people of God, so the church also must consider them as the people of God, and stand with them in their efforts to resist oppression and exclusion in society. The church, in its mission and ministry, should consider Dalits as the dialogue partners in the process of empowering/saving human communities. Their issues must become point of departure for the dialogue (mission and ministry).[21] Thirdly, the focus of mission and ministry must be shifted from 'soul-saving alone' to 'whole salvation.' It must touch the questions of 'life after death' and 'life after birth.' For Dalits, the issues and challenges of 'life after birth' need immediate attention than 'life after death.' Jesus equally addressed both dimensions of life. He started to deal with the issues of this life and proceeded to address the questions of 'life after death.' The church must follow this approach in the missional and ministerial engagement with Dalits. Finally, the issues of Dalits must become the issues of the church as Jesus risked his life for addressing the questions of the poor in society. For Dalits, caste discrimination and economic disempowerment are the most important challenges they face in India.[22] The church's missional and ministerial involvement with Dalits must address those challenges that place them in disadvantaged social position. The Christian mission and ministry get new meaning and new expression when it practically interacts with the life realities and issues of Dalits. The issue of reservation for Dalit Christians is a case in point. The mission/ministry as dialogue with the Dalit realities also implies expressing solidarity with Dalits. The sacraments lay the foundation for the praxis of dialogue.

Sacraments

The word 'sacrament' is derived from the Latin word, 'sacramentum,' which means 'a sacred oath.' It primarily points to the religious rituals performed in faith communities. Tertullian, who introduced this word into Christian theology, meant it in two ways. Firstly, it refers to the mystery of God's salvation. Secondly, it is a symbol or ritual related to the understanding of salvation. For Augustine, sacraments are signs of invisible grace. According to Martin Luther sacraments are divine signs which contain the promise of the forgiveness of sins.[23] While there are seven sacraments in Catholic tradition, two sacraments (Baptism and Eucharist) are observed in Protestant tradition. As symbols/signs or rituals, the sacraments play an important role in expressing Christian faith in community life. The symbolic/ritualistic and faith dimensions of sacraments become meaningful in a context if they are observed with contextual significance. The ritualistic dimension of the sacraments should be accompanied by the praxis of faith element involved in the sacraments. While acknowledging the ritualistic and symbolic value of sacraments, Dalit theologizing brings out the social meaning of sacraments in Indian context.

Baptism basically symbolizes the process of dying and rising with Christ. It is an act which involves the public declaration of the beginning of new life in Christ. Christians believe that a person becomes a child of God, a new creation through the ritual of baptism. The baptism facilitates him/her to become member of the Christian community, a new community built on the life and teachings of Jesus Christ.[24] On the one hand, baptism demands the believers to live a new life in Jesus Christ; on the other hand it calls for them to be part of Jesus' life and mission. In fact, baptism changes the identity of every baptized person. Therefore St. Paul stated that a baptized person is clothed with Jesus Christ (Gal 3: 27). The vow s/he takes at the time of baptism requires him/her to express the identity of Jesus in society. When a person dies with Jesus in the baptismal experience (Rom 6: 3), s/he dies with his/her old identity. In Indian context, a person primarily buries his/her caste identity in baptism. S/he is supposed to be no longer known by his/her caste identity, rather by his/her faith identity based on the life of Jesus Christ. Since baptism destroys all walls of separation created by caste, all baptized persons are equal in status and privilege in faith community (Galatians 3: 28).[25] Thus, baptism builds up a community of Jesus, a sign of the kingdom of God. In this community, caste consciousness is replaced by the consciousness of right relationship, equality and justice. For Dalits, baptism becomes meaningful in Indian context if it leads to the death of caste consciousness in the life of baptized believers. It is a ritual that proclaims not only salvation in Jesus Christ but also announces the annihilation of caste in his/her life. In the rite of baptism, they are actually baptized in the waters of kingdom values taught by Jesus Christ. It naturally leads them to involve in the praxis which affirms life in societal life. The unity of believers in Christ achieved through baptism should reflect in the united actions (actions in solidarity) against the life-negating forces and practices in church and society. If baptism does not create a new community beyond caste/ethnic assertions, it has no meaning for the margins in society. The baptism remains as a symbol/ritual than an instrument of change if it does not remove the obstacles which prevent the baptized persons from becoming a new creation. In fact, every Christian has to derive energy from the practice and meaning of baptism and use that energy to take bold initiatives in transforming church and society. The baptism actually gives birth to a new person with new perspective for building up an alternative community in society. For Dalits, baptism is not merely one of the rituals to be performed in faith communities but an experience of denouncing old disempowered life and of beginning a new life in Jesus whose life became a beacon of hope for those who were discriminated and excluded in society.

At the Eucharist, the Christians primarily remember the sufferings and death of Jesus Christ. When Eucharist was instituted Jesus instructed his disciples to observe it in remembrance of him. In fact, it is a memorial of what Jesus has done for the salvation of humanity. Today, it is observed as a rite which helps the believers experience God' grace and forgiveness of sins. Though it has a symbolic and spiritual value, the social and communitarian value of Eucharist is important for Dalits in India. As a sacrament, Eucharist facilitates the unity of believers in Christ. But in the context of caste, Eucharist demands the unity of believers beyond caste identities.[26] The Eucharistic unity fundamentally invalidates overt and covert forms of caste solidarity. As a symbol of faith, Eucharist points to the social responsibility of the believers. It teaches that unity achieved through faith has to be reflected in the social relations too. Jesus' table fellowship, primal form of Eucharist, was a table of empowerment and inclusion. It invited everyone who experienced discrimination and exclusion in society and empowered them to start a new journey in life. It was a symbol of reaching out to the outcastes of His time.[27] For Dalits, participation in the Eucharistic table is a liberative gesture. Once they were excluded from the social meals and religious rituals of Brahmanic Hinduism. In the Eucharistic community, they are no longer excluded but equal partakers in the 'holy meal.' The social praxis of this equality leads to the creation of a new community. It demolishes all walls of separations and brings forth a community of equals and solidarity. "Sharing the bread and one cup implies the breaking of all social divisions based upon racial, ethnic or caste system."[28] The Eucharist also reminds the believers about the social responsibility of sharing the resources with those who are not able to meet their basic needs of food, clothing and shelter. Unfortunately, majority who belong to this category are Dalits. Sharing the resources with the poor is a Eucharistic experience. It makes Eucharist more meaningful in society. The celebration of Eucharist without sharing the resources is meaningless to Dalits and other marginalized communities. Through sharing, a sense of community and solidarity is experienced among the believers, particularly the margins among them. And those who practice caste do not have right to take part in Eucharist. While caste perpetuates social inequity, Eucharist promotes equality. The partakers cannot follow the rule of caste but the rule of Eucharist: all are equal. As a sacrament of unity and reconciliation, Eucharist also calls for the unity and reconciliation of Dalits and non-Dalits in faith communities.[29] Thus, a new community of Jesus will be born in context. This community will be committed to the poor and the marginalized and stands in solidarity with those who strive for the celebration of life in its fullness. The sacraments prepare the believers to be a community of solidarity which is always in dialogue with *pain-pathos* of oppressed communities like Dalits.

Endnotes

[1] Alister E. Mcgrath, *Christian Theology, An Introduction* (Oxford: Blackwell Publishing, 2001 Third Edition), 476.

[2] Alister E. Mcgrath, *Christian Theology, An Introduction*, 479.

[3] Alister E. Mcgrath, *Christian Theology, An Introduction*, 481.

[4] James Massey, "Christianity to be Renewed? Rethink Theology," in *Rethinking Theology in India: Christianity in the Twenty-first Century*, edited by James Massey and T.K. John SJ (New Delhi: CDS & Manohar, 2013), 68.

[5] James Massey, "Church in Dialogue with the Dalits," *NCC Review* cxxvii/3 (April, 2007): 51-61 at 57

[6] James Massey, "Christianity to be Renewed? Rethink Theology," 69-70.

[7] James Massey, "On Being a New Community and Ecclesia of Justice and Peace," in *On Being a New Community and Ecclesia of Justice and Peace*, edited by James Massey and NOH, Jong Sun (Bangalore: BTESSC/SATHRI, 2010), 20-23.

[8] Francis Gonsalves, "Vision of Pope Francis to Renew Church and Society," in *The Emerging Challenges to Christian Mission Today*, edited by S.M. Michael and Jose Joseph (Pune: Ishvani Kendra and New Delhi: Christian World Imprints, 2016), 222.

[9] Jose Maliekal, *Standstill Utopias? Dalits Encountering Christianity* (Delhi: ISPCK, 2017), 216.

[10] Theological (missional) expositions/articulations which ignore the temporal concerns and overemphasize the 'other-worldly' life.

[11] M.M. Thomas, *Salvation and Humanization* (Madras: The CLS, 1971), 10.

[12] Israel Selvanayagam, *Samuel Amirtham's Living Theology* (Bangalore: BTESSC\ SATHRI, 2007), 442.

[13]Arvind P. Nirmal, "A Dialogue with Dalit Literature," in *Towards a Dalit Theology*, edited by M.E. Prabhakar (Delhi: ISPCK, 1989),76; Sathianathan Clarke, "Dalit Theology: An Introductory and Interpretative Theological exposition," in *Dalit Theology in the Twenty-first Century*, edited by Sathianathan Clarke, Deenabandhu Manchala and Philip Vinod Peacock (New Delhi: Oxford University Press, 2010), 22.

[14] AP Nirmal, "Towards a Christian Dalit Theology," in *A Reader in Dalit Theology*, edited by Arvind P. Nirmal (Madras: Gurukul/ UELCI, 1991), 63-64& 65-69; V. Devasahayam, "Doing Theology: Basic Assumptions," in *Frontiers of Dalit Theology*, edited by V. Devasahayam (New Delhi: ISPCK and Chennai: Gurukul, 1997), 277.

[15] James Massey, *Dalit Bible Commentary, Old Testament Vol. 2, Exodus* (New Delhi: CDS, 2010), 24.

[16] James Massey, *Dalit Bible Commentary, Old Testament Vol. 2, Exodus*, 43-44.

[17] James Massey, *Dalit Bible Commentary, Old Testament Vol. 5, Judges* (New Delhi: CDS, 2012), 85.

[18] James Massey, *Introducing Dalit Theology* (New Delhi: Centre for Dalit Studies, 2004), 27.

[19] James Massey, "Church in Dialogue with the Dalits," *NCC Review* cxxvii/3 (April, 2007): 51-61 at 52.

[20] James Massey, "Church in Dialogue with the Dalits," 55-56.

[21] Deepak Seth, ed., *From Truth to Truth, A Journey Through Faiths: A Selection of Representative Essays by Dr. James Massey* (New Delhi: CDS and Noida: Academy Press, 2008), 77-78.

[22] James Massey, "On Being a New Community and Ecclesia of Justice and Peace," 33-34.

[23] Alister E. Mcgrath, *Christian Theology: An Introduction*, 510-511 & 518.

[24] M. Amaladoss, "The Eucharist and the Christian Community," *VJTR* 68/10 (October, 2004): 721-735 at 724.

[25] James Massey, "On Being a New Community and Ecclesia of Justice and Peace," 28-29.

[26] Keith Hebden, *Dalit Theology and Christian Anarchism* (Farnham, Surrey, England: Ashgate, 2011), 146-147.

[27] Michael Amaladoss, *Life in Freedom: Liberation Theologies from Asia* (Oregon: WIPF and Stock Publishers, 2014), 29.

[28] James Massey, "On Being a New Community and Ecclesia of Justice and Peace," 23.

[29] M. Amaladoss, "The Eucharist and the Christian Community," *VJTR* 68/10 (October, 2004): 721-735 at 730-731.

Chapter 7

Dalit-Bahujan: Indian Subalterns[1]

The idea of subaltern has its roots in the British military system. 'Subaltern,' a military term basically stands for a junior officer below the rank of Captain in British army. Its literal meaning is 'subordinate.' In adjective form, it means 'of lower status.'[2] It was Antonio Gramsci, an Italian Marxist leader who first popularized the expression 'subaltern' in the ideological discourses. As an academic and ideological term it appeared first in his prison notes when he was imprisoned between 1929 and 1935. Antonio Gramsci was born in 1891 in the small town of Ales in Sardinia. He was the general secretary of the Communist Party in Italy. He was put behind the bars by Benito Mussolini in 1929. While in jail, he wrote 2,848 pages of notes on various subjects such as Italian history, education, politics, state, civil society, the philosophy of praxis, etc. He used the expression 'subaltern' in section two of his notes on 'Italian History' and 'The Philosophy of Praxis.' Selected portions of the prison notes of Antonio Gramsci in Italian language were translated and published in different languages. *Selections from the Prison Notebooks of Antonio Gramsci* is the edited version of his prison notes in English.[3]

Since, the publication of the prison notes of Antonio Gramsci the expression 'subaltern' has been used as a tool/concept in the academic discourses. It was Ranajit Guha and a group of thinkers who first initiated an extensive study on subaltern in Indian academia. Within the framework of their definition of the expression 'subaltern,' they have published a number of volumes which deal with South Asian History and Society under the research scheme of *Subaltern Studies*[4] from subaltern perspective.[5] The 'subaltern' expression is conspicuous by its presence in the theological discourses in India also. James Massey, Sathianathan Clarke, V.V. Thomas etc.[6] have employed it in their respective areas of study and reflection. Since Antonio Gramsci, the expression 'subaltern' has been defined and understood, and widened its scope and space by many scholars in different contexts.

Selections from the Prison Notebooks of Antonio Gramsci gives the basic understanding of the expression 'subaltern' by Antonio Gramsci. 'Subaltern' is an ideological construct emerged in the socio-economic-political context of Europe in the first part of 20th century. Before locating the subalterns in respective contexts, we need to be aware of the limitations or complications involved in the prison notes of Gramsci. It is very much clear in the words of the editors of *Selections from the Prison Notebooks of Antonio Gramsci*, "The problem of making a selection from Gramsci's *Prison Notebooks* is complicated by two factors: the fragmentary character of the writings and the uncertain status of the Notebooks in Gramsci's intentions."[7] Though the prison notes have its own inadequacies to explain the expression 'subaltern' unambiguously it is not much difficult to understand to whom Gramsci applied it.

Antonio Gramsci understood 'subaltern' in relation with the term 'hegemonic.' For him, "'hegemonic' is …to designate an historical phase in which a given group moves beyond a position of corporate existence and defense of its economic position and aspires to a position of leadership in the political and social arena."[8] Gramsci called non-hegemonic groups as 'subordinate,' 'subaltern' or sometimes 'instrumental' though it is difficult to distinguish any systematic difference between subaltern and subordinate in his discourse.[9] It can be interpreted that non-hegemonic groups are those who are not only dominated by other group/s but also unable to create space in the socio-political spheres of life. They are the ones who cannot move beyond their present existence, be it social, political, economic or religious, and advance in life. It means the subalterns are non-hegemonic people in particular social context. They may be politically powerless, socially voiceless and disempowered and economically exploited because of the supremacy of hegemonic forces/groups in society. In Gramsci's context, working class/proletariat was the subalterns. Since the subalterns are contextual in nature, the contextual factors help to identify and name who are subalterns.

The Subaltern Studies Group, who articulated on the expression 'subaltern' in Indian academic circle, has taken the meaning 'of inferior rank' given in the Concise Oxford Dictionary to categorize who are subalterns. Accordingly, they framed the subaltern groups in Indian society: those who are of inferior status. For them, the expression, 'subaltern' stands for the general attribute of subordination in South Asian society. It means subalternity can be in terms of class, caste, age, gender, office or in any other way. Any category/group which has the status 'of inferior rank' in particular location or field can be considered as subaltern. They also argue that subordination can be understood only in a binary relationship: subordination and dominance, for 'subaltern groups are always subject to the activity of ruling groups, even when they rebel and rise up.'[10]

In their attempt to study South Asian History and Society from the subaltern perspective, the Subaltern Study Group clarifies the usage of the expression 'subaltern' and its binary categories. For them, the term 'elite' refers to the dominant groups which consist of both foreign and indigenous. All non-Indians mainly the British officials, foreign industrialists, merchants, financiers, planters, land lords and missionaries belong to the category of foreign elite. The dominant indigenous groups are operating at two levels: all-India and regional and local. The biggest feudal magnates and native bureaucrats constitute the class of dominant indigenous groups at the national level. The members of the dominant class in all-India level and the groups who are inferior to the dominant all-India groups in the social hierarchy belong to the category of elites in the regional and local level. The last category of the elite is heterogeneous in its existence due to the nature of regional and social developments. While dominant in one region the same group/class may be the dominated in another location.

The Subaltern Study Group also explains the groups that may come in the category of subaltern class: the lowest strata of the rural gentry, impoverished landlords, rich peasants, and upper-middle peasants. These groups are identified not only as 'subaltern' but also as 'people.' Moreover, they also caution that though aforementioned groups are 'naturally' subalterns some of these classes may act for the elites or as the elites in some local or regional settings.[11]

Identifying the subalterns within the framework of the meaning 'of inferior rank/status' does not bring out the real subalterns if it contradicts the social reality of Indian society. Though the Subaltern Study Group in their project of South Asian Society and History tried to understand the subalterns in terms of class, caste, age, gender, office, etc, they kept the door of subaltern category open by giving option for interpreting 'of inferior rank' 'in any other way.'

For them, those who experience 'inferior status' in terms of social standing, economic condition, religious identity and status, political power, administrative hierarchy etc can be named as subalterns. This approach brings more groups under the umbrella of subaltern category without considering the social context of India, which is characterized by caste system. Throughout the centuries, the socially poor have been economically, politically, religiously non-hegemonic groups. The synonymous use of 'people' and 'subaltern' gives more ambiguity than clarity in identifying the real subaltern groups. 'People' can be referred to any community who may or may not be poor or non-hegemonic in status and power. The subaltern categorization by Subaltern Study Group is more or less economic than social cataloging. In fact, they homogenized the subaltern groups though they are heterogeneous by caste. In their profiling, any group of people can be defined as subalterns if they are of inferior status/category in particular region/field even though they belong to different castes. This generalization requires identification of specific groups who qualify to be called as subalterns in Indian social setting.

Sathianathan Clarke in his book, *Dalits and Christianity: Subaltern Religion and Liberation Theology in India* attempts to situate Dalits in the subaltern space. He gives a critique of the attempt of the homogenization of subalterns by putting together all categories of differentiation in terms of caste, class, age, gender, offices and any other way. He takes departure from the generalization of subaltern class to the identification of subalternity in particular community. He argues that many groups may share equal disabilities at one level in society. Nevertheless all may not face same degree of handicaps and oppressions in all facets of societal life. Any attempt of unifying different groups with different struggles and aspirations under one category may lead to the unjustifiable generalization. Therefore, he tried to concentrate the caste dimension of subalternity to categorize subalterns in Indian context. He views that categorization of subalterns in terms of caste is not to deny any other class or group which share the condition of subalternity. The institution and ideology of caste plays a big role in determining the contextual manifestation of subalternity in the caste-ridden Indian context. Since the caste has religious sanction its role cannot be overlooked.[12] Clarke quotes the words of Partha Chatterjee to substantiate his argument, "No matter how we choose to characterize it, subaltern consciousness in the specific cultural context of India cannot but contain caste as a central element in its constitution."[13] If caste is the determining factor for subalternity in Indian context, for Clarke, it is Dalits who deserved to be called subalterns. Indeed they are subalterns in all sense. He says, "The subaltern, thus, are the communities (Dalits) that are cumulatively and comprehensively disadvantaged and subordinated through the caste system, which operates to benefit the dominant groups."[14] Dalits are subalterns because they have been considered and treated as people 'of inferior rank/status' in the caste-ridden society. They have been deprived of equal rights and equal distribution of justice, and subordinated by the ruling class and caste people for many centuries. If caste is placed as the criterion to find the subaltern group then one cannot avoid the possibility of including other communities, who are discriminated because of caste identity, within subaltern category.

James Massey proposes Dalit-Bahujan as subalterns in Indian context. Though he accepts the possibility of using the expression, 'subaltern' in constructing new theoretical and theological formulations he does not admit it without a critique and caution. For him, the expression 'subaltern' is a European construct emerged in a particular context. In academic discourses, it has travelled from European class context to Indian caste context. Therefore, he cautions that since each context is different in its nature and function it is important that one should know whether this expression can be applied in our context. According to Massey, Gramsci used this expression in a very general sense to make a distinction between ruling classes and non-ruling classes.[15] He also argues that Gramsci's reflections inform us that the expression 'subaltern' is a political construct because in his writings subalterns are discussed in relation to the politically dominated/powerful group, the ruling class of his time. He continues that Gramsci's understanding of subaltern is also the product of socio-economic factors of his time and context.[16] Hence, the expression 'subaltern' cannot be used without taking the contextual realties into consideration.

James Massey is also critical of the Subaltern Study Group led by Ranajit Guha. For him, their views which categorized and interpreted the subaltern are very much generalized. Their understanding of subaltern include all categories of people both 'caste people' and 'non-caste people' as they are defined on the basis of 'class, caste, age, gender and office or in any other way.' Therefore, the views of Ranajit Guha and his colleagues are more suitable and applicable to the European context. Since, Indian context is basically rooted in and shaped by caste system any attempt of the generalization of subalterns without applying caste will not work well. The caste factor makes Indian context different from the European class context.[17] In this regard Massey tends to agree more with Sathianathan Clarke's view on the caste dimension of subalternity that: "This is not to deny that collectives held together by commonalities of age, gender, class and office do share in the state of subalternity. The institution and ideology of caste engenders contextual manifestation of subalternity, which is intrinsically tied up to religion in India."[18] Often, the people who belong to the lower strata of society are identified with the expressions like 'people,' 'public' or 'poor.' They are not nameless and faceless. They are Dalits, Tribals and Other Backward Classes. And their religious identity is not limited to Hinduism alone. Every religion in India has their membership.[19] This scenario broadens the understanding of subaltern in India.

In his attempt to understand 'subaltern' in terms of caste, James Massey goes beyond Clarke and includes more communities in the frame of subalternity. He affirms that caste gives birth to subalternity in India. Caste is the main factor in the formation of subaltern consciousness. Majority of Indian population has the history of discriminations and disabilities inflicted by the caste.[20] The report of the Mandal Commission proves that majority of Indian population falls in the category of backward communities. Their social and economic backwardness is caused by the caste system in society.[21] There is no sign of reducing its influence even today.

According to James Massey, "the problem of the Indian subaltern groups ... is that their rank in society are fixed by birth, which also decides their social, educational, cultural, religious, political and economic status."[22] The permanency of social status by birth is also underlined in the report of Mandal Commission, "The ranks and their respective duties, ordained by God for humanity, were intended to remain fixed and immutable. Like the limbs of the body, they cannot properly exchange either their place or function."[23] Actually, this rank or status is fixed by birth in a particular caste. Thus, the phenomenon of caste decides Indian subalterns and their space in society. They should be called by a contextual name to unify them as a social group. Though the expression 'Dalit' has been understood and interpreted as subaltern, 'Bahujan' (Other Backward Classes, Religious Minorities of lower caste origin) can also be added to it. Thus, the subalterns in India can be called as Dalit-Bahujan. For Massey Dalit-Bahujan (Dalits-Tribals-OBCs-Religious Minorities of OBC/Dalit origin) constitute majority of the population. They have been historically victimized by the caste system. They are of inferior status because of their low caste/outcaste identity, which has been imposed upon them by the oppressive caste system.[24]

The Dalit-Bahujan, the historical victims of caste, was not completely non-resistant people in the past. They raised their movements in different historical periods against the caste and religious hegemony. Religious and non-religious movements have contributed to the empowerment of Dalit-Bahujan. Present Dalit-Bahujan movements owe to those movements which sowed the seeds of resistance against any form of hegemony. Jainism and Buddhism, which challenged the supremacy of Brahmanism, contributed to the emergence of Dalit-Bahujan movements. Bhakti movement in the medieval period, led by caste and non-caste people, also influenced the Dalit-Bahujan to raise their voice against their social disabilities. The movements initiated by Jyothirao Phule and B.R. Ambedkar also awakened the critical consciousness of Dalit-Bahujan. Mass conversions, particularly to Christianity, played an important role in empowering the Dalit-Bahujan in Indian society. British legal systems, land policy, new education policy etc also contributed to the awakening of Dalit-Bahujan in later period. For the Dalit-Bahujan, their movements are closely connected because of two reasons: common history and common oppressor. They have common history because they are the historical victims of caste. Their ancestors equally suffered due to the oppressive caste system in the past, and they continue to face the challenge of caste in social life. They also have common oppressor, the caste people, who treat Dalit-Bahujan as inferior and block their upward social mobility. It demands the solidarity of Dalit-Bahujan in their efforts to achieve complete liberation.[25] Dalit-Bahujan is not only an Indian expression of subalterns but also an embodiment of solidarity. Though Dalit-Bahujan is numerically majority in India, they are defeated by the lack of solidarity among them. If they come together beyond religious and ideological affiliations, then only they can challenge the hegemony of oppressive life-negating forces. Often their solidarity is broken up by the divisive politics of the caste people also. Therefore, their empowerment depends on the level of solidarity they build up in their journey of resistance and collective consciousness.

Endnotes

[1] In this chapter, James Massey is placed along with other scholars of subaltern discourses.

[2] Catherine Soanes and Angus Stevenson, eds., *Concise Oxford English Dictionary, Indian Edition* (New Delhi: Oxford University Press, 2007), 1434.

[3] Antonio Gramsci, *Selections from the Prison Notebooks of Antonio Gramsci*, edited and translated by Quintin Hoare and Geoffrey Nowell Smith (Chennai: Orient Longman, 1996), xvii ff.

[4] *Subaltern Studies* is a collection of edited works which attempted to understand South Asian History and Society from subaltern perspective. A group of scholars such as Ranajit Guha, Partha Chatterjee, Gyanendra Pandey, David Arnold, David Hardiman, Dipesh Chakrabarthy, Gautam Bhadra etc edited the multi-voluminous work.

[5] James Massey, "Subaltern People and the Rise of their Movements," in *A Vision of Mission in the New Millennium*, edited by Thomas Malipurathu and L. Stanislaus (Mumbai: St. Paul's, 2001), 24-25; James Massey, *Caste-Class Victims and Their Assertion for Justice* (New Delhi: Centre for Dalit/Subaltern Studies, 2013), 12-13.

[6] James Massey, "Subaltern People and the Rise of their Movements," in *A Vision of Mission in the New Millennium*, edited by Thomas Malipurathu and L. Stanislaus (Mumbai: St. Paul's, 2001); James Massey, *Caste-Class Victims and Their Assertion for Justice* (New Delhi: Centre for Dalit/Subaltern Studies, 2013); Sathianathan Clarke, *Dalits and Christianity: Subaltern Religion and Liberation Theology in India* (Delhi: Oxford University Press, 1998); V.V. Thomas, *Dalit Pentecostalism* (Bangalore: ATC, 2008).

[7] Antonio Gramsci, *Selections from the Prison Notebooks of Antonio Gramsci*, x.

[8] Antonio Gramsci, *Selections from the Prison Notebooks of Antonio Gramsci*, xiv.

[9] Antonio Gramsci, *Selections from the Prison Notebooks of Antonio Gramsci*, xiv.

[10] Ranajit Guha, "Preface," in *Subaltern Studies* Vol. I, edited by Ranajit Guha (Delhi: Oxford University Press, 1994), vii.

[11] Ranajit Guha, "On Some Aspects of the Historiography of Colonial India," in *Subaltern Studies* Vol. I, edited by Ranajit Guha (Delhi: Oxford University Press, 1994), 8.

[12] Sathianathan Clarke, *Dalits and Christianity: Subaltern Religion and Liberation Theology in India*, 7.

[13] Quoted from Partha Chatterjee, "Caste and Subaltern Consciousness," in *Subaltern Studies* Vol. VI, edited by Ranajit Guha (New Delhi: Oxford University Press, 1989), 169 in Sathianathan Clarke, *Dalits and Christianity: Subaltern Religion and Liberation Theology in India*, 7.

[14] Sathianathan Clarke, *Dalits and Christianity: Subaltern Religion and Liberation Theology in India*, 7.

[15] James Massey, "Subaltern People and the Rise of their Movements" 24-25; James Massey, *Caste-Class Victims and Their Assertion for Justice*, 12-13.

[16] James Massey, "Subaltern People and the Rise of their Movements," 25.

[17] James Massey, "Subaltern People and the Rise of their Movements," 26; James Massey, "Journal of Subaltern and Cultural Theology, Editorial," *Journal of Subaltern and Cultural Theology* (Inaugural Issue, 2013): 7-12 at 9-10.

[18] Quoted from Sathianathan Clarke, *Dalits and Christianity: Subaltern Religion and Liberation Theology in India*, 7 in James Massey, "Subaltern People and the Rise of their Movements," 26.

[19] James Massey, "Christianity to be Renewed? Rethink Theology," in *Rethinking Theology in India: Christianity in the Twenty-first Century*, edited by James Massey and T.K. John SJ (New Delhi: CDS & Manohar, 2013), 35.

[20] James Massey, *Caste-Class Victims and Their Assertion for Justice*, 14-15; James Massey, "Journal of Subaltern and Cultural Theology, Editorial," *Journal of Subaltern and Cultural Theology* (Inaugural Issue, 2013): 7-12 at 10.

[21] *Reservations for Backward Classes, Mandal Commission Report of the Backward Classes Commission, 1980* (Along with Introduction) (New Delhi: Akalank Publications, 1990), 61.

[22] James Massey, *Caste-Class Victims and Their Assertion for Justice*, 15.

[23] Quoted from *Reservations for Backward Classes Mandal Commission Report of the Backward Classes Commission, 1980* (Along with Introduction), 19 in James Massey, *Caste-Class Victims and Their Assertion for Justice*, 15.

[24] James Massey, "Subaltern People and the Rise of their Movements," 27-29.

[25] Deepak Seth, ed., *From Truth to Truth, A Journey Through Faiths: A Selection of Representative Essays by Dr. James Massey* (New Delhi: CDS and NOIDA: Academy Press, 2008), 149-160.

Chapter 8

Ecumenism and Justice

Ecumenism is generally understood as the unity of churches for the welfare of Christian community. It aims to promote the fellowship of different churches and addresses common issues of Christians in different contexts. It facilitates the sharing of resources, developing common Christian response to the issues in society, raising voice of protest against the violation of rights, promoting mission etc. Often, the concerns of ecumenism do not go beyond the boundaries of the church/denominations. The involvement of ecumenical movement in responding to the societal realties is also shrinking today in the national and international levels. The approach of ecumenical movement in India sometimes seems to be communal in nature too because of limiting its space within the Christian community. It often fails to identify with the people of other faiths. It becomes active when the rights and privileges of Christian community are challenged. One of the reasons for shrinking the space of ecumenical movement in India is the political atmosphere of the country. The communal politics views the involvement of ecumenical movements in raising the issues related to social justice and economic development as anti-national. Even in the international level, the space of ecumenical movement is reducing considerably. It is not able to create much impact in the countries where Christians constitute majority of the population. Instead of becoming a voice of justice for all, ecumenical movement has become a formal fellowship of churches practically limited to the ecclesial life. James Massey reflected on ecumenism within the frame work of justice. He argued that ecumenism means justice. Some of his thoughts on ecumenism are explained in this chapter.

The ecumenical movements work in local, regional, national and international levels. They help the churches come together on common platform and celebrate the unity of faith in Christ. However, according to James Massey, the sad part of the story is that they are unable to lead the Christian community, particularly in India, to overcome the 'disjointed' situation. The Christian community in India is not simply divided but 'disjointed' in every area of life. They are not able to move forward with common goal and to stand for the issues equally affect the community.[1] This disjointed situation cannot be easily healed because they are badly gripped by strong denominationalism, casteism and regionalism. They face more divergences than convergences. The areas where they can genuinely stand together are lesser than the areas of disagreement in societal and ecclesial life.

James Massey argues that there is lack of inclusiveness in the approach of the concerns and programs of ecumenical movements. The World Council of Churches is a case in point. When WCC was formed, two-third of its member churches represented the Christians in European and North American countries. They actually influenced the programmes of WCC too. Majority programs were designed mainly to address the issues and needs of Christians in those countries. The issues of Christian communities outside the European and North American countries were not adequately addressed in the early programs of WCC. Even after the increase in the number of member Churches from Asian and African countries, the role and nature of WCC has not changed. Still major programs and discussions are centered on the issues of first world countries. One example of such preferential treatment is the work of the particular desk of WCC which addresses the concerns of inter-religious relationship/dialogue. It is observed that the programmes of this desk are focused more on the Semitic religions like Christianity, Judaism and Islam. These religions are more concerned because they are somewhat present in the Northern countries. Moreover, they also have historical relations with Christianity.[2] Another reason for considering Semitic religions in inter-faith programs is that the resources for such programs mainly come from Northern countries. Though the number of member Churches from Asian and African countries increased, religious traditions in those countries have not received considerable attention. Hinduism, Buddhism, Jainism, Confucianism and other religious traditions of Asia, particularly of China and Japan do not get equal importance as the Semitic Religions get in the programs of inter-religious relationship.[3] Even the Busan Assembly of WCC in 2013 has not addressed the contextual of issues of Southern countries.[4] The lack of inclusiveness is evident not only in international ecumenical forum but also in national ecumenical forums. There are voices in the ecumenical forums regarding the scope of ecumenical involvement. Some argue that ecumenical councils in different levels should address only the issues related to the member churches. It not only fixes the boundaries of ecumenical initiatives but also questions the real purpose of ecumenical movement. An authentic ecumenical movement should primarily address the concerns of entire Christian community and stand for the cause of justice in respective society.[5] The exclusive character of ecumenical movement in terms of prioritizing the issues and concerns reduces the space of ecumenical movement. Though ecumenical movements stand for the unity of Christians in public domain, the inner conflicts and disagreements make them ineffective to address the pertinent issues of Christians in society.

Ecumenical movements attempt to live out a vision of the unity of Christian communities/churches. Often, they do not get the co-operation of churches to achieve the goal of unity. Many Christian groups are even hesitant to the idea of ecumenism because they think that once they are part of ecumenical movements they have to compromise their doctrinal positions. The unity of Christians has to be understood in the context of the mushrooming of local/regional Christian groups. They may not have ecclesial structure of established churches. However, unlike established Churches, they attract people from other churches and religious traditions. They also have to be part of ecumenical movements. They may enter into ecumenical fraternity if ecumenical movements emphasize issue-based unity and programs than doctrinal unity.[6] Issue-based unity brings more Christian communities into ecumenical movements and thereby the unity of Christians can be fulfilled.

The 'organic unity' has been main focus of ecumenical movements throughout the world even though there is no symptom of such unity among the Churches. The proponents of 'organic unity' believe that ecumenical initiatives will ultimately lead to the formation of one Christian community devoid of denominational boundaries. It is a fact that ecumenical movements spend a lot of energy and resources to achieve the goal of 'organic unity.' While this is an ideal goal to achieve, the initiatives and programs centered on 'organic unity' could not stop the emergence of new denominations. It has also failed to bring many Churches even into spiritual communion. The over-emphasis on 'organic unity' has not only weakened the ecumenical movements but also kept many Churches away from the ecumenical movements. Many Churches approach 'organic unity' with suspicion. They are not encouraged by the idea of 'organic unity' which destroys their ecclesial identities. 'Organic unity' is not a suitable approach in today's context which is characterized by the emergence of new denominations and faith communities.[7] Ecumenical movements can be successful if they focus on 'Programmatic unity' than 'Organic unity.' Issue-based programs can bring more churches into the ecumenical world. The Churches/denominations will be more comfortable to join hands with others to address the issues of Christian community in society than to sort out doctrinal differences.

For Massey, the 'programmatic unity' enlarges the space of ecumenical movements in society. It provides new partners into the ventures of ecumenism. It gives space for all those who can stand for the issues of justice and peace apart from the general wellbeing of Christian community. The 'programmatic unity' has to be initiated on the basis of Ephesians 1:10 and vertical and horizontal experiences of unity as indicated by John 1:21. The 'programmatic unity' of ecumenical movements has two dimensions. Firstly, it addresses the issues related to the Christian community. In this stage, the ecumenical partners work together for a common cause of the community. Secondly, it addresses the common issues of society by joining hands with others who belong to different religious and ideological backgrounds. In this stage, the space of ecumenical movement is enlarged beyond ecclesial boundaries. The programmatic unity encourages the ecumenical movements to work with the people, movements and community who promote justice, peace and freedom. Here, ecumenical movement becomes inclusive rather than exclusive and gets new meaning for the expression 'ecumenical.' While standing for the common cause of society, ecumenical movements do not lose their identity as Christian movements. When ecumenical movements focus on programmatic unity, they are getting liberated from institutional captivity. On the one hand ecumenical movements come out of the institutional functioning of ecumenism which emphasizes the issues of member churches and focuses on doctrinal unity; on the other hand they break the culture of limiting ecumenical endeavors within the Christian community.[8] The programmatic unity helps more Churches become part of ecumenical movements and brings new partners from other religious traditions. It makes Christian witness meaningful in society. While strengthening the unity of Christians, programmatic unity opens new avenues of partnership for addressing the issues both within and outside the community.

According to James Massey, the issues of oppressed communities all over the world should be addressed by the ecumenical movements. The broken life-realties of the oppressed are one of the challenges of ecumenical witness in society. In many countries, the oppressed constitute majority of Christian population. For example, in India majority Christians are drawn from Dalit communities. They are historical victims of injustice perpetuated by caste system. The ecumenical movements cannot overlook their societal issues while attempting to unite the Christians in India. The Minjungs of Korea, Buraku of Japan, and Adivasis of India are other examples of oppressed people groups who need special attention of World Council of Churches and regional ecumenical movements. Often the issues of oppressed communities are discussed in the ecumenical forums to deliver a statement on the struggles of people. Nothing goes beyond a statement. Practically, the issues of the oppressed are not addressed on the grass root level. The ecumenical movement enters into another level of its existence when it identifies with the oppressed communities in the world.[9] The issue-based programs related to Dalits, Tribals and Women may attract sincere co-operation among the churches in India. The issues of personal law, religious freedom and human rights are other areas where Indian Churches can come together and share the resources.[10] Unfortunately, the involvement of ecumenical movements in the struggles of people is very much limited. Therefore, the space of ecumenical movements in society is also not getting enlarged.

Globalization is another challenge before ecumenical movements. The negative impact of globalization has to be addressed at all levels of ecumenical endeavor. Since Churches are part of society, they cannot remain aloof from the issues that emerge out of the process of globalization. Majority victims of globalization are socially and economically disempowered people in society. Their issues must be attended as part of ecumenical initiatives. The ecumenical movements become symbols of hope if they care for the concerns of those who are victimized by the process of globalization. Apart from the challenge of globalization, the world particularly third world countries face the threat of developing New World Order. This is initiated by the first world countries. One of the components of this process is use of military power. It is destructive and threat to the entire creation. The so-called super powers use their military strength to bring the weak countries under their control and exploit their natural resources. The attacks of USA and its allies on middle-eastern countries in the last few decades are examples of preparing the world towards new world order under super powers. The war on terrorism has created chaotic situations in some countries and still they are struggling to come back to the normal state. The worst victims of the military interferences are children and women. The quantity of nuclear weapons developed by the countries irrespective of continents pose a great threat to entire creation. In such situation, ecumenical movements have moral and theological responsibility to respond to the issues of militarization and neuclearization of this world. Possibility of nuclear war hangs over the creation. The ecumenical movements must come out of their traditional understanding of ecumenism and invite new partners from other religious traditions to respond to the growing menaces of globalization and militarization going on under the supervision of first world countries. When new partners are included in the ecumenical endeavors, ecumenism gets new meaning and opens new avenues of engagement in society.[11] Christians alone cannot tackle the issues of entire world. It means, ecumenical movements cannot effectively respond to the pertinent issues of the world unless they expand their boundaries by joining hands with those who equally concerned with the issues of the world.

The nature of issues in the present world and the necessity of larger participation of the churches to tackle those issues points towards the idea of wider ecumenism. It means ecumenism should not be limited to the unity of Christians alone. It should go beyond religious and ideological boundaries. The wider ecumenism is a biblical idea based on Ephesians 1:9-11. This passage talks about God's wider plan of cosmic unity in Christ. If cosmic unity is God's will, then ecumenism must be redefined as an attempt to achieve the unity of entire creation. The wider ecumenism invites people from all walks of life to participate in the cosmic plan of God. The vision of cosmic unity breaks all walls of separation and embraces every created being into plan of God.[12] The universal harmony of entire creation in Christ is the ultimate plan of God. The wider ecumenism brings a shift in the approach of ecumenical movements. It encourages them to shift the focus from 'organic unity' to programmatic unity.' God's plan of cosmic unity in Christ can be achieved through 'programmatic unity.' Cosmic unity informs that unity of entire creation is the final destiny of ecumenism.[13] The wider ecumenism does not nullify the ecumenical vision of Churches but opens new pathways of experiencing the unity of entire creation.

Ecumenism becomes real venture of unity if it initiates the process of cosmic unity.

Massey also connects ecumenism with social justice. For him, social justice occupies an important place in the mission of Church. The efforts to raise voice for social justice in the past led to the formation of Christian communities in many parts of the world particularly in India. Churches were established among the oppressed communities because missionaries also worked for social justice. They considered social justice as part of Christian mission. While propagating the faith they stood against the tendencies of oppression and exploitation in society. Social justice is Biblical mandate too. Therefore the ecumenical movements also have to address the issue of social justice. The model for such endeavor is the incarnational model. This model is summarized in John 1:14 and Luke 2:1-7. This model demands the churches (ecumenical movements) to identify with the victims of injustice. In the incarnational model God identified with the oppressed by becoming an ordinary human being in Jesus Christ. He lived among the people and confronted their broken life realities. He appeared as ordinary human being in society and participated in the social struggles of people. The solidarity of God with human beings through Jesus Christ set a new paradigm for the ecumenical movements in the world to express their solidarity with the people who fight for social justice. As God completely identified with the poor and the oppressed in the incarnational act, so the ecumenical movements have to stand with the people who are deprived of justice in society. The incarnational act for ecumenical movements means taking part in the struggles of the oppressed and journeying with them and enabling them to celebrate life in its fullness.[14] The incarnational model actually places the ecumenical movements in the sites of social injustice and inequality. It demands them to walk an extra mile with the oppressed communities and stand for their rights.

According to the incarnational model, the ecumenical engagements cannot be limited within the Christian community. They have to engage with all people irrespective of religious traditions. In the incarnational act, God participated in the sufferings of entire humanity through Jesus Christ. Therefore, the churches which are involved in ecumenical endeavors have to re-interpret who are the 'people of God.' The incarnational act of God informs that the 'people of God' is composed of entire humanity. It opens the doors of ecumenism to develop partnership with the people who are willing to take side with the poor and the oppressed. While inviting others as 'people of God' to participate in the ecumenical engagements on behalf of the oppressed, the ecumenical movements have to be aware of the mission role of their different institutes and programs. In order to respond to the life realities of the oppressed, the mission of the Church should be re-defined. A shift in the approach of mission is necessitated by the changing context of the world, particularly the context of third world countries. The shift should be from the understanding of mission as 'soul saving' to the mission as holistic empowerment. The mission of the churches should be the mission of ecumenical bodies and institutions. Apart from reaching the unreached, the mission must take care of the upward social and economic mobility of the people, particularly the oppressed. It has to address the issues of human rights violations, educational rights, freedom of religion, minority rights etc. The ecumenical movements have to design programs in tune with the mission of holistic empowerment: spiritual and material. The understanding of mission as holistic empowerment reminds the churches that they cannot limit their work only within the religious sphere of societal life.[15] They have to come into the public space and activate their faith in Jesus in whom God completely identified with the suffering humanity. When they participate in the journey of suffering people, they enter into the process of the 'authentic imitation of Christ.' The ecumenical movements whose mission is God's mission in Jesus must express their solidarity with the least ones within and outside the Church. The unity of Churches must reflect in the praxis of Good News in society.[16] An authentic and productive ecumenism will emerge if the churches can initiative bold steps to carry out the incarnational mission among the people.

The initiatives that are taken by different ecumenical bodies in the past demonstrate their genuine concern for the oppressed communities. They are the initial signs of the incarnational act of the Churches. For example, World Council of Churches and the Christian Conference of Asia organized a global Dalit conference in Bangkok in 2009. It was a bold step taken by the ecumenical bodies exclusively to discuss the issues related to one of the oppressed communities in the world. It helped to bring the Dalit issue into international level and to develop global solidarity among the oppressed communities. This conference had some impact among the Indian Churches. The National Council of Churches in India (NCCI) urged the Indian churches to be 'caste-free zones.' This call is actually contradictory to the very nature and essence of the church which is not supposed to be 'caste-zones.' It once again underlines the fact that Indian Church could not resist the entry of caste into its psyche.[17] The call for 'caste-fee-zones' is at least one step closer to the aim of identifying with the victims of caste in Indian society. While emphasizing the 'caste-free-zones' the ecumenical movements have to start thinking Christian communities as 'denominational-free-zones.' The disunity among the Christians often blocks their upward social mobility and fails them as witnessing community in Indian society.[18] The idea of 'denominational-free-zones' can be practiced at least in rendering services to the Christians irrespective of denominations. The denominational consciousness among the Christians often restricts their services within the respective communities. Some denominations are willing to share their resources with non-Christians in the name of mission, but not with fellow Christians in another denomination. The ecumenical endeavors of creating churches as 'caste-free-zones' and Christian communities as 'denominational-free-zones' contributes to the empowerment of oppressed communities and the meaningful witness of Christians in society.

It is true that ecumenical movements have acknowledged the issues of oppressed communities all over the world and have taken a few initiatives to internalize their issues. They also have attempted to develop some programs for bringing them into mainstream of society. However, for Massey, the assembly of World Council of Churches (the last assembly he attended before his death) held on 3-8 November, 2013, in Busan, South Korea throws a question, 'wither ecumenical movement?' This question is emerged in the light of the failure of Indian ecumenical representatives to get Dalit issue included in the statement of World Council of Churches. The question of justice for the oppressed communities was addressed in the previous statements of WCC. But the disunity and caste-cum-denominational consciousness of Indian leaders worked against the inclusion of Dalit issue in the statement of WCC in 2013. In the 7th Assembly of WCC in Canberra in 1991, the final statement of the assembly acknowledged the Dalit issue, "We affirm the growing consciousness of the indigenous peoples' struggle for freedom, including Dalits in India." It has to be noted that though there was not a single staff from Dalit background in WCC in 1991, Dalit issue was included in the final statement. In spite of having two staff from Dalit background and one from Tribal background from India in WCC in 2013, Dalit issue did not get entry into the statement. There were also twenty official delegates who had right to raise voice for the oppressed communities in India. The Indian delegates were not those who did not know about the Dalit issues. But they have failed the Dalits who constitute majority Indian Christians. Dalit issue was excluded from the final statement because it could not meet the necessary criterion for the statement. If three official delegates from India had endorsed the Dalit issue with their signatures, Dalit issue would have been included in the final statement. If 7th Assembly of WCC included Dalit issue in the statement, 10th Assembly said, "A Statement of Dalit Christians and Dalit Muslims in India: did not meet the necessary criteria."[19] The question is whether the necessary criterion decides the importance of Dalit's or any oppressed community's issue? If the answer is affirmative, then ecumenical movement has started to wither.

In the 10th Assembly of WCC, Dalit issue was dropped from the statement on technical grounds. It was not only the failure of Indian ecumenical leaders but also the failure of WCC. It shows the withering of an international ecumenical forum. Instead of standing for the oppressed communities, it stood by the technical reasons.[20] The so-called ecumenical leaders are still comfortable to their respective denominations. That is why they are not able to take the issues of oppressed communities who are spread in different denominations. They are hesitant to touch the issues of people who are either absent or less in their denominations. The Busan Assembly of WCC emphasized the 'necessary criterion' than 'justice' to the suffering people. Acknowledging the issue of justice is the starting of ensuring justice to the oppressed.

It is paradox that exclusion of Dalit issue from the final statement happened in 10th Assembly of WCC which deliberated on various issues in the light of the theme, "God of life lead us to justice and peace." Dalits are one of the oppressed communities in

India who face different forms of injustice even today. They are the historical victims of oppressed social structures and customs. It is quite natural that they should been considered in the statement made out of the discussions on the theme, "God of life lead us to justice and peace." The mind-set of ecumenical leaders towards the oppressed communities still has not radically changed. When some Dalit delegates approached the head of an Indian Church to endorse the cause of Dalits in the Assembly he refused to sign the document, and was reported that he said, "It is your Dalit issue; so you Dalits deal with it."[21] If this statement is true, he is an uncaring shepherd to the wounded sheep. The response of the head of the church shows utter disregard exists among the ecumenical/church leaders towards the issues of the oppressed communities. If the ecumenical movements and its leaders cannot stand for the cause of justice, themes such as "God of life lead us to justice and peace" are irrelevant not only in the life of churches but also for the oppressed. If God of life leads everyone to justice and peace, then ecumenism also should lead entire creation towards justice and peace. It means ecumenism must attempt to bring justice to everyone, particularly those who are denied of justice. Therefore, ecumenism practically means justice. The idea of *oikoumene* basically considers all human beings as God's people and invites whole created world to experience justice and peace.[22] The ultimate aim of ecumenism is to accomplish God's plan of comic unity in which every creature enjoy justice and peace. The unity of churches is part of the process of cosmic unity.

Endnotes

[1] James Massey, *Ecumenism Means Justice* (Matiala, New Delhi: CDS, 2014), 104.

[2] James Massey, *Ecumenism Means Justice*, 106; James Massey, "Alternative Approaches to the Ecumenical Movement," in *Ecumenism in India Today*, edited by James Massey (Bangalore: BTESSC/SATHRI, 2008), 60.

[3] James Massey, *Ecumenism Means Justice*, 107.

[4] James Massey, *Ecumenism Means Justice*, 117.

[5] James Massey, "Alternative Approaches to the Ecumenical Movement," 61.

[6] James Massey, *Ecumenism Means Justice*, 107.

[7] James Massey, *Ecumenism Means Justice*, 108.

[8] James Massey, *Ecumenism Means Justice*, 109; James Massey, "Alternative Approaches to the Ecumenical Movement," 62.

[9] James Massey, *Ecumenism Means Justice*, 110; James Massey, "Alternative Approaches to the Ecumenical Movement," 62.

[10] James Massey, *Ecumenism Means Justice*, 117.

[11] James Massey, *Ecumenism Means Justice*, 111; James Massey, "Alternative Approaches to the Ecumenical Movement," 64.

[12] James Massey, *Ecumenism Means Justice*, 116; James Massey, "Alternative Approaches to the Ecumenical Movement," 59.

[13] James Massey, *Ecumenism Means Justice*, 117; James Massey, "Alternative Approaches to the Ecumenical Movement," 60.

[14] James Massey, *Ecumenism Means Justice*, 122.

[15] James Massey, *Ecumenism Means Justice*, 123-124.

[16] James Massey, *Ecumenism Means Justice*, 124-125.

[17] James Massey, *Ecumenism Means Justice*, 167.

[18] James Massey, *Ecumenism Means Justice*, 168-169.

[19] James Massey, *Ecumenism Means Justice*, 172-173.

[20] James Massey, *Ecumenism Means Justice*, 162.

[21] James Massey, *Ecumenism Means Justice*, 9.

[22] James Massey, *Ecumenism Means Justice*, 10.

Chapter 9

Dalits, Christianity and Missionary Theology

The native Christians have largely contributed to the formation of Christian communities in India. Among the natives, the Dalit communities played an important role in the development of Christianity in this nation. They largely responded to the message of the Gospel and became instruments of establishing Christian communities. Their response to the call by the Spirit of God led to the formation of the Body of Christ in India. They have contributed to the qualitative and quantitative development of Christianity. The history of the origin of Christianity, particularly Protestant Christianity, in many places informs of the Dalit roots of Indian Christianity. While the conversion of Dalits increased the number of Christians the works of early Dalit leaders and missionaries established Christian communities throughout the country. The stories of Christian movements testify the work of Holy Spirit through Dalit communities.[1] The Dalit stories of Christianity tell us that Dalits were not mere recipients of faith but pioneers of spreading the faith among various communities. In spite of adverse social circumstances, they used their resources and opportunities to propagate the faith and establish Christian communities. However,

James Massey observes that, the early missionary theologies which mainly focused on conversion and otherworldly salvation, to an extent, contributed to the disempowered social life of Dalit Christians. This chapter looks at the Dalit roots of Indian Christianity and the impact of early missionary theology upon the life of Dalits.

Dalit Roots of Indian Christianity and Spirit Movements

Before we get into the stories of the development of Christianity in India, we need to see the approach of majority missionaries in the process of evangelization. They initially focused on the upper caste people and attempted to propagate Christian faith among them. The place of upper castes in the hierarchy of caste system and the status and privileges they enjoyed in society might have influenced the missionaries to begin their ministry with the caste people. They might have thought that the conversion of caste people would naturally lead to the conversion of lower caste people who constituted majority of the population. When they failed to bring upper caste people into Christian fold, they shifted their focus to the lower caste people. The statement of Andrew Gordon who was a missionary of the United Presbyterian Church of U.S.A. to Punjab underlines this shift. After thirty years of missionary work, he says in his book, *Our India Mission* that "In concluding these remarks, about my own evangelistic work in the last decade, I may say briefly, that I began with my eyes upon the large towns and cities, but have been later led from them to the country's villages. I began with the educated classes and people of good social position, but ended up among the poor."[2] The upper caste based evangelism approach was not successful according to the historical data available. The number of conversions during the early period of Christian evangelistic work in Punjab is a case in point. The missionaries who focused the upper caste people could not see increase in the number of conversions. It is recorded that from 1834 to 1885, there were only 477 communicant members. It is interesting to note that many of them were not Punjabi Christians. The upper caste focus of evangelism is very much evident in the nature of first baptism. The first person who was baptized in Ludhiana on 30th April 1837 was a Bengali upper caste Hindu. It was quite natural for the missionaries to expect more conversions among the caste people and the steady growth of Christianity. Unfortunately, such movement did not take roots among the caste people. But the growth of Christianity in Punjab began with the baptism of Ditt, a Dalit. After his conversion in 1885, the number of Christians increased in Punjab particularly among Dalits and other oppressed communities. This change was the result of shift in the approach of missionaries who were hesitant to baptize the lower caste people.[3] Some missionaries were literally disturbed by the large scale conversions of Dalits. The letter of J.C.R Ewing shows utter displeasure over the conversion of poor, illiterate and lower caste people into Christianity. In his letter to the mission board, he described the trend of lower caste conversions as 'raking in rubbish into the Church.' For him, the poor people whom Jesus showed his concern was 'rubbish.' This was the mind-set of many missionaries towards the conversion of lower caste people. They were described as 'common villagers' or 'illiterate menials' in missionary reports. They were not called 'coverts,' the title reserved for upper caste Christians. This negative approach reflected in the later stage of the Christianity in Punjab. Perhaps, it is true in other places also. The presence of a few upper caste Christians forced the missionaries to build separate Churches or to serve the Eucharist first to the caste Christians.[4] But the history of Indian Christianity shows that it was those 'rubbish' people who contributed to the establishment of Christian communities in different parts of the nation. Some of the stories which James Massey narrated in his writings are given in the following sections.

The arrival of Protestant Christianity into the kingdom of Tanjore was facilitated by a person named Rajanaiken. He was a Pariah by caste. While serving as a non-commissioned officer in the army of Tanjore in 1727, he requested the Tranquebar mission to send a catechist to Tanjore. The mission centre assigned Aaron for the new mission field. He got permission to enter the kingdom and preach the Gospel.[5] The role played by Rajanaiken is noteworthy. First of all he invited the missionary into the kingdom where he was serving in the army. Though it was risky, he took the initiative to bring a missionary into a place which was predominantly Hindu. Secondly, Aaron got permission with the help of Rajanaiken. If he had not approached the king, Aaron would not have been allowed to enter the kingdom. The permission granted to the missionary shows that Rajanaiken was either influential or closer to the administration. He became instrumental to establish a Christian community later in Tanjore. In fact, his missionary mind brought Christian faith into the kingdom of Tanjore. As an army officer, he used his influence and resources to the expansion of Christian mission. The story of Rajanaiken primarily explains the Dalit roots of Christianity in Tanjore.

The history of Christianity in Sialkot region in Punjab before independence has an important mission history. The main role played in that mission history was Ditt, a dealer in hides. His conversion led to the establishment of Christian community in the region of Sialkot. Ditt was born in 1843 in a small village named Shahabdike in Sialkot, presently in Pakistan. Rev. Andrew Gordon describes him as "…a man of the low and much despised chura tribe, by the name Ditt, a dark man, lame of one leg, quiet and modest in his manners, with sincerity and earnestness, well expressed in his face, and at that time about thirty years of age." He became Christian because of his contact with Nattu, a Jat who was baptized by Rev. J.S. Barr.

Ditt learned about Jesus Christ from Nattu and gradually accepted Jesus Christ and decided to receive baptism. He was baptized by the missionary in Sialkot. The missionary was initially hesitant to baptize him. In those days, new converts were asked to stay with the missionary for some time or till they were placed in safe place. This practice was followed because of two reasons. Firstly, they were taught the basic catechism by the missionary during their stay. Secondly, they were protected from the immediate opposition of their relatives, landlords or caste people. But Ditt did not stay with the missionary. He came back to his village and started to witness his new faith to his relatives and others in society. His decision to return to his village after baptism was a starting point of Christian movement among the Churas, one of the Dalit communities in Punjab. Though he faced opposition from relatives and caste people, he boldly stood for his new faith and used every opportunity to share the Gospel to the people. His witness began to draw people into new faith. Three months after his baptism in August 1873, his wife, daughter and two neighbors came forward to receive baptism. He took them to Sialkot and introduced them to the missionaries. They had to walk 30 miles to reach the mission station. This shows the passion for mission that had been brewing in his mind since his conversion to Christian faith. His job of buying hides also gave him opportunities to share the Gospel of Jesus Christ. He used to visit many villages to buy hides. Wherever he went, he boldly preached about Christ. By 1884, after eleven years of his baptism, more than five hundred people came to Christian faith because of his job-cum-evangelism method. The movement he started progressed step by step. By 1900, more than half of his community became Christians. More people continued to add into Church, and by 1915 majority of Churas of Sialkot became Christians whose descendents are now spread in both Indian and Pakistan sides of Punjab region.[6] The conversion and mission of work of Ditt set a new precedent in the history of mission. Firstly, he overlooked the protection offered by the missionary in mission compound. If he had continued under the protection of missionary, there would not have emerged a strong Christian community in Sialkot, particularly among the Churas. He boldly confronted the opposition and continued to stay in his village. Secondly, he used every opportunity that came through his job to preach about the new faith. He achieved what a missionary could not achieve within a limited span of time. This is another story of Dalit roots of Christianity.

The history of Protestant Christianity in South Travancore is indebted to Vedamanickam. He was born in a Dalit family in Mailady, a village near to Cape Comorin. He belonged to Sambavar community, one of the Dalit communities in Travancore. His mother was pious woman who provided her son basic education and led him into family religious life. He used to worship his family god and even built one temple for his family god. As a religious man, Vedamanickam used to read religious books like Puranas. He also used to go on pilgrimage. Once he undertook a pilgrimage to the temple of Chidambaram with his nephew. He began his journey with hope that he would be spiritually satisfied. But the situation in the temple, particularly the life style of priests, discouraged him and decided to go back home. While returning, he and his nephew visited his sister's family in Tanjore. They were Christians, and Vedamanickam heard about Christ first time from them. One Sunday he visited the church there and heard the message from outside the church. After the service, he shared about his search of truth and pilgrimage to the missionary. The missionary gave him a small booklet about Jesus Christ. He experienced joy and satisfaction while reading the booklet. He continued to stay there for some more days and read more literature about Christian faith and

Jesus Christ. Finally, he accepted Jesus Christ as the true Savior of humanity.[7] Upon his conviction of faith, he was given baptism. After receiving further instructions regarding Christian faith and life, he returned home. His family members and relatives were expecting the gift of the Lord of Chidambaram and holy ashes. When they asked holy gifts, he showed a copy of the Gospels in his hand and said this was the Holy Gift of the Lord of all worlds!' He had to face strong opposition from the Hindu community in his village. He was even excommunicated from his community.[8] In spite of adverse circumstances, he stood by his faith and started to preach the Gospel to his family members and relatives. Gradually a few of them accepted Jesus Christ. This was the beginning of the formation of Christian community in Travancore. He continued to preach the Gospel to people irrespective of caste and creed. While doing his ministry in Mailady he continued his contact with the missionaries in Tanjore. When he came to know that William Tobias Ringeltaube, a missionary of London Mission Society after his language study, was thinking of selecting a mission field Vedamanickam invited him to Mailady. Ringeltaube accepted the invitation and arrived in Mailady on 25th April, 1806. This was another turning point in the history of Travancore Christianity. When he came, there was a group of people prepared by Vedamanickam for baptism. He baptized them and placed them under Vedamanickam. As a catechist and co-worker, Vedamanickam worked with Ringeltaube till 1816. When Ringeltaube left Travancore due to bad health conditions, Vedamanickam was made in-charge of the mission field. He led the local Christian community till the arrival of Rev. Charles Mead, a new missionary assigned to south Travancore, in December 1817. After some time, due to health reasons, Vedamanickam had withdrawn from active mission work. The mission work, which he started among his community, was later spread to other oppressed communities in Travancore.[9] A search for truth in the life of Vedamanickam gave birth to a Christian movement in later years. In fact, he laid the foundation of an influential Christian community today. He had no hesitation to hand over the mission to a foreign missionary and work under him. His greatness lies in the risk he had taken for introducing new faith in the unfavorable social and religious context

The story of Venkayya (1811-1891) is another leaf in the history of Christian mission initiated by a Dalit. He was from Krishna district of Andhra Pradesh. He became Christian in 1849. He was baptized by Mr. Darling, a missionary of Church Missionary Society. J. Waskon Pickett informs that there was not a single covert during the first seven years of Mr. Darling's ministry in Krishna district. He focused on the conversion of upper castes as other missionaries followed in their mission fields. This approach did not contribute to the formation of a Christian community. But after the conversion of Venkayya in 1849, the number of Christians began to increase in Krishna District. There was a strong movement among the oppressed communities particularly among the Dalits. His conversion attracted his own community members and other marginalized sections of society. Gradually a strong Christian community was emerged in Krishna district. Indeed, Venkayya, a Dalit was the founder of that Christian community, not Mr. Darling.[10] The mission story of Krishna district shows again the fact that Church began to grow when the missionaries implemented a shift in their mission approach: from the caste people to the oppressed communities. Above mentioned stories provide us new perspective in defining the role of native Christians in the development of Christianity in India. They encourage us to dig out the forgotten histories of the people who took adventurous steps to introduce Christian faith in new contexts. J. Waskon Pickett gives a clue to read the history of

Christianity from new perspective when he says, "The real founder of Church in Travancore was not Ringeltaube, but Vedamanickam. In Krishna it was not Darling, but Venkayya. In Sialkot, it was not Gordon, but Ditt." [11]

The conversions and mission works of Rajanaiken, Ditt, Vedamanickam and Venkayya are a few examples of the Dalit roots of Christianity in India. They loudly speak of the contributions of Dalits to the formation of Christian communities in different parts of the country. Their conversions and mission initiatives prove that God's Spirit was working through them. Therefore, the movements which they initiated can be called as 'Spirit Movements.' Instead of using the caste people and missionaries, God used these socially low people as founders of Christian communities. It shows God's preferential option for the weak and the downtrodden in society. The missionaries were initially hesitant to accept the oppressed into Christian community. For them, the arrival of Dalits and other oppressed communities was not a happy sign.[12] The Spirit of God who worked through these lowly people actually disturbed the missionaries. It is often true that God's Spirit works through insignificant people against the expectations of the dominant. The missionaries thought that the caste people would embrace Christian faith but just opposite happened in their mission journey. The missionaries called the conversions of Dalits and other oppressed communities as 'mass movement.' They were not ready to accept them as 'Spirit Movement.' For them, the poor became Christians because of the material prosperity attached to the conversions.[13] Actually, 'mass movements' were 'Spirit Movements.' They were the movements of Spirit among the people.[14] The poor and lowly became powerful instruments of God's Spirit to establish Christian communities in a social context where they were socially inferior, economically deprived and religiously impure.

Early Missionary Theology and 'Religion' Factor on Dalit Christians' Life

The numerical growth of Christianity in India is mainly contributed by the conversion of Dalits and other socially backward communities in 19th and 20th centuries. Though Christianity has contributed to the social advancement of Dalit Christians, they still face different forms of disempowerment in society. There are some root causes which continue to play certain role behind the problems of Dalit Christians. The life-style of early missionaries created a negative image of Christianity among the people. They gave 'elitist' image or identity to Indian Christianity despite the fact that majority of Christians come from Dalit-Tribal-OBC origin. The elitist image not only kept many Dalits from Christianity but also created an impression among the caste people that Dalit Christians could avail the resources of the church for their social empowerment. It gradually led to the complete exclusion of Dalit Christians from the legal and social protection of scheduled caste status. The early missionaries also directly or indirectly supported the oppressive social and cultural practices, particularly of the caste system which denied the equal status of Dalits in society. In the name of accommodating the local practices, many missionaries consciously or unconsciously compromised their communitarian faith principles with the existing social relationships based on caste system. In fact, it gave strength to the oppressive caste system within the church. It continues to haunt Dalit Christians even today. The missionaries shifted their focus towards the Dalit communities when they failed to get converts from upper castes. The early missionary approach which preferred the upper castes actually looked down the Dalits. This approach was literally the social approach of the upper castes. It further contributed to the oppressed condition of Dalits and the hegemonic outlook of caste people.[15] Along with the caste system, these factors also functioned as the root causes of the problems of Dalit Christians in India today.

Theological background and teachings of early missionaries also contributed to the problems of Dalits Christians. The early Catholic missionaries like Francs Xavier focused on the conversion of people, and taught them some moral teachings, Lord's Prayer and Ten Commandments. They limited their works to the religious life than the holistic development of converts in society. The protestant missionaries like Ziegenbalg, Plutschau and Schwartz also followed the same mission pattern. They were basically trained in the pietistic religious background. They primarily emphasized the infallibility of the Scripture, personal holiness and otherworldly life. Though they believed in doing charity and social empowerment of people they prioritized the otherworldly salvation.[16] Theological background of those missionaries influenced their mission agenda. The 'soul saving' mission approach of early missionaries overlooked the social issues of people particularly the Dalits and other marginalized communities. The absence of bold social vision and mission in the early missionary initiatives has led to the accommodation of local oppressive social practices and to the negligence of addressing the social issues of the time.

The theological emphasis of early missionaries was centered on 'otherworldly' salvation which ignored the social realities of early converts. It prevented the upward social mobility of converts, particularly the Dalits. The 'otherworldly' salvation which was preached and taught among them had given them 'half salvation' only. It is 'half-salvation' because it did not address the worldly issues of the people. Salvation is primarily holistic in nature, and touches every aspect of human life in this world also. The moral teachings, personal holiness and other-worldly spirituality taught by the missionaries did not lead them to social empowerment. It has to be noted that majority of the people who accepted the Christian faith in the beginning stage of missionary Christianity in India were illiterate and socially poor. They genuinely believed what the missionaries taught them. They could not understand the social implications of their faith which was introduced as the way to heaven. They were theologically molded by the teachings on otherworldly salvation. It has been continued throughout the centuries. Still majority of Dalit Christians are shaped by the theological thinking of 'otherworldly' salvation. It has two main consequences. Firstly, Dalit Christians themselves ignore the issues which question their identity and dignity. The internalization of 'otherworldly' salvation makes them non-resistant to the forces of oppression and marginalization in society. It also prepares them to accept any kind of suffering caused by their social identity. Secondly, non-Dalits, who are influenced by the 'otherworldly' salvation, are not guilty of practicing caste in church and society because caste is 'this-worldly' reality.[17] Thus, theological thinking of early missionaries and converts has also contributed to the present conditions of Dalit Christians in India.

Christian faith generally encourages its adherents to fight against injustice and equality and teaches them to establish an egalitarian society in this world. Instead of encouraging the Dalits to achieve their equal human dignity, the other-worldly salvation approach continuously keeps them in the bondage of oppressive forces in society. The problem with theological emphasis on individualistic and otherworldly salvation is that it promotes escapism of Dalits from their actual wretched conditions in this world and makes them passive recipients of the social evils of caste system. In such situation they do not even feel that they are victims of this-worldly powers of oppression and exploitation.[18]

The influence of caste can be seen in the methodology of early missionaries. They believed that the conversion of upper castes would lead other communities into Christian faith. Therefore, they initially focused on the upper castes. But they could not create impact among the upper castes except few conversions hither and thither. They also failed to understand the influence of caste system which provided superior status to the upper castes in society. The missionaries were also divided in their approach towards the conversion of lower castes in the later period. One group encouraged the conversion of lower castes for the sake of increasing the number of converts. Another group resisted the large scale conversion of people from the lower strata of society. And some missionaries even had racial superiority that kept them away from the lower castes, particularly the Dalits.[19] The approach of early missionaries towards the conversion of lower castes in fact prevented the liberation of Dalits from the captivity of caste system. It also influenced the outlook of native Christian leaders in later period.[20]

Majority Indian Christians are today influenced by the otherworldly salvation theology taught by the missionaries in the past. They are least concerned about social issues particularly the issues of Dalits and other marginalized communities. Among them, Dalits live in a condition in which they themselves have forgotten their problem of Dalitness. The social realities of majority Christians, particularly the Dalits are often not considered in framing the approach of Christian witness in society. For instance, Christian educational institutions prefer to have more non-Christians than Christians. They serve the interests of upper class/castes than the poor Christians, majority of them come from the lower strata of society. It also shows the influence of otherworldly salvation theology which ignores the issues of this-world including social and educational empowerment of people. It is also evident in the approach taken by the Christian representatives in the Constituent Assembly which framed the Constitution of India. All Christian representatives in the Assembly were belonged to the upper castes/ classes. They were H.C. Mookerjee, a high-caste Bengali convert, Rajkumari Amrit Kaur, a Panjabi convert from a royal background and Jerome D'Souza, a Jesuit belonging to the upper class. They represented the Christian community but failed to represent the real need and condition of majority Christians. While drafting the constitution, the question of certain socio-economic privileges like free education and reservation in jobs for the poor who belonged to the lower strata of society was discussed. When the Christian representatives were asked if they desired to have such privileges to empower the poor within the community, they declined the offer even though majority of Christians were socially and economically poor. They failed to represent majority Christians who really needed special privileges to achieve upward social and economic mobility in society. The stand taken by the upper caste/class Christian representatives later influenced the Presidential Order of 1950 which denied Scheduled Caste status to the Dalit Christians. Since then, Dalit Christians have been deprived of the benefits of reservation and legal protections which they deserve to enjoy in society.[21] This denial of justice is partly contributed by the influence of other worldly salvation theology inherited from the missionaries.

It is a fact that Dalit Christians face discrimination common with other Dalits who belong to other religious traditions. Dalits irrespective of faiths are discriminated in social, economic and political areas of life. This is the first level of Dalit discrimination. They face discrimination in terms of dwelling place, job, social relations etc. For instance, Dalits are historically forced to live in segregated parts of the society. Except few changes, still it is common throughout the country.[22] The social discrimination of Dalit Christians continues in the Church also. This is second level of discrimination. Though they practice the same faith, they are discriminated within the faith community because of their social identity. The co-religionists, particularly the upper caste Christians, treat them as inferior even though the Christian faith teaches egalitarianism.[23] Third level of discrimination is the denial of Constitutional rights. The Presidential Order 1950 denied them Scheduled Caste status because of their religion. According to the said order, Dalit Christians are not entitled to get the constitutional provisions exclusively granted to the Dalits in India. It directly contradicts the fundament right, the Right to Equality (Article 14) guaranteed in the Constitution.[24] The irony is that though the Constitution guarantees equality of every citizen irrespective of religion, Dalit Christians face discrimination in the name of religion. The Presidential Order 1950 also prevents Dalit Christians to enjoy the special legal protection given to the Dalits who belong to Hindu, Sikh and Buddhist religions. The religious identity keeps Dalit Christians outside the ambit of the Protection of Civil Rights Act 1955; Protection of Civil Rights Rules, 1977; and the Scheduled Castes and Scheduled Tribes (Prevention of Atrocities) Act, 1989. Though Dalit Christians share same social identity of other Dalits, they are not protected under these laws.[25] The Presidential Order 1950 denies Dalit Christians not only 'the right to equality' and 'special legal protection' granted to Dalits but also the rights granted in the Articles 330, 332, 335 and 338 concerning jobs, education and participation in the governance of the country. Dalit Christians face third level of discrimination mainly from the government.[26] The life realities of Dalit Christians strongly substantiate the demand that they must be granted Scheduled Caste status based on their social identity. The religious identity of Dalit Christians has not completely eliminated the social discrimination they face in church and society. The social life of Dalit Christians also shows that social identity and religious identity together keep them in disempowered condition. It is observed that "religious factor, it seems, becomes for the Christian Dalits more a source of problems or bondage than a source of liberation."[27] Different levels of discrimination faced by Dalit Christians are the result of the historical perpetuation of caste system. It is primarily caste system which led them into new religious faith and subsequent denial of rights.

The history of the denial of scheduled caste status to the Dalit Christians goes back to the Government of India (Scheduled Castes) Order, 1936 which says "no Indian Christian...should be deemed a member of a Scheduled Caste." By this order, 'religion' became a criterion for defining Scheduled Caste. Though Dalits (Scheduled Castes) were defined in terms of religion, it did not affect the Dalit Christians because they were enjoying the status of minority community during that time. Thus, they were not deprived of any right which would socially and economically empower them. The minority rights compensated the privileges of scheduled caste status.[28] But after independence, Government of India applied 'religion' criterion followed in the Government of India (Scheduled Castes) Order, 1936, to define Scheduled Caste. Thus the Presidential Order 1950 completely excluded Dalit Christians from the constitutional protection and privileges extended to other Dalits. Another historical reason for the present unprivileged condition of Dalit Christians is the position taken by the representatives of Indian Christians in the Constituent Assembly which drafted the Constitution of India. They informed the Assembly that Indian Christians were satisfied with the fundamental rights and willing to forgo the minority rights they enjoyed till 1947. It is Dalit Christians who face the consequences of such decision even today. While the existing minority rights do not compensate the denial of civil rights (Scheduled Caste Status) because of their religious faith,[29] Dalit Christians still continue to uphold their faith which promised them salvation/liberation. The different levels of discriminations they face in society are not only because of their social and religious identities but also because of the historical mistakes committed by the colonial masters and native Christian leaders who were influenced by early missionary theologies. In short, the journey of Dalit Christians shows that the impact of early missionary theology and the 'religion' factor in defining Scheduled Castes have largely contributed to the present disempowered condition of majority Dalit Christians. Dalit theology stands as a theological correction to the early missionary theologies which poorly responded to the worldly issues of Dalits. As they contributed to the establishment of Christianity in India, so the present Christianity has to express its solidarity with Dalit Christians to come out of their disempowered condition.

Endnotes

[1] James Massey, *Dalit Theology: History, Context, Text and Whole Salvation* (New Delhi: Manohar, 2013), 98-99; James Massey, "Dalit Roots of Indian Christianity," in *Frontiers of Dalit Theology*, edited by V. Devasahayam (Chennai: ISPCK/Gurukul, 1997), 191-192.

[2] Quoted in James Massey, "Dalit Roots of Indian Christianity," 193.

[3] James Massey, "Dalit Roots of Indian Christianity," 193; James Massey, *Dalit Theology: History, Context, Text and Whole Salvation*, 100.

[4] James Massey, *Dalit Theology: History, Context, Text and Whole Salvation*, 101.

[5] James Massey, "History and Dalit Theology," in *Frontiers of Dalit Theology*, edited by V. Devasahayam (Chennai: ISPCK/Gurukul, 1997), 161-162.

[6] James Massey, "Dalit Roots of Indian Christianity," 183-184; James Massey, *Dalit Theology: History, Context, Text and Whole Salvation*, 93-94.

[7] James Massey, *Dalit Theology: History, Context, Text and Whole Salvation*, 95; James Massey, "Dalit Roots of Indian Christianity," 185.

[8] James Massey, *Dalit Theology: History, Context, Text and Whole Salvation*, 96; James Massey, "Dalit Roots of Indian Christianity," 186.

[9] James Massey, "Dalit Roots of Indian Christianity," 187; James Massey, *Dalit Theology: History, Context, Text and Whole Salvation*, 97.

[10] James Massey, "Dalit Roots of Indian Christianity," 195-196; James Massey, *Dalit Theology: History, Context, Text and Whole Salvation*, 103.

[11] James Massey, "Dalit Roots of Indian Christianity," 196.

[12] James Massey, "Dalit Roots of Indian Christianity," 193.

[13] James Massey, *Dalit Theology: History, Context, Text and Whole Salvation*, 243.

[14] James Massey, *Dalit Bible Commentary, New Testament Vol. 5, Acts of Apostles* (New Delhi: CDS, 2008), 26 & 116.

[15] James Massey, *Dalits in India: Religion as a Source of Bondage or Liberation with Special Reference to Christians* (New Delhi: Manohar, 2009 Reprint), 98.

[16] James Massey, *Dalit Theology: History, Context, Text and Whole Salvation*, 77 & 79; James Massey, *Dalits in India: Religion as a Source of Bondage or Liberation with Special Reference to Christians*, 99; James Massey, "Need of a Dalit Theological Expression," in *Confronting Life: Theology out of the Context*, edited by M.P. Joseph (Delhi: ISPCK, 1995), 194.

[17] James Massey, *Dalit Theology: History, Context, Text and Whole Salvation*, 83; James Massey, "Dalit Theology: Response to Dalit Context," in *Dalit Issue in Today's Theological Debate*, edited by James Massey and S. Lourduswamy (New Delhi: CDS, 2003), 123; James Massey, "Dalit Roots of Indian Christianity," 201.

[18] James Massey, *Dalits in India: Religion as a Source of Bondage or Liberation with Special Reference to Christians*, 113; James Massey, *Dalit Theology: History, Context, Text and Whole Salvation*, 88.

[19] James Massey, *Dalit Theology: History, Context, Text and Whole Salvation*, 84-85; James Massey, *Dalits in India: Religion as a Source of Bondage or Liberation with Special Reference to Christians*, 100-101.

[20] James Massey, *Dalits in India: Religion as a Source of Bondage or Liberation with Special Reference to Christians*, 112.

[21] James Massey, *Dalit Theology: History, Context, Text and Whole Salvation*, 87-88.

[22] James Massey, *Dalit Theology: History, Context, Text and Whole Salvation*, 127; James Massey, "An Analysis of the Dalit Situation with Special Reference to Dalit Christians and Dalit Theology," *Religion and Society*, Vol 52/No 3-4 (September-December 2007): 57-86 at 71

[23] James Massey, *Dalit Theology: History, Context, Text and Whole Salvation*, 128-129; James Massey, "An Analysis of the Dalit Situation with Special Reference to Dalit Christians and Dalit Theology," 73-75.

[24] James Massey, *Dalits in India: Religion as a Source of Bondage or Liberation with Special Reference to Christians*, 98; James Massey, "An Analysis of the Dalit Situation with Special Reference to Dalit Christians and Dalit Theology," 71-73.

[25] James Massey, *Dalit Theology: History, Context, Text and Whole Salvation*, 130-131; James Massey, *Dalits in India: Religion as a Source of Bondage or Liberation with Special Reference to Christians*, 142.

[26] James Massey, *Dalit Theology: History, Context, Text and Whole Salvation*, 132; James Massey, "Dalits and Human Rights," *Religion and Society* Vol 49/No 2& 3 (June and September 2004): 1-9 at 4-5.

[27] James Massey, *Dalits in India: Religion as a Source of Bondage or Liberation with Special Reference to Christians*, 144.

[28] James Massey, *Dalit Theology: History, Context, Text and Whole Salvation*, 133; James Massey, *Dalits in India: Religion as a Source of Bondage or Liberation with Special Reference to Christians*, 132 & 140.

[29] James Massey, *Dalit Theology: History, Context, Text and Whole Salvation*, 135.

Chapter 10

Peace, Reconciliation and Justice

Generally, 'peace' is understood as 'absence of war' or 'absence of organized violence.' According to James Massey,[1] it has another dimension which is more related to the marginalized peoples, particularly Dalits in India. It is the question of 'justice' in the context of 'structural injustices.' The structural injustice or inequality primarily destroys the peaceful life of Dalits. Caste system is the root cause of any structural injustice in social life. Dalits are the primary victims of structural injustice perpetuated by caste system. Their life realities define peace as 'absence of injustice.' It tells the fact that 'peace' and 'justice' is integrally related; the former cannot be established without addressing the latter. While 'absence of war' is 'negative peace,' 'absence of injustice' is 'positive peace,' which is authentic and real peace. For Dalits, authentic peace basically comes from an experience of just life, a life not victimized by oppressive structures.[2] In fact, peaceful life is fruit of the establishment of justice in society. Dalits enjoy peace when they are liberated from structural injustices.[3] Assertion of justice helps both the oppressed and the oppressor live a life of peace. While structural injustice destroys the peace of oppressed communities, resistance to structural injustice may disturb the peace of the oppressors.

Caste is not only unjust structure but also violent structure. It perpetuates injustice in social relations and encourages physical and psychological violence. What is needed for Dalits is peace that seeks justice.[4] Poverty is another form of structural injustice and violence. Dalits constitute majority of the poor who struggle to get resources needed for their survival.[5] Poverty is the result of unequal economic structure historically developed by caste system. That is why Dalits remain as primary victims of poverty too.

Dalits carry their 'injured psyche' created by the structure of caste. It is far more than their economic deprivations. The pain (*peeran*) they experience in different forms makes them peaceless in all aspects of life. The 'wholeness of their lives' is measured by the peace they experience in personal and community life in relation to others who perpetuate structural injustice. 'Peace as absence of injustice' should be a point of departure for Dalit liberation.[6] Dalits experience peace when *peeran* is eased in their 'injured psyche.' *Peeran* cannot be alleviated without restoring justice to them. Since Dalit *peeran* is community *peeran*, justice has be rendered to the community. When community enjoys 'absence of injustice', 'absence of *peeram*,' it reflects in the peaceful dignified life of individuals.[7] For Dalits, peace is nothing less than experiencing social justice in par with others in society.

The community dimension of *peeran* comes from caste system which promotes community/caste rights than individual rights. The social order based on caste system gives importance to a particular caste than an individual. Unlike Universal Declaration of Human Rights which places individual rights over community rights, the caste system defines individual rights within the framework of caste duties and rights. Each caste is given specific privileges and rights. An individual enjoys his/her rights solely based on his/her membership to a particular caste. There is no right an individual can claim apart from his/her caste. It also implies that if an individual is deprived of any right, it is because of his/her birth in a particular caste. If s/he experiences *peeran* because of the deprivation of justice, it is not his/her problem but s/he belongs to a particular caste. [8] Therefore, structural violence and injustice faced by Dalits in India is not individual in nature but communitarian.

One of the worst realities in Dalit life is that they are made to internalize their broken social conditions as their destiny. They are also conditioned to think 'injustice' as normal in social relations shaped by caste system. Thus caste system has been successful to keep Dalits 'ritually impure,' 'socially inferior,' 'economically poor,' and 'politically powerless.' Indeed, by denying justice, caste system has placed Dalits in the site of pain and peacelessness.[9] Instead of being active in responding to the 'structural injustices' they are made passive and 'non-people.'[10]

The liberation of Dalits from structural inequalities is centered on the basic requirement of 'justice.' They believe that justice alone can remove all inequalities they experience in society. Massey provides two suggestions in this direction. Firstly, Dalits should be educated about the nature and causes of injustices and inequalities inflicted upon them. 'Education for justice' should enable them be critically conscious of their wretched situation. This critical consciousness is the first step towards liberation. Secondly, they should be taught of their equal rights with others. Awareness of their rights helps them to resist exploitation and marginalization. They also should be educated how to organize themselves to fight against the unjust behavior of their oppressors. 'Reservation' in education and jobs is one of the means to remove social injustice in the life of Dalits, the historical victims of caste.[11]

The awareness of rights is part of the process of empowerment. It is often reflected in different forms. Though the frequent physical, sexual, emotional atrocities against Dalits are primarily structural in nature, they are manifestations of upper caste intolerance against the growing awareness of rights among the Dalits.[12] When Dalits assert their rights by modifying their life style and improving their economic, social, educational conditions, violent response is a common phenomenon in many rural and urban societies in India. In the light of the atrocities against Dalits, 'peace' is also meant as absence of "any structural violence of one group against the other in a society."[13] The atrocities not only put them in peaceless situation but also drain their hard earned resources because of legal struggle, physical injury, loss of accommodation etc.

Two approaches are proposed to achieve genuine peace in the life of Dalits. One is dialogical approach. It aims to bring a total change in the existing social stricture which perpetuates the pain of Dalits in social life. Dialogue with Dalits means an active participation in their struggles for full humanhood and social empowerment. It is an intentional engagement with the broken life-realities of Dalits and an attempt of moral correction from non-Dalits. Dialogical approach demands the dialogue partners (non-Dalits) to be nonjudgmental in their approach towards Dalits. Before entering into dialogue with Dalits, there are three prerequisites. Firstly, dialogue should not be considered as gift to the Dalits. It should be an attempt to rectify what was unjustly done to the Dalits. Secondly, it should help Dalits achieve their lost dignity and humanhood. Once they were free human beings who had enjoyed full freedom in all aspects of life. They lost their freedom with the emergence of caste structure in society. Thirdly, dialogue must lead to total change in the present condition of Dalits.[14] It primarily implies an attitudinal change of caste people and upward social mobility of Dalits.

Second approach is Holistic Approach. Firstly, since the structural injustice and violence affected the whole life of Dalits, the issues which destroy peaceful life of Dalits have to be dealt holistically. A genuine peace can be brought forth through a holistic approach than treating part by part. Holistic approach has significance in the life of Dalits because every Dalit problem is primarily connected with caste structure. Secondly, this approach argues that every human being has to involve in the process of establishing genuine peace. It derives from the meaning of 'holistic' that "an organic or integrated whole has a reality independent of and greater than the sum of its parts." In fact, the entire society is responsible for achieving and maintaining peace. Since caste-based social order destroys peaceful life of all human beings one way or other, holistic approach demands all human beings to break the structures and systems which oppress them.[15] For Dalits, it is caste-based behavior of non-Dalits that obstructs their upward social mobility and keeps them in unpeaceful situation. It is caste structure that shapes oppressive behavior and denies justice to Dalits. Thus, entire society has to combat against oppressive structures and root out their influence in social life.

The holistic approach is biblical approach. The Hebrew word for 'peace' in the Bible means 'completeness' or 'wholeness.' It also gives the clue that holistic approach is always practical approach to achieve peace in society. Peaceful society/individual is characterized by an experience of 'fullness' or 'wholeness' in all aspects of life. It lacks nothing in terms of resources, potential, opportunities and rights. Prophet Isaiah talks about the coming of a future King and his rule (9: 6-7). That King is addressed as 'Prince of Peace.' His reign will witness endless peace on earth. He will establish and uphold peace with justice and righteousness (9: 7). The foundation of His reign will be righteousness and justice (Chapter 32), which facilitates 'fullness of life.' The prophet also says peace is the fruit of righteousness (right relationship).[16] For Dalits, peace can be established if there is right relationship between human beings. Caste structure does not allow people to live in right relationship and enjoy peace. Therefore, it must be countered by all. Right relationship gives birth to just society where everyone celebrates life in its fullness.

Jesus' approach was also holistic in nature. His Nazareth manifesto testifies it. He announced liberation for both oppressed and oppressor.[17] He wanted to liberate entire society from the bondage of different oppressive structures. He offered a life which experiences 'absence of structural injustices.' He also invited everyone to participate in the process of building up Kingdom of God.

For Massey, peace has to be understood along with reconciliation also. Reconciliation is the starting point of establishing authentic peace. If communities or individuals are not reconciled, peace will not be restored in society. In a social context where caste-based social order exists, 'repentance' and 'justice' are two essential requirements of reconciliation. Reconciliation happens when the oppressors repent for their social sins and participate in the struggles of the oppressed for the restoration of rights. For Dalits, the non-Dalits have to shun their oppressive hegemonic behavior emanates from caste consciousness. This caste consciousness hinders reconciliation and prevents the restoration of rights, the restoration of justice. The repentance of caste people may restore 'justice' denied to the Dalits for centuries. Dalits basically long for their social restoration. It is possible if both individuals and communities are renewed (Jeremiah 24:7, 31:31f, 32: 38f; Ezekiel 11:19, 36:25-27, 37:1-14). It demands renewed understanding of human life and social justice. The renewal of society manifests in the changed behavior of the oppressors and in the celebration of the full humanhood of the oppressed. Then, the real reconciliation happens between the oppressors and the oppressed. It will ultimately lead to genuine peace, the absence of structural injustice and violence.[18]

Reconciliation basically points to the removal of enmity, the enmity between communities and individuals. In Indian context, what kind of enmity Dalits face is enmity based on caste. For them, caste-based enmity has to be completely removed for their social reconciliation and restoration of justice. The removal of enmity between Dalits and caste people contributes to the establishment of peace in social relations, particularly in the life of Dalits. Enmity cannot be fully removed unless the root cause of enmity is removed. Dalit understanding of reconciliation informs that caste consciousness is the root cause of enmity between Dalits and non-Dalits.[19]

Authentic peace comes out of the process of reconciliation centered on justice. "The test of 'authentic peace' is the freedom from threat to the powerless of society."[20] Dalits experience 'authentic peace' when they enjoy freedom from the threat of oppression and marginalization. The process of reconciliation, social reconciliation, can produce authentic peace. But reconciliation without justice is meaningless for Dalits.[21] Justice is the basic principle of the Dalit perception of reconciliation and peace. Without justice, both remain abstract ideas in social life.

What is needed to achieve genuine peace is prophetic spirituality which breaks all walls of separation and calls for repentance. It confronts all forms of structural injustices and violence and nourishes the spirit of reconciliation among human beings. Prophetic spirituality denounces any kind of oppression and announces the good news of salvation. It demands a shift from 'ambulance ministry' to a 'ministry of involvement and participation' in the struggles of marginalized communities. They can think of peace only with justice.

They long for a just society patterned after Kingdom of God in which they will celebrate life in its fullness-life with 'redeemed dignity and recovered humanity.'[22] Understanding peace and reconciliation within the framework of justice is the sign of prophetic spirituality. The peace and reconciliation based on justice reflects the Divine solidarity with humanity which was climaxed in Jesus Christ. This solidarity has to be manifested again to break the barriers that prevent to achieve authentic peace in the life of Dalits. We are the site of such solidarity.

Endnotes

[1] This chapter narrates James Massey's reflections on Peace and Reconciliation within the framework of justice.

[2] James Massey, *Ecumenism Means Justice* (Matiala, New Delhi: CDS, 2014), 55.

[3] James Massey, *Caste-Class Victims and Their Assertion for Justice* (New Delhi: CDS, 2013), 73.

[4] James Massey, *Ecumenism Means Justice*, 150.

[5] Deepak Seth, ed., *From Truth to Truth, A Journey through Faiths: A Selection of Representative Essays by Dr. James Massey* (New Delhi: CDS and NOIDA: Academy Press, 2008), 133.

[6] James Massey, *Ecumenism Means Justice*, 57.

[7] James Massey, *Ecumenism Means Justice*, 58; James Massey, *Caste-Class Victims and Their Assertion for Justic*, 96

[8] Deepak Seth, ed., *From Truth to Truth, A Journey Through Faiths: A Selection of Representative Essays by Dr. James Massey*, 134.

[9] James Massey, *Ecumenism Means Justice*, 65.

[10] James Massey, *Ecumenism Means Justice*, 66.

[11] James Massey, *Ecumenism Means Justice*, 73.

[12] Deepak Seth, ed., *From Truth to Truth, A Journey Through Faiths: A Selection of Representative Essays by Dr. James Massey*, 132-133.

[13] James Massey, "On Being a New Community and Ecclesia of Justice and Peace," in *On Being a New Community and Ecclesia of Justice and Peace*, edited by James Massey and NOH, Jong Sun (Bangalore: BTESSC/SATHRI, 2010), 13.

[14] Deepak Seth, ed., *From Truth to Truth, A Journey through Faiths: A Selection of Representative Essays by Dr. James Massey*, 142.

[15] James Massey, "Approaches to the Whole Issue of Peace," in *Towards Justice and Peace: A Subaltern Initiative*, edited by Monodeep Daniel and Yangkahao Vashum (Jorhart: TCS/WSC, Nagpur: CNI Desk on Dalit and Tribal Concerns & New Delhi: CDS, 2010), 117; Deepak Seth, ed., *From Truth to Truth, A Journey through Faiths: A Selection of Representative Essays by Dr. James Massey*, 143.

[16] James Massey, *Dalit Theology: History, Context, Text and Whole Salvation* (New Delhi: Manohar, 2013), 169; James Massey, "Approaches to the Whole Issue of Peace," 117; James Massey, "On Being a New Community and Ecclesia of Justice and Peace," 27.

[17] James Massey, *Ecumenism Means Justice*, 61; James Massey, *Caste-Class Victims and Their Assertion for Justice*, 96.

[18] James Massey, *Ecumenism Means Justice*, 151.

[19] James Massey, *Dalit Theology: History, Context, Text and Whole Salvation*, 162.

[20] James Massey, *Ecumenism Means Justice*, 158.

[21] James Massey, *Dalit Theology: History, Context, Text and Whole Salvation*, 170; James Massey, "Approaches to the Whole Issue of Peace," 118.

[22] James Massey, *Dalit Theology: History, Context, Text and Whole Salvation*, 171-172.

Chapter 11

Dalits:
Roots, Spirituality and Leadership

Every community has a history. It may be a history of triumph or history of subjugation or history of oppression. It does not mean that history of every community is well documented or written. Previously, the histories of dominant and privileged in society were the focus of traditional historical narrations. The histories of subalterns in respective contexts were either unwritten or ignored in the attempts of historicizing process. In the Indian context, the history was once meant only the history of rulers and the high castes. The lower castes, the Dalits and the women, particularly the Dalits among them were outside the traditional ambit of history. James Massey argues that though it was not properly documented, the history of Dalits begins before the coming of Aryans who later oppressed them for centuries. Today, their history has become the history of oppression which spans many centuries. They had their own religious heritage and traditions of spirituality. Massey has attempted to bring out the roots of Dalit identity, their religious heritage and historical problem in his writings. Some of his views in this direction are discussed in this chapter. In order to build up empowered Dalit communities, he also proposes different models for Dalit leadership. They are also narrated in the following sections.

Dalits

The term 'dalit' has etymological relation with Sanskrit word, 'dal' which means 'to crack', 'split', 'be broken' or 'torn asunder', 'trodden down', 'scattered', 'crushed', 'destroyed.' It is used in noun and adjective forms to refer masculine, feminine and neuter genders. Though the term was used in the past to denote the people who did not belong to the caste hierarchy, it got popularity with the emergence of Dalit Panthers in Maharashtra in 1970's.[1] The term 'dalit' primarily refers to a condition/state of affairs into which a group of people have been reduced through the mechanism of caste system in India. It also exclusively points neither to the name of a 'caste', nor to the economically poor condition. It basically expresses the 'broken or 'downtrodden' condition of the people.[2] Though the seeds of the concept of Dalit can be seen in the writings of Mahatma Jyotirao Phule and B.R. Ambedkar, it was conceptually defined by the Dalit Panthers Movement. In its manifesto, Dalits are defined as "Members of Scheduled Castes and Tribes, neo-Buddhists, the working people, the landless and the poor peasants, women and all those who are being exploited politically, economically and in the name of religion."[3] In the present context, 'Dalit' is not just a word or name; rather it is an 'assertion of pride' by the people who were considered as 'untouchables' in the social history of India. For them, Dalit is a 'sign' of being conscious of their historical victimhood, a sign of the rejection of oppression and a sign of liberation.[4] The beauty of the use of this term is that Dalits have adopted it as a title for themselves against the titles given by the caste people in the past. On the one hand it implies the condition of oppression or brokenness; on the other hand, the people who are oppressed. This term stands as a title of self-assertion in the midst of those titles given by their oppressors. Dalits were given the titles/names such as Dasa, Dasyu, Raksasa, Asura, Avarna, Nisada, Panchama, Mleccha, Chandala, Achuta, Exterior Castes, Depressed classes, Scheduled Castes, Harijan, Untouchables etc. They were also addressed by the titles in regional languages such as Churas, Bhangi, Paraiyan etc. These titles were the titles of contempt.[5] Therefore, asserting the identity with new name/title is a liberating action.

Dalits claim that their ancestors are indigenous people of this land. The historical oppression of Dalits began around 1500 BC, and it continues even today in different forms. The Dalits have lost their primary identity as indigenous people and free human beings because of the long years of oppression and have fully internalized 'oppressive condition' as normal condition in their lives. Physically and psychologically they are made to think that 'suffering' is their social privilege.[6] "It is the acceptance of oppression, not oppression itself, which destroys people. This is exactly what has happened to the Dalits/Subaltern community: they have accepted the inferior status imposed by their colonizers."[7] However, there was a time Dalits were free people enjoying full human dignity and ownership of the land. They were indigenous people and had glorious past before the arrival of Aryans.[8] The historical traditions in Rigveda and archeological findings points to the indigenous identity of Dalits. Ramprasad Chanda observes that many Rigvedic hymns (e.g., hymn 51 of Mandala book one, and hymn 34 of Mandala three) give the idea of the existence of two hostile people groups in the land of Rigveda. While one group was Arya/Aryans who worshipped *deva*, the other was Dasyu or Dasa who were *deva*-less and rite-less people. The authors of Vedic Index of Names and Subjects argue that Arya was the earlier designation of Aryan who was later identified with Brahman, Kshatriya, or Vaishya *varnas*. They stood in opposition to the Dasyu/Dasa. Rigveda passages like 1.51.8, 103.3; 2.18.19; 3.34.9 etc. give the space to believe that Dasyu were indigenous people. Moreover, in Rigveda, they were addressed with negative features like *anaso* (without face), *anas* (noseless), etc.[9] The archeological findings at Mohenjodaro and Harappa also established the existence of two groups. While one group was considered as early settlers (indigenous people); the other was foreigners who attempted to occupy the space through invasions. The Dasyus as indigenous people must been the early settlers of the land.[10] The inferior status attributed to the Dasyus/Dasas in the later period of Brahmanic socio-religious traditions points to the fact that these Dasyus were the ancestors of Dalits who have been oppressed for centuries.

History of Dalit Problem

According to James Massey, the present problem of Dalits (discriminated condition of Dalits) has more than 3500 years of history. The root cause of their discrimination lies with the *Purusasukta* hymn in the Rigveda, which narrates the origin and existence of four-fold divisions (castes) of humanity. This hymn later led to the formation of *varna dharma*, the primal form of present caste system. In fact, Dalit problem was begun during the Rigvedic period starting with the hostility between Aryas and Dasas and the creation hymn in Purusasukta. Since Rigveda was considered as the earliest religious text, the people believed the content of the creation hymn in it and practically followed the hierarchy of creation in social life. There started the inferior social status of Dalits.[11] During the period of Upanishads, the condition of Dalits was worsened. It is very evident in the Chandogya Upanishad which compared Chandala (Dalit) with a dog or a swine.[12] The period of Epics further strengthened the mechanism of *varna dharma*. The story of Sambuka in Valmiki Ramayana and the story of Ekalavya explain the condition of Shudras and Adivasis of that time. The degraded

condition of Dalits can be inferred from the stories of Sambuka
and Ekalavya even though they were not Dalits. The affirmation
of *chaturvarna* (four varnas) by the Lord Krishna in Gita also
contributed to the discriminated condition of Dalits and other
oppressed communities.[13] The gradual degradation of Dalits reached
its climax during the period of Manusmriti. The Manusmriti actually
negated the existence of Dalits by recognizing only the four varnas.
It considered the people who did not belong to the four *varnas* as
children of inter-caste/mixed (*varna*) marriages. They were called as
Chandala and Sapaka and numerous restrictions imposed on their
mobility, housing, dress code, food etc. By the time, Manusmriti
was compiled in AD 700, Dalits had already experienced many
years of oppression and humiliation at the hands of four *varnas*.
The period between Rigveda and Manusmriti (Brahmanic Period)
was a period of institutionalizing the caste system which established
the problem of Dalits. Rest of the period of Dalit oppression can be
divided into three: Muslim period (AD 700 to 1700), British Period
(AD 1700 to 1947) and Post-Independence period (Since 1947).[14]

The social condition of Dalits was not changed even during the
period of Muslim rule in India. The hegemony of caste continued
undisturbed even though the religion of the rulers (Islam) taught
the principle of equality. The condition of Dalits during this period
was very evidently narrated by Al-Beruni in his travel account.
Dalits, who were then called as Chandala, Hadi, Doma etc, were
not treated as a caste group. They were mainly involved in the job
of cleaning villages which they even continue today and rendered
different services to other communities. People of that time believed
that Dalits were outcastes because their ancestors were born out of
the illegitimate relationship between a Sudra father and a Brahmin
mother. In the later period of Muslim rule, the emergence of Bhakti
movements under the leadership of non-Brahmins (some of them

were Dalits), contributed to the upliftment of Dalits at least in spiritual realm.[15] Though the British rule maintained the policy of non-interference in social and religious practices, the work of Christian missionaries influenced the outlook of people. They questioned some of the dehumanizing customs and practices that existed in society and challenged the religious communities and leaders to initiate bold steps to remove the social and religious disabilities of Dalits. However, silent recognition of caste system within the church does not completely exonerate the missionaries from the sin of perpetuating an inhuman social institution. The British period also witnessed the emergence of certain reform movements which directly or indirectly addressed the life realities of Dalits. The movements of Jyoti Rao Phule and B.R. Ambedkar played a significant role in addressing the issues of Dalits. Nevertheless, the Bhakti movements of this time were more interested in reforming the existing socio-religious practices than in facilitating radical change in the outlook of people in social relations.[16] The post-independence period also has not seen adequate change not only in the life of Dalits but also in the social outlook of people towards caste and Dalits.[17] Though many liberative principles were incorporated into the Constitution of India and much progressive legislations were made, still the influence of caste continues in all aspects of Indian social life. This situation perpetuates the problems of Dalits in India. They continue to face different forms of discrimination and negation even today.

Dalit in Biblical Narratives

The meaning of term 'Dalit,' according to James Massey, has linguistic relationship not only with the Sanskrit word 'dal' but also with the Hebrew word 'dall' which means 'to hang down,' 'to be languid,' 'be low,' 'be feeble.' 'dall' is closely related to the Akkadian term 'dalulu,' (be weak) and the Assyrian 'dalulu' (be weak or humble). The word 'dall' is used in different forms in the Bible. Its perfect form, *dalote*, is used in psalms 116: 6, 142: 7 etc. *y-dal*, an imperfect verb form of *dall* is employed in Isaiah 17: 4. It is used to explain the condition of people groups also. *dal* is the basic adjective of *dall*. *dalem, dalot,* and *dalah* are its masculine plural, feminine plural and feminine singular respectively. *dal* is generally translated in English as low, weak or poor. In Genesis 41:19, Exodus 23:3, Leviticus 14:21, Judges 6:15, Isaiah 11:4, Jeremiah 40:7, Amos 2:7, Ruth 3:10, 2 Samuel 13:4, Job 5:15, Psalms 41:1, Proverbs 10:15, Zephaniah 3:12, etc the examples of such translations can been seen. The collective use of the feminine plural constructed from the *dal* and *dalot* in II Kings 24:14, 25:12, Jeremiah 40:7, 52:15-16 have been translated as 'the poorest people of the land' and 'the poorest of the people' in most of the translations in English and Indian languages. But, the term *dal* or *dalot* takes the meaning of the 'poor' beyond the physical or economic condition. It also refers to the psychological inability of the people and the helpless condition in which they are placed. Therefore, the English word 'poor' cannot fully express the multiple disabilities of these *dal* or *dalot* people. Nevertheless, the Hebrew words used to denote the 'poor' and their meanings in the Bible bring them closer to the word 'Dalit' and its meaning in Indian context, and points to the existence of Dalits in the Biblical world. The expressions like *weha-dal* (Ex. 30: 15) *dalim* (Job 31: 16) and *dal* (Psalms 82: 3-4) also establishes the fact that Dalits were part of biblical society.[18]

The derivatives of *dal* are used in the same way/sense the term 'Dalit' has been employed to refer to the condition of people who are called Dalits. They are used in physical, economic, political, judicial and religious senses. Though *dalot* (poor) is literally used in Genesis 41: 19, it is used to refer to the physical condition of a person in II Samuel 13: 4. In Ruth 3: 10, *dal* implies the economic status of people. The term *w-dalim* in II Samuel 3: 1 conveys the position of politically weak people. In Proverbs 29: 14, *dalim* signifies the condition of the poor people who often do not get justice from the king. Isaiah 25: 4 portrays God as a refugee to the poor (*la-dal*). It indicates, what is God to the people who are not cared in society. The derivatives of *dal* are used not only to explain the condition of people (Dalits) but also to tell the process through which they are pushed into oppressed situations. Job 20: 18-19 says that the *dalim* are oppressed and abandoned. 'We have been brought very low (*dalonu*)" (Psalm 79:8) speaks of a process of being oppressed. The expression, 'Those who oppress *dal* (poor)' in Proverbs 14: 31 underlines the practice of oppression. The Bible also talks about communities who were reduced to condition of 'dalitness.' In Genesis 46: 34 Joseph explains how 'every shepherd is an abomination to the Egyptians.' This shepherd community later became slaves in Egypt (Exodus 1). When they were liberated from the bondage of slavery, they also pushed some communities into the state of Dalitness. The Gibeonites were made as wood cutters and water carriers for the Israelites (Joshua 9: 3-27). The Israelites also subdued the communities like Canaanites and the Amorites and made them to live under tribute (Judges 1: 28, 30 and 35).[19] In short, the term 'Dalit' and its meaning in different contexts are closely connected with Hebrew words used to explain the condition and identity of 'Dalits' in Biblical times. Moreover, in the history of Bible translations in India, Yesu Das Tewari was the first to use the word *dalito* ('dalit' in Hindi) for the 'oppressed/downtrodden' in Nazareth Manifesto (Luke 4: 18) in his Hindi translation of New Testament.[20] Today, the term 'Dalit' is widely used as synonym for the 'oppressed' in secular and theological literatures.

Dalit Religious Traditions and Spirituality

As indigenous people of India, Massey argues that, Dalits have their own religious traditions even before the arrival and establishment of Brahmanic religious traditions. Unfortunately, many of them were either lost or co-opted into the dominant Hindu traditions. However, some of them are still preserved by the Dalits in different parts of the nation. Scholars of religion call those traditions as 'little traditions' and the traditions of Aryans as 'great traditions.' Dalits worshipped nature, earth, water, trees and animals. They practiced community worship in open space on the contrary to the worship in temples. Still such open worships are practiced among the Dalits. For example, Dalits in a village called Zafferwal in Punjab worship 'a human-made dome-shaped mound of earth, called Bala Shah.' It is normally seen under a tree or in an open space. An earthen lamp will be placed over it, and a red flag will be kept at the top of the earth mound. They believe that the lamp and the flag protect them from the attack of evil powers. Songs having liberative elements are another characteristic of Dalit religious traditions. They used to sing songs while worship their Gods. One of the famous songs of Pulayas in North Malabar in Kerala is 'Tottom (song) of Pottan Teyyam.' This song was sung to worship their god, Pottan Teyyam. The content of the song is basically a critique of caste discrimination. It shows that Dalit religious traditions resisted the caste hierarchy and its hegemony throughout the centuries. The spirituality of Dalits is based on the liberative values upheld in their traditions. The spirituality of liberation is clearly articulated in the traditions of Bhakti Saints like Ravidas, Kabir and Namdev who questioned the caste narratives on inferior or superior birth and taught the equality of human beings before God. Though they were respected by the caste people for their spirituality, they never failed to condemn the caste consciousness of people through their literacy works.[21] The writings of Marathi Dalit Buddhists like Lanjewar, Limbale who emphasized the subjecthood and rights of Dalits explain another level of Dalit Spirituality. Kavi Jashuva, Telugu poet, in his poem questioned the Brahminical story of creation in Rigveda and vehemently criticized the caste laws which allowed a Bat to enter a temple, but not a Dalit. For these writers, spirituality is an experience of fight for 'freedom, justice and human dignity.'[22] In short, the spirituality in Dalit religious traditions is liberative in nature and upholds the values that affirm the dignity and freedom of every human being irrespective of caste in society. The spirituality of liberation naturally involves spirituality of combat also. Therefore, for Dalits, spirituality is not limited to the worship of a deity alone, but an experience of combating against life-negating customs and practices too.

Models for Dalit Leadership

James Massey provides some Biblical models for Dalit leadership. They are Moses model, Gideon model and Jesus model.

The Moses Model

The liberation of Israel from the slavery of Egypt and their community formation in the later stage stands as a strong pointer to the liberation of Dalits from the slavery of caste system and their empowerment in Indian society. The leadership of Moses in the process of Israel's liberation provides insights for Dalit leadership in today's context. A divine-human partnership was worked in the liberative exodus of Israel.[23] The most important human role in the form of leadership was played by Moses. He strictly followed the instructions of God while leading his people towards liberation. Moses as a leader conscientized his people of their oppressive condition under the Egyptians and began to take initiatives of liberative process.[24] The consciousness of the oppressed condition is the first step in the process of liberation and community formation.[25] It motivates the community to challenge the forces that keep them subjugated and oppressed. The oppressed also must have an urge to break the chains of exploitation. This urge derives its energy from the consciousness of oppressed condition. The liberation starts from the point of taking initiatives motivated by the consciousness of being broken and oppressed.[26]

The role of a leader does not end with the liberation of a community from its historical bondage-political, social, religious and economic. Community formation after liberation is crucial for the upward social mobility of respective community. Moses as a leader was aware of this fact and commenced the process of community formation. His method of community formation was based on 'memory'-past experiences of suffering and liberation. Moses might have understood the value of history in the formation of a community. He instituted Passover as the central festival of the people of Israel and asked them to celebrate it annually to remember their liberation from Egyptian slavery. It primarily contained the memory of their inhuman sufferings under Egyptians and God's historic intervention in their enslaved life. Certain rules were also given regarding the cerebration of the Passover. By celebrating it, the people of Israel were reminded of their historical experiences and strengthened in their community consciousness. The memories are important for unifying a community in the initial stage of their formation. Apart from instituting the festival of Passover, Moses also gave certain rules to be followed in the community life. They were asked to build up their community life within the framework of Ten Commandments given by God. In fact, the Ten Commandments were not simply rules, rather worked as an 'ideology' or 'theology' in the process of community formation.[27]

While the first part of the Ten Commandments (first four commandments) constituted the faith statement of the community,

the second part (last six commandments) contained the inter-
personal relationship of the community members. The first
commandment demanded the people of Israel an undivided loyalty
to the God who liberated them from slavery. It also reminded
them of their slave condition and of their liberative historical
experience. Therefore, they were strictly prohibited to worship any
idol (second commandment). As part of their undivided loyalty
to God, they were instructed not to misuse the name of the Lord
(Third commandment). The observance of fourth commandment is
a visible manifestation of community's identity as followers of the
God who created the whole universe and rested on the seventh day.
In fact, the observance of these four commandments was sign of a
collective action of the people of Israel and gave them an identity
of God's people. Next six commandments were centered on the
familial and societal relationships of community members.[28] The Ten
Commandments underline the fact that community as whole and
every individual have role in the process of community formation.
The commitment to God and the commitment to fellow community
members are important for building up a strong community life.
Moses also realized the importance of a 'central worship place' (Ex
25: 1-31) in the process of community formation. It also provided
them a sense of unity and common (religious) identity. As a leader,
Moses must have been aware that the community which was broken
in all aspects of life could not be restored without a festival (present
consciousness of past) and Ten Commandments (tools of ordering
the community in initial stage) and a central worship place (place/
symbol of inculcating sense of unity and identity).[29] Moses model
demands a Dalit leader not only to facilitate the liberation of his
people but also to take bold initiatives in building up his community.
Both are equally important in the journey of a community who
was oppressed for centuries. Liberative period (period of resistance

and freedom from the bondage) is often riskier than formative period. While liberative period faces external (oppressive) threats, formative period faces internal (community) threats. The success of a leader depends on how s/he handles these threats diplomatically, ideologically and futuristically.

The Gideon model

The story of Gideon is portrayed in the Book of Judges (Chapter 6-8). He was challenged by a divine messenger (angel of the Lord) to fight against the Midianites who were ruining the agriculture and livestock of his people. The Midianites were literally destroying Israel's sources of survival. While his people were going through an oppressive situation, an angel appeared to him and encouraged him with a positive note that "The Lord is with you, you mighty warrior." When he was asked to go against the Midianites, Gideon expressed his inability by revealing his identity among the Israelites. His encounter with the angel of the Lord reminded him of his community's historical experiences in which God miraculously liberated the people of Israel from the Egyptian slavery. This recollection of historical liberative events encouraged Gideon to take up the challenge of the angel of the Lord against the Midianites. When he sought divine help, he was assured that 'I will be with you, and you shall strike down the Midianites.' God said to him, 'Go in this might of yours and deliver Israel from the hand of Midian; I hereby commission you' (Judges 6:14). In the beginning, he was hesitant to go and fight against the Midianites because of his low (caste) social position among the Israelites. It is very much clear when he says, "O my Lord, how can I save Israel? My clan is the weakest (ha-dal) in Manasseh (a tribe) and I am the least in my family' (Judges 6:25). He expressed his community's social position through the Hebrew expression 'ha-dal,' which also means 'dalit.' Gideon's question was a typical question of a Dalit when s/he is encountered to take up the responsibility of challenging the dominant in caste society. A Dalit might say, 'I am a Dalit, how can I undertake such a great responsibility?'[30] Though he belonged to a 'ha-dal' clan in a community which was living in an oppressive condition, he decided to fight against the powerful Midianites. In Indian social setting, what Gideon says is that though he is a Dalit, he can fight against the caste people who have been oppressing his community for centuries. Dalit leaders in India must have such confidence to question the hegemony of the dominant as many of them do today. The story of Gideon informs that it is not the social identity which determines the leadership but the energy that derives from the condition of people and the assurance of God in the journey of combating the oppressive forces.

Gideon was very much aware of his social condition and identity. He did not try to hide his identity as many present Dalits do because of impending stigma. His awareness of low social status did not prevent divine intervention in the life of his community but once again proved that Biblical God always sided with the oppressed. And it also must have encouraged Gideon to seize the opportunity of divine encounter in his life to liberate his community. Like Gideon, Dalits must assert their identity in society. The assertion of identity is the first step towards an empowered life. A Dalit does not become a leader unless s/he asserts his/her identity and inspire his/her people to assert the same. Many Dalits, who think and behave like Gideon who was timid in the initial time of divine encounter, need positive energy as the angel of the Lord provided to him. The role of a Dalit leader becomes crucial for such Dalits who have been psychologically conditioned to think that they cannot save their community. The episode of Gideon teaches that a Dalit leader must think like Gideon who was empowered after divine encounter and motivate his people with the positive energy to come out of their inferior mind-set. This is applicable to a pastor/church leader who is working among Dalits too. S/he must combine the role of both Gideon and the angel who encountered Gideon. In Gideon's life, a divine-human partnership in the liberation of people also can be seen. He took up the challenge of the angel of the Lord and move forwarded with his task of liberating his people. But the sad part of the episode is that the Israelites could not continue with the liberation they achieved through divine-human partnership in Gideon. After the death of Gideon, the Israelites did not remain faithful to their faith commitment (Ideology) and gain fell into the hands of another oppressor.[31] It reminds the Dalits about the need of being committed to the faith/ideology which provided them full/partial liberation in respective context. Ideological commitment helps the community stay alert and united to fight against the forces of subjugation. Dalit leadership should not be centered on a person than an ideology though person (s) is needed to carry forward the ideology (faith). If it is fully centered on a person, after the death of that person the community may lose the ideological foundations upon which the community attempted to contest the oppressive narratives. It also points to the need of raising ideologically shaped leadership in each stage of community's life. On the one hand Gideon model provides blueprint for Dalit liberative leadership, on the other hand reminds of the possible decline of ideological commitment among the people if ideologically sound new leadership is not formed.

Jesus Model

Jesus Christ primarily embodies a perfect model for 'divine-human partnership' in the process of liberation. Three main principles can be discerned in Jesus model of leadership. The first principle is 'incarnational' principle. In order to liberate humanity from the bondage of sin, God became human being in Jesus Christ. God himself took up the divine challenge of becoming human being.

Through this incarnational act (John 1: 14), on the one hand God identified himself with the humanity, on the other hand God participated in human history. God came to this world in human form and lived among human beings and shared the identity of poor in the society. In his incarnational act, God abandoned his other worldly identity and adopted authentic human identity to accomplish the goal of human liberation. The life of Jesus Christ, God's incarnation in human form, put forth a basic leadership principle for the liberation and community formation of Dalits. Those who desire to work among Dalits should identify with them and live among them. In fact, s/he must become one among them. Jesus started the process of liberation from identifying with the least ones in society. The second principle is public declaration of the manifesto of leadership (Vision and Mission). Jesus started his ministry with a declaration of a manifesto in his village called Nazareth. He publicly announced what he was going to do (Luke 4: 18-19). He clearly narrated the goal and scope of his ministry (leadership). It means leaders must have clarity of vision and mission which is intelligible to the people. Third principle is organizational development. In order to carry out his mission, Jesus Christ organized a group of disciples. He equipped them with His vision and mission and taught them the values of His Kingdom. After selecting twelve people as his immediate disciples, he also selected another seventy-two and trained them with a clear goal of building up an alternative community on this earth. As part of community formation, he also instituted a ritual of Lord Supper with the intention of maintaining faith (ideological) commitment and solidarity among his followers in future.[32] The liberation and community formation of Dalits require the actualization of these leadership principles.

Jesus' life and ministry reflected what he announced (Nazareth Manifesto) when he started his ministry. Jesus model of leadership was the culmination of Moses model and Gideon model. This must be a model for the leaders who stand for the cause of Dalits. His manifesto did not die with its announcement but was materialized for which he had to risk his life. Many Dalit leaders paid the price for taking bold stand against caste oppression as Jesus positioned against the religious hegemony which blocked the empowerment of least ones in his society. The nature of Jesus' selection of disciples shows the need of organizational planning for achieving the vision of Dalit liberation. The words of Ambedkar echo the action of Jesus: 'educate, agitate and organize.' Dalit leadership must be guided by Jesus model of leadership and Dalit spirituality of liberation in process of addressing the historical problem of Dalits. The common feature of the different biblical models of leadership narrated above is the call for solidarity with Dalits.

Endnotes

[1] James Massey, "Historical Roots," in *Indigenous People: Dalits*, edited by James Massey (Delhi: ISPCK, Reprint 2006), 6.

[2] James Massey, *Dalit Theology: History, Context, Text and Whole Salvation* (New Delhi: Manohar, 2013), 28.

[3] James Massey, *Dalits in India: Religion as a Source of Bondage or Liberation with Special Reference to Christians* (New Delhi: Manohar, 2009 Reprint), 15.

[4] James Massey, *Dalits in India: Religion as a Source of Bondage or Liberation with Special Reference to Christians*, 16.

[5] James Massey, "Historical Roots," 7.

[6] James Massey, *Dalit Theology: History, Context, Text and Whole Salvation*, 65-66.

[7] James Massey, *Dalit Bible Commentary, New Testament Vol. 3, The Gospel According to Luke* (New Delhi: CDS, 2007), 24.

[8] James Massey, *Dalit Theology: History, Context, Text and Whole Salvation*, 148.

[9] James Massey, *Dalits in India: Religion as a Source of Bondage or Liberation with Special Reference to Christians*, 25-27.

[10] James Massey, "Historical Roots," 26-27.

[11] James Massey, *Dalit Theology: History, Context, Text and Whole Salvation*, 47.

[12] James Massey, *Dalits in India: Religion as a Source of Bondage or Liberation with Special Reference to Christians*, 40.

[13] James Massey, "Historical Roots," 29-30.

[14] James Massey, *Dalit Theology: History, Context, Text and Whole Salvation*, 49-51.

[15] James Massey, *Dalits in India: Religion as a Source of Bondage or Liberation with Special Reference to Christians*, 44.

[16] James Massey, "Historical Roots," 34.

[17] James Massey, *Dalit Theology: History, Context, Text and Whole Salvation*, 60.

[18] James Massey, *Dalit Theology: History, Context, Text and Whole Salvation*, 17-20.

[19] James Massey, *Dalit Theology: History, Context, Text and Whole Salvation*, 21-23.

[20] James Massey, *Dalit Theology: History, Context, Text and Whole Salvation*, 28.

[21] James Massey, *Dalit Theology: History, Context, Text and Whole Salvation*, 149-151 & 240.

[22] James Massey, *Dalit Theology: History, Context, Text and Whole Salvation*, 241-243.

[23] James Massey, *Ecumenism Means Justice* (Matiala, New Delhi: CDS, 2014), 38.

[24] James Massey, "Theology for a New Community: Looking Ahead," in *Theology for a New Community*, edited by James Massey (New Delhi: CDS, 2013), 303.

[25] James Massey, *Dalit Bible Commentary, Old Testament Vol. 2, Exodus* (New Delhi: CDS, 2010), 22.

[26] James Massey, *Dalit Bible Commentary, Old Testament Vol. 2, Exodus*, 24.

[27] James Massey, *Ecumenism Means Justice*, 40-42.

[28] James Massey, *Dalit Theology: History, Context, Text and Whole Salvation*, 180; James Massey, "Theology for a New Community: Looking Ahead," 305.

[29] James Massey, *Dalit Theology: History, Context, Text and Whole Salvation*, 177 & 180.

[30] James Massey, *Dalit Theology: History, Context, Text and Whole Salvation*, 182-183.

[31] James Massey, *Dalit Theology: History, Context, Text and Whole Salvation*, 184-185.

[32] James Massey, *Ecumenism Means Justice*, 43-49.

Chapter 12
Dalits, Globalization and Civil Society

Globalization is generally considered as a process which brings people of different regions closer in terms of economic, social, cultural, religious aspects of human life. It is more or less understood in relation to economic advancement, and creating and accessing opportunities beyond geographical boundaries. It is often argued that developed countries are the main beneficiaries of globalization. It may be true because of the large presence of multi-national companies owned by the first world citizens in third world countries. Then question remains-who are the real beneficiaries of globalization in India. James Massey argues that the social and economic situation of Dalits tells the story of a disempowered community which struggles to face the challenges of globalization process in India. Dalits remain unable to tap the benefits of globalization because majority of them lack quality education, an important tool to access the opportunities created by globalization. Quality education enhances the socio-economic situation of people. Since the upper caste people have access to the quality education now available only in private institutions, they reap the benefits of globalization in India. They are well placed in multi-national companies and occupy high profile jobs and assignments. The education, which they received, enables them to meet the challenge of globalization.[1] Historically, they have full access to education because of caste system which also controlled economic resources of the country. The economic resources not only enabled them to get quality education but also equipped them to become beneficiaries of globalised economic system. This chapter offers a narration of James Massey's reflections on globalization from Dalit perspective and the role of civil societies in enabling Dalits to face the challenges of globalization.

According to James Massey, Dalits, the historical victims of caste are the losers of globalization. Caste system placed them in disadvantaged social and economic position which blocked their educational opportunities for upward social mobility. They have not come out of the impact of the historical denial of education in the past. Though government claims that Dalits have improved in education, very few among them are able to get quality education and go for higher education which may place them in better positions in the globalized world. They are neither able to tap the benefits of globalization in the form of jobs nor to be part of it in the form of getting resources and starting new ventures. Dalits are losers because they are not people with assets, high skills, professional-managerial-technical education and economic capital. They are people who struggle to survive with meager wage, dependent on creditors, lacking skills to get into the technologically advanced labor market.[2] They are involved in odd jobs which are seasonal in nature and are not equipped to take up jobs/assignments which contribute to their social and economic advancement.

Globalization from Dalit point of view tells us that globalization have created two categories of people: losers and winners. The peculiarity of this classification has historical dimension-victims of caste and victors of caste. In the traditional Indian social order, the victims were Dalits and other oppressed communities and the victors or privileged were caste people. This equation still continues in the globalized economic order. As noted earlier, the victims of caste continue to be losers and the victors continue to be winners in the process of economic globalization. Privatization and liberalization actually keep the Dalits disempowered in the areas of employment, education, social welfare and politics. Moreover, it is caste which keeps the Dalits as casual laborers even in the liberal economic society.[3] The limited access of Dalits to the opportunities created by globalization shows that it could not overcome the influence of caste. Apart from the negative economic impact of globalization upon the weaker sections of society, Dalits also face the challenges of overt and covert influence of caste in the globalization process in India.

Globalization has already become a reality in today's society. No one can escape from the impact of globalization. Though Dalits are losers of globalization, they cannot be mute spectators to the changing economic and social life. Ultimately, they have to face the challenge of globalization in the context in which they are oppressed for centuries. Massey suggests that, first of all, they must be aware of the negative impact of globalization in their lives. The awareness of negative impact will enable them to resist the exploitative behavior of globalization. Secondly, they have to prepare themselves to face the challenge of globalization. It has two aspects. On the one hand they must be educated to save themselves from the negative effects of globalization; on the other hand they must be taught to tap its benefits. Dalit engagement with globalization involves resistance and appropriation of the resources available to move forward in life. To engage with the process of globalization, they have to be empowered with education. It will help them to participate in the process and get their share in the competitive world.[4] No community will wait for the Dalits to miss their chance in the globalized world.

If Dalits do not prepare themselves, then they will continue to be losers. Though fight is tough, they have to define the strategies to get empowered in life.

The globalization helps Dalits to be part of global civil society and internationalize the 'Dalit issue.' It facilitates them to come out of their traditional caste boundaries and get resources and moral support to fight against their disabilities. The global attention of Dalit issue may influence the attitude of caste people towards Dalits. The global civil societies can contribute to the empowerment of Dalits by raising their issues in international forums. Their involvement can open new horizons of Dalit struggle and enlarge the space of Dalits in society. The caste people who are beneficiaries of globalization cannot evade the questions of justice, equality and human rights. Dalit stories of unemployment, illiteracy, violation of human rights etc in the era of globalization will definitely question the integrity of caste people in international level. They can ignore the issues of Dalits in India, but when they represent India in the globalized world as successful entrepreneurs they cannot just boast of their economic advancement. They have to answer why globalization fails to address the issues of Dalits in India. The issue of caste gets more exposure when Dalit stories of exploitation and discrimination are globally discussed. Naming and shaming the caste is one of the ways to get liberated from the bondage of caste. In order to break the control of caste, Dalits use opportunities opened by globalization and expose the caste atrocities globally. It is like 'using a weapon of the enemy against the enemy.'[5] The caste people love to talk and perpetuate caste in India. But in international forum, they love to cover up the issue of caste and attempt to project India as land of equality and justice. Thus, globalization provides at least an opportunity to take up the issue of caste outside India and to get global partners in countering the forces of oppression.

Though globalization provides space for engaging with Dalit issues, it also creates anxiety among Dalits. One of the areas where Dalits express their concern is the protection of constitutional rights. The Constitution of India guarantees reservation of seats for Dalits (Scheduled Castes) in the state legislative assemblies and in the Parliament (Articles 330-4). Dalits are also offered reservation of jobs in government departments and public undertakings (Articles 16, 320, 353). Another constitutional provision which protects the rights of Dalits is prohibition of any kind of forced labor (Article 23). Though this article protects every citizen of the country, it has more significance in the life of Dalits because they were subjected to forced labor in the past than any other communities. It is not that they have completely come out of the menace of forced labor. Still they face direct or indirect forms of forced labor in society. Economically, prohibition of forced labor is comparatively relief for Dalits because it offers freedom to do any job they like. There is also special provision in the constitution (Article 46) which promotes the educational, economic and social welfare of the Dalits. Though these constitutional rights are intended to protect and promote the life of Dalits, the scope of those rights is very much limited now. Reservation policy is a case in point. Firstly, reservation policy is limited to the government departments and public enterprises. There is no provision for reservation in private enterprises which currently generate majority job opportunities in the context of globalization. Secondly, reservation benefits are available to the Dalits who are Hindus, Buddhists and Sikhs by faith. Dalit Christians and Muslims are excluded from the reservation policy. Religious faith has become the criterion for availing reservation benefits. Thirdly, many eligible Dalits have not yet received the benefits of reservation.[6] Apart from these limitations of reservation policy, globalization affects the reservation through the process of privatization.

Privatization, one of the important recommendations of the Structural Adjustment Programme (SAP) in the process of globalization, is a major threat to the constitutional rights of Dalits. Reservation has helped Dalits to improve their social condition through jobs in government departments and other public enterprises. According to Massey, if privatization is encouraged, then it is Dalits who are going to be affected more because reservation is not applicable in private sector. If government privatizes public enterprises, Dalits lose their job opportunities guaranteed by the constitution. In the name of economic growth and structural adjustment program, government also sells the shares of public enterprises to the private shareholders. One of the direct examples is formation of Disinvestment Ministry. It finds out so-called 'sick' government enterprises and sells/reduces the share of government and hand over to private investors. Many government services also have been outsourced to the private companies. When a public enterprise goes into the hands of private investors or government service is outsourced, then the job opportunities of Dalits are badly reduced because reservation is not followed in the private sector. Instead of protecting those public enterprises, government/ state directly involves in the process of privatization.[7] For Dalits, privatization takes away their constitutional right of reservation in jobs. The state/government involvement in privatization keeps Dalits more vulnerable in relation to the constitutional protection of their economic rights and jobs. They are socially and economically not in a position to face the challenge of privatization because they do not have social capital and economic capital.

Privatization affects not only the prospects of the employment of Dalits but also their educational opportunities. Globalization has made the role of the state much easier in the field of education. Now, major portion of the educational institutions in our country are located in private sector. The government has almost, if not completely, withdrawn from education sector. Even many government schools are handed over to the private groups in the name of public-private partnership. There is no chance that those institutions will come back into the complete control of the government. Here also the problem of the privatization of education is that reservation policy is not followed in higher education. It affects the Dalits who come from economically disadvantaged position. Often they are not able to meet the requirements of admission in private educational institutions. They cannot afford the fees and other requirements in those institutions. On the one hand they are deprived of opportunities; on the other hand they are unable to face the challenge of privatization. Majority dropouts in school and higher education levels are Dalit students. The percentage of Dalits in higher education is very less compared to other communities.[8] Privatization of education sector will reduce the speed of the educational advancement of Dalits in the era of globalization if the government does not strengthen the public education sector. In the midst of all these challenges, Dalits need moral and political support to move forward with their aim of community empowerment. There comes the role of civil society in the life of Dalits.

The civil society has an important role to play in the process of globalization. The Dalits and other oppressed communities continue to live in disempowered condition, according to the Human Development Report 2001, because of the inefficiency of the administration of public sectors and poor governance. Since these issues are directly related to the government, civil society groups can raise those issues in public space and help Dalits to face the challenge of globalization and tap the opportunities. Though globalization affects the life of Dalits due to the specific social condition in India, it has potential to enhance the condition of Dalits also. But the whole process of globalization is controlled by the upper castes who are least concerned about the constitutional rights of Dalits and other oppressed communities. While attempting to avail the benefits of globalization process, what they need is the involvement of civil society in their struggles to protect their constitutional rights. The importance of civil society in the empowerment of Dalits lays in its efforts to uphold the values of freedom and equality. Civil society defends the liberties of human beings and resists the oppressive structures. Often civil societies emerge when violations of human rights are reported. Instead of being seasonal in nature, civil societies should shape the mind-set of people towards the creation of a society where justice, liberty, equality, fraternity prevails in every area of life. Formation of such society is the vision of Indian Constitution. It is a society where the rights of Dalits and other oppressed communities are protected and dignity and opportunity of every citizen is guarded.[9] The negative impact of globalization can be checked by building up such societies.

The civil society also includes media, social organizations, NGOs etc. Any person or organization automatically becomes part of a civil society when s/he works to bring changes in the existing oppressive structure in society. One of the main obstacles to the formation of civil society in Indian context is caste system. As pressure groups, civil societies cannot address any issue without challenging caste. If they raise any issue of Dalits and oppressed communities, the caste also has to be challenged because caste is directly or indirectly related to their problems. Moreover, the process of globalization talks about human development. But in India, human development is incomplete without social justice. The question of social justice as part of human development brings the civil societies in direct encounter with oppressive structures. How far the civil societies comprised of caste people can actively be involved in the struggles of Dalits and other oppressed communities to materialize social justice in the age of globalization. It does not mean that the caste people cannot express their solidarity with Dalits and participate in their struggles. There are caste people who actively journey with Dalits. But all may not be ready to counter the caste dimension of the issues of Dalits. This situation demands the emergence of civil societies comprised of the historical victims of caste-Dalits and other oppressed communities. It needs solidarity among Dalits and between Dalits and other oppressed communities. Then, they can connect with other oppressed communities in the world to influence the forces of globalization to include social justice as part of human development. A global solidarity is the need of the hour to counter the negative impact of globalization. Those who fight against the oppressive and exploitative structures should be brought into the global solidarity. This global solidarity will enable them to develop alternative approaches to get quality education and to formulate solutions to their problems in the globalized world. [10] In short, while enabling them to avail the benefits of globalization Dalits need to be equipped to protect their constitutional rights in society. Theology of Solidarity reminds the need of expressing solidarity with Dalits to enable them to achieve whole salvation in this globalized world. The human solidarity leads to experience salvation in this world, which is to be culminated in the experience of ultimate Salvation offered in Jesus Christ.

Endnotes

[1] James Massey, *Ecumenism Means Justice* (Matiala, New Delhi: CDS, 2014), 68-69; James Massey, "Dalit Theology: Response to Dalit Context," in *Dalit Issue in Today's Theological Debate*, edited by James Massey and S. Lourduswamy (New Delhi: CDS, 2003), 117.

[2] James Massey, *Dalit Theology: History, Context, Text and Whole Salvation* (New Delhi: Manohar, 2013), 115; James Massey, "On Being a New Community

and Ecclesia of Justice and Peace," in *On Being a New Community and Ecclesia of Justice and Peace*, edited by James Massey and NOH, Jong Sun (Bangalore: BTESSC/SATHRI, 2010), 17.

[3] James Massey, *Dalit Theology: History, Context, Text and Whole Salvation*, 116; Deepak Seth, ed., *From Truth to Truth, A Journey Through Faiths: A Selection of Representative Essays by Dr. James Massey* (New Delhi: CDS and NOIDA: Academy Press, 2008), 167; James Massey, "On Being a New Community and Ecclesia of Justice and Peace," 15.

[4] Deepak Seth, ed., *From Truth to Truth, A Journey Through Faiths: A Selection of Representative Essays by Dr. James Massey*, 167-168; James Massey, "An Analysis of the Dalit Situation with Special Reference to Dalit Christians and Dalit Theology," *Religion and Society*, Vol 52/No 3-4 (September-December 2007): 57-86 at 65.

[5] James Massey, *Dalit Theology: History, Context, Text and Whole Salvation*, 117; Deepak Seth, ed., *From Truth to Truth, A Journey Through Faiths: A Selection of Representative Essays by Dr. James Massey*, 168.

[6] James Massey, *Dalit Theology: History, Context, Text and Whole Salvation*, 118; James Massey, "On Being a New Community and Ecclesia of Justice and Peace," 18; Deepak Seth, ed., *From Truth to Truth, A Journey Through Faiths: A Selection of Representative Essays by Dr. James Massey*, 168-170; James Massey, "An Analysis of the Dalit Situation with Special Reference to Dalit Christians and Dalit Theology," 66.

[7] James Massey, *Dalit Theology: History, Context, Text and Whole Salvation*, 119-120; Deepak Seth, ed., *From Truth to Truth, A Journey Through Faiths: A Selection of Representative Essays by Dr. James Massey*, 170-171; James Massey, "On Being a New Community and Ecclesia of Justice and Peace," 19; James Massey, "An Analysis of the Dalit Situation with Special Reference to Dalit Christians and Dalit Theology,"67

[8] James Massey, *Dalit Theology: History, Context, Text and Whole Salvation*, 122; Deepak Seth, ed., *From Truth to Truth, A Journey through Faiths: A Selection of Representative Essays by Dr. James Massey*, 173; James Massey, "An Analysis of the Dalit Situation with Special Reference to Dalit Christians and Dalit Theology," 70.

[9] James Massey, *Dalit Theology: History, Context, Text and Whole Salvation*, 123; Deepak Seth, ed., *From Truth to Truth, A Journey Through Faiths: A Selection of Representative Essays by Dr. James Massey*, 174; James Massey, "An Analysis of the Dalit Situation with Special Reference to Dalit Christians and Dalit Theology," 77-78.

[10] James Massey, *Dalit Theology: History, Context, Text and Whole Salvation*, 124-125; Deepak Seth, ed., *From Truth to Truth, A Journey Through Faiths: A Selection of Representative Essays by Dr. James Massey*, 175; James Massey, "An Analysis of the Dalit Situation with Special Reference to Dalit Christians and Dalit Theology," 78-79.

Bibliography

Books

Amaladoss, Michael. *Life in Freedom: Liberation Theologies from Asia*. Oregon: WIPF and Stock Publishers, 2014.

Buhler, G. (tr.). *Sacred Books of the East Edited by F. Max Muller Vol. 25, The Laws of Manu*. Delhi: Motilal Banarsidass, 1988.

Clarke, Sathianathan. *Dalits and Christianity: Subaltern Religion and Liberation Theology in India*. Delhi: Oxford University Press, 1998.

Chakkalakal, Pauline. *Discipleship: A Space for Women's Leadership*. Mumbai: Pauline Publications, 2004.

Deshpande, Satish and Geetika Bapna. *Dalits in Muslim and Christian Communities*. New Delhi: CDS, CBCI and NCCI, 2010.

Dr. Babasaheb Ambedkar: Writings and Speeches Vol 5. Compiled by Vasant Moon. Bombay: Education Department, Government of Maharashtra, 1989.

Gramsci, Antonio. *Selections from the Prison Notebooks of Antonio Gramsci*. Edited and Translated by Quintin Hoare and Geoffrey Nowell Smith. Chennai: Orient Longman, 1996.

Griffith, Ralph T.II. (tr. & cr.). *The Hymns of the Rigveda*, New Revised Edition. Delhi: Motilal Banarsidass, 1986.

Ghurye, G.S. *Caste and Race in India*. London: Routledge and Kegan Paul, 1932; Reprint of Fifth Edition, Bombay: Popular Prakashan, 1994.

Hebden, Keith. *Dalit Theology and Christian Anarchism*. Farnham, Surrey, England: Ashgate, 2011.

Logan, William. *Malabar Vol I*. Madras: Government Press, 1887; Reprint, Trivandrum: Charithram Publications, 1981.

Lourduswamy, S. *Towards Empowerment of Dalit Christians*. New Delhi: Centre for Dalit/ Subaltern Studies, 2005.

Maliekal, Jose. *Standstill Utopias? Dalits Encountering Christianity*. Delhi: ISPCK, 2017.

Massey, James. *Minorities and Religious Freedom in a Democracy*. New Delhi: New Delhi: Manohar & CDS, 2003.

Massey, James. *Introducing Dalit Theology*. New Delhi: Centre for Dalit Studies, 2004.

Massey, James. *Dalit Bible Commentary, New Testament Vol. 3, The Gospel According to Luke*. New Delhi: CDS, 2007.

Massey, James. *Dalit Roots of Christianity, Theology and Spirituality*. New Delhi: CDS, 2008.

Massey, James. *Dalit Bible Commentary, New Testament Vol. 5, Acts of Apostles*. New Delhi: CDS, 2008.

Massey, James. *Dalits in India: Religion as a Source of Bondage or Liberation with Special Reference to Christians*. New Delhi: Manohar, 2009 Reprint.

Massey, James. *Dalit Bible Commentary, Old Testament Vol. 2, Exodus*. New Delhi: CDS, 2010.

Massey, James. *Dalit Bible Commentary: A Challenge Response*. New Delhi: CDS, 2011.

Massey, James. *Dalit Bible Commentary, Old Testament Vol. 5, Judges*. New Delhi: CDS, 2012.

Massey, James. *Dalit Bible Commentary, Old Testament Vol. 17, Jeremiah, Lamentations, Baruch*. New Delhi: CDS, 2012.

Massey, James. *Dalit Bible Commentary, Old Testament Vol. 9, 1 & 2 Chronicles*. New Delhi: CDS, 2012.

Massey, James. *Caste-Class Victims and Their Assertion for Justice*. New Delhi: CDS, 2013.

Massey, James and T.K. John, Eds. *Christians of Scheduled Caste Origin in India*. New Delhi: Centre for Dalit Subaltern Studies, 2013.

Massey, James. *Dalit Bible Commentary, Old Testament Vol. 10, Ezra, Nehemiah and Tobit*. New Delhi: CDS, 2013.

Massey, James. *Dalit Theology: History, Context, Text and Whole Salvation*. New Delhi: Manohar, 2013.

Massey, James. *Ecumenism Means Justice*. New Delhi: CDS, 2014.

Massey, James. General Editor, *Dalit Heritage and Liberative Traditions in India*. New Delhi: CDS, 2015.

Mateer, Samuel. *Land of Charity*. London: John Snow & Co, 1871.

Mcgrath, Alister E. *Christian Theology, An Introduction*. Oxford: Blackwell Publishing, 2001 Third Edition.

Mustafa, Faizan and Anurag Sharma. *Conversion: Constitutional and Legal Implications*. New Delhi: Kanishka Publishers, 2003.

Parkhe, Camil. *Dalit Christians: Right to Reservations*. Delhi: ISPCK, 2007.

Rajpramukh, K.E. *Dalit Christians of Andhra*. New Delhi: Serials Publications, 2008.

Reservations for Backward Classes, Mandal Commission Report of the Backward Classes Commission, 1980. Delhi: Akalank Publications, 1990.

Selvanayagam, Israel. *Samuel Amirtham's Living Theology*. Bangalore: BTESSC\ SATHRI, 2007.

Sen, Amartya. *Identity and* Violence. New Delhi: Allen Lane (Penguin Books), 2006.

Seth, Deepak. Ed. *From Truth to Truth, A Journey Through Faiths: A Selection of Representative Essays by Dr. James Massey*. New Delhi: CDS and NOIDA: Academy Press, 2008.

Srinivas, M. N. *Social Change in Modern India*. New Delhi, Orient Longman Limited, 2000.

The Constitution of India. Ministry of Law and Justice. Government of India, 1989.

Thomas, M.M. *Salvation and Humanization*. Madras: The CLS, 1971.

Thomas, V.V. *Dalit Pentecostalism*. Bangalore: ATC, 2008.

Webster, John C.B. *The Dalit Christians: A History*. New Delhi: ISPCK, 2009.

Wilfred, Felix. *Asian Public Theology*. New Delhi: ISPCK, 2010.

Articles in Books

Chinnappa, A.M. "Inaugural Speech by the President of CDS (T) at the Inaugural Function of Centre for Dalit Studies (Theology), ISI, New Delhi, 28th September 2001." In *A Theology from Dalit Perspective*. Edited by James Massey and S. Lourduswamy. New Delhi: CDS, 2001.

Clarke, Sathianathan. "Dalit Theology: An Introductory and Interpretative Theological exposition." In *Dalit Theology in the Twenty-first Century*. Edited by Sathianathan Clarke, Deenabandhu Manchala and Philip Vinod Peacock. New Delhi: Oxford University Press, 2010.

Devasahayam, V. "Doing Theology: Basic Assumptions." In *Frontiers of Dalit Theology*. Edited by V. Devasahayam. New Delhi: ISPCK and Chennai: Gurukul, 1997.

Gonsalves, Francis. "Vision of Pope Francis to Renew Church and Society." In *The Emerging Challenges to Christian Mission Today*. Edited by S.M. Michael and Jose Joseph. Pune: Ishvani Kendra and New Delhi: Christian World Imprints, 2016.

Guha, Ranajit. "Preface." In *Subaltern Studies* Vol. I. Edited by Ranajit Guha. Delhi: Oxford University Press, 1994.

Guha, Ranajit. "On Some Aspects of the Historiography of Colonial India." In *Subaltern Studies* Vol. I. Edited by Ranajit Guha. Delhi: Oxford University Press, 1994.

Lourduswamy, S. "Catholic Church and Dalit-Tribal Movements in India." In *Rethinking Theology in India*. Edited by James Massey and T.K. John. New Delhi: Manohar and Centre for Dalit/Subaltern Studies, 2013.

Massey, James. "Ingredients for a Dalit Theology." In *A Reader in Dalit Theology*. Edited by Arvind P. Nirmal. Chennai: GLTC & RC, 2007 Reprint; "Ingredients for a Dalit Theology," in *Indigenous People: Dalits*. Edited by James Massey. Delhi: ISPCK, 2006 Reprint.

Massey, James. "Need of a Dalit Theological Expression." In *Confronting Life: Theology out of the Context*. Edited by M.P. Joseph. Delhi: ISPCK, 1995.

Massey, James. "History and Dalit Theology." In *Frontiers of Dalit Theology*. Edited by V. Devasahayam. Chennai: ISPCK/Gurukul, 1997.

Massey, James. "Dalit Roots of Indian Christianity." In *Frontiers of Dalit Theology*. Edited by V. Devasahayam. Chennai: ISPCK/Gurukul, 1997.

Massey, James. "Subaltern People and the Rise of their Movements." In *A Vision of Mission in the New Millennium*. Edited by Thomas Malipurathu and L. Stanislaus. Mumbai: St. Paul's, 2001.

Massey, James and S. Lourduswamy. "Preface." In *A Theology from Dalit Perspective*. Edited by James Massey and S. Lourduswamy. New Delhi: CDS, 2001.

Massey, James. "Vision and Role of Dalit Theology." In *A Theology from Dalit Perspective*. Edited by James Massey and S. Lourduswamy. New Delhi: CDS, 2001.

Massey, James. "Centre for Dalit Studies (Theology): An Introduction." In *A Theology from Dalit Perspective*. Edited by James Massey and S. Lourduswamy. New Delhi: CDS, 2001.

Massey, James. "Dalit Theology: Response to Dalit Context." In *Dalit Issue in Today's Theological Debate*. Edited by James Massey and S. Lourduswamy. New Delhi: CDS, 2003.

Massey, James. "Education for All." In *Education for Empowerment of Dalits: Perspectives and Priorities*. Edited by S. Lourduswamy. New Delhi: CDS, 2004.

Massey, James. "Forward." In *Globalization and Its Impact on Dalits: A Theological Response*. Edited by James Massey. New Delhi: CDS, 2004.

Massey, James. "Historical Roots." In *Indigenous People: Dalits*. Edited by James Massey. Delhi: ISPCK, 2006 Reprint.

Massey, James. "A Review of Dalit Theology." In *Dalit and Minjung Theologies: A Dialogue*. Edited by Samson Prabhakar and Jinkwan Kwon. Bangalore: BTESSC/SATHRI, 2006.

Massey, James. "Preface." In *Breaking Theoretical Grounds for Dalit Studies*. Edited by James Massey, S. Lourduswamy and I. John Mohan Razu. New Delhi: CDS, 2006.

Massey, James. "A Fresh Look at Mission with Special Reference to the Case of Case." In *Mission with the Marginalized*. Edited by Samuel W. Meshack. Tiruvalla: CSS, 2007.

Massey, James. "Vision, Nature and Method of Dalit Theology." In *Dalit-Tribal Theological Interface*. Edited by James Massey and Shimreingam Shimray. New Delhi: CDS & Jorhart: TSC/WSC, 2007.

Massey, James. "Introduction." In *Dalit World-Biblical World: An Encounter*. Edited by Leonard Fernando SJ and James Massey. New Delhi: CDS and Vidyajyoti College of Theology, 2007.

Massey, James. "Revisiting and Resignifying the Methodology for Dalit Theology." In *Revisiting and Resignifying the Methodology for Dalit Theology*. Edited by James Massey and I. John Mohan Razu. New Delhi: CDS & Bangalore: UTC, 2008.

Massey, James. "A Church According to the Best and Earliest Traditions of the Church." In *Church of North India According to the Best and Earliest Traditions of the Church*. Edited by James Massey. New Delhi: Evaluation Commission CNI, 2008.

Massey, James. "Alternative Approaches to the Ecumenical Movement." In *Ecumenism in India Today*. Edited by James Massey. Bangalore: BTESSC/SATHRI, 2008.

Massey, James. "Counterculture in Dalit Thought and Life." In *Deciphering the Subaltern Terrain*. Edited by James Massey. Bangalore: BTESSC/SATHRI, 2009.

Massey, James. "Approaches to the Whole Issue of Peace." In *Towards Justice and Peace: A Subaltern Initiative*. Edited by Monodeep Daniel and Yangkahao Vashum. Jorhart: TCS/WSC, Nagpur: CNI Desk on Dalit and Tribal Concerns & New Delhi: CDS, 2010.

Massey, James. "Present State of Theological Education in South Asia: Response of SSC and BTESSC." In *Partnership between Churches and Theological Institutions*. Edited by James Massey, Bangalore: BTESSC/SATHRI, 2010.

Massey, James. "On Being a New Community and Ecclesia of Justice and Peace." In *On Being a New Community and Ecclesia of Justice and Peace*. Edited by James Massey and NOH, Jong Sun. Bangalore: BTESSC/SATHRI, 2010.

Massey, James. "Christianity to be Renewed? Rethink Theology." In *Rethinking Theology in India: Christianity in the Twenty-first Century*. Edited by James Massey and T.K. John SJ. New Delhi: CDS & Manohar, 2013.

Massey, James and T.K. John "Common Task for Tomorrow." In *Rethinking Theology in India: Christianity in the Twenty-first Century*. Edited by James Massey and T.K. John SJ. New Delhi: CDS & Manohar, 2013.

Massey, James. "Theology for a New Community: Looking Ahead." In *Theology for a New Community*. Edited by James Massey. New Delhi: CDS, 2013.

Mohan Razu, Indukuri John. "Towards a Critical Theology of Risk Taking: The Changing Landscape and Discourse." In *Rethinking Theology in India*. Edited by James Massey and T.K. John. New Delhi: Manohar and Centre for Dalit/Subaltern Studies, 2013.

Mulackal, Shalini. "Women: Theology and Feminist Movements in India." In *Rethinking Theology in India*. Edited by James Massey and T.K. John. New Delhi: Manohar and Centre for Dalit/Subaltern Studies, 2013.

Nirmal, Arvind P. "A Dialogue with Dalit Literature." In *Towards a Dalit Theology*. Edited by M.E. Prabhakar. Delhi: ISPCK, 1989.

Nirmal, Arvind P. "Towards a Christian Dalit Theology." In *A Reader in Dalit Theology*. Edited by Arvind P. Nirmal. Madras: Gurukul/ UELCI, 1991.

Nirmal, Arvind P. "Introduction." In *A Reader in Dalit Theology*. Edited by Arvind P. Nirmal. Chennai: GLTC & RC, 2007 Reprint.

Prabhakar, M.E. "Introduction." In *Towards a Dalit Theology*. Edited by M.E. Prabhakar. Delhi: ISPCK, 1989.

Prabhakar, M.E. "The Search for a Dalit Theology." In *Towards a Dalit Theology*. Edited by M.E. Prabhakar. Delhi: ISPCK, 1989.

Seth, Deepak. "Preface." In *From Truth to Truth, A Journey through Faiths: A Selection of Representative Essays by Dr. James Massey*. Edited by Deepak Seth. New Delhi: CDS and NOIDA: Academy Press, 2008.

Yong-Bock, Kim. "Forward." In James Massey, *Ecumenism Means Justice*. New Delhi: CDS, 2014.

Articles in Journals

Amaladoss, M. "The Eucharist and the Christian Community." *VJTR* 68/10 (October, 2004): 721-735.

Anthony, Prem. "Church, State and the Civil Society." *VJTR*, Vol 78/no 2 (March, 2014): 166-182.

Bama, "Dalit Christian Women Today, Their Struggles and Prospects for Future." *Jeevadhara* Vol. XLI/No.241 (January, 2011): 35-44.

Doniger, Wendy. "The Hindu Code in Vanishing Ink." *Outlook* (24th February 2014, New Delhi): 16-18

Jamir, Imti. "Scripture through the Eyes of Disempowered People." *Journal of Subaltern and Cultural Theology*, Inaugural Issue (June, 2013): 74-81.

Gahilote, Prarthna. "Some Old Footfalls?" *Outlook* (24th February 2014, New Delhi): 14.

Jesurathnam, K. "Yerraguntala Peraiah: An Honorable Dalit Christian Missionary." *Journal of Subaltern and Cultural Theology* (2013): 20-24.

Indian Currents XXVII, no. 36 (September, 2015): 26-28.

Lourduswamy, S. "Dalit Christians: Has Anything Changed?" *Jeevadhara* Vol. XLI/No.241 (January, 2011): 7-13.

Massey, James. "Mandal Commission Report: A Christian Perspective." *Religion and Society* Vol XXXVII/No. 4 (December, 1990): 40-49.

Massey, James. "Minority Rights." *NCC Review* cxxi/2 (February-March, 2001): 119-144.

Massey, James. "Dalits and Human Rights." *Religion and Society* Vol 49/No 2& 3 (June and September 2004): 1-9.

Massey, James. "Why Fundamental Rights of Dalit Christians Should be Restored?" *NCC Review* cxxv/3 (April, 2005): 114-120.

Massey, James. "Church in Dialogue with the Dalits." *NCC Review* cxxvii/3 (April, 2007): 51-61.

Massey, James. "An Analysis of the Dalit Situation with Special Reference to Dalit Christians and Dalit Theology." *Religion and Society*, Vol 52/No 3-4 (September-December 2007): 57-86.

Massey, James. "The Office and the Function of Episcopate: An Appraisal." *NCC Review* cxxviii/5 (June, 2008): 243-260.

Massey, James. "Journal of Subaltern and Cultural Theology, Editorial." *Journal of Subaltern and Cultural Theology* (Inaugural Issue, 2013): 7-12.

Naqvi, Saba. "We need Ambedkar-Now urgently..." *Outlook* (10 March 2014, New Delhi): 29-30.

People's Reporter Vol. 26/No. 24 (Mumbai, December 25-January 10, 2014): 1.

Pradhan, Kunal. "Riot for Vote." *India Today* (September 23, 2013): 26.

Purie, Aroon. "From the Editor-in-Chief." *India Today* (September 23, 2013): 1.

Thomas, M.J. "Dalit Heritage and Liberative Tradition in North India: Towards Breaking the Silence." *Journal of Subaltern and Cultural Theology*, Inaugural Issue (June, 2013): 92-98.

Varma, Pavan K. "A Deeply Sorry Game." In *The Times Of India* (15th February 2014, New Delhi): 20.

Wilson, Viju. "Victims of Caste and Wounded Sheep of the Church." *Journal of Subaltern and Cultural Theology*, Inaugural Issue (June, 2013): 82-91.

Wilfred, Felix. "Editorial," *Jeevadhara* Vol. XLI/No.241 (January, 2011): 3-5.

Wilfred, Felix. "What Can 'Upper Caste' Christians Learn from Dalit Christians?" *Jeevadhara* Vol. XLI/No.241 (January, 2011): 66-76.

Wilfred, Felix. "Create Opportunities for Dalit Christians." An Interview with Archbishop A.M. Chinnappa, *Jeevadhara* Vol. XLI/No.241 (January, 2011): 77-84.

Xavier, Francis P. "Anatomy of Humiliation and Signs of Hope." *Jeevadhara* Vol. XLI/No.241 (January, 2011): 26-34.

Reports/Booklet

Annual Activity Report, Centre for Dalit/Subaltern Studies, 2009-2010. New Delhi: CDS, 2010.

Profile: James Massey. New Delhi: CDS, 2010.

Dictionary

Soanes, Catherine and Angus Stevenson. Eds. *Concise Oxford English Dictionary, Indian Edition.* New Delhi: Oxford University Press, 2007.

News Paper

The Hindu (Vijayawada), Friday September 23, 2016.

The Times of India (New Delhi) March 21, 2014.

Online Sources

http://www.indianexpress.com/news/scs-sts-form-25--of-population-says-census-2011-data/1109988

http://www.pewforum.org/2017/4/11/global-restrictions-on-religion-rise-modestly-in-2015-revesing-downward-trend/

www.firstpost.com Feb 6, 2018

https://www.ramakrishna.org/chicgfull.htm

Index